Double Entry

Double Entry

Published by Empty Tank Press, Stoneham, Mass. 02180

©2017 Donald N. Sweeney
all rights reserved

ISBN 978-1-946731-02-9

PCIP: (Author)   Sweeney, Donald N.
        (Title)   Double Entry
        (Subject Headings)
              (1) Mystery Fiction
              (2) Crime
              (3) Thriller, Legal
              (4) Boston, Massachusetts

Cover design by Robin Ludwig Design Inc.
Cover photo by Shutterstock

Legal Thriller

Following a two-year suspension of his law license for unethical conduct, living-on-the-edge criminal defense attorney Mike Ratigan defends burglar Frank Maguire from charges of murder committed during a burglary. But with his client in jail, Mike quickly becomes carnally enmeshed in a torrid affair with Maguire's paramour, Elaine Fowler. Ultimately convinced of his client's innocence of murder, Mike confronts the challenge of whether to win the case—or the woman.

Courtroom high drama ensues.

———

"An involving tale with a protagonist who's both compassionate and disreputable." This novel is "more than simply a legal thriller, as it rivetingly focuses on Mike's personal life as well."

Kirkus Reviews

"This legal thriller is a rollicking tale with twists and turns, brimful of sex, an up-down, all around roller-coaster ride with plenty of laughs. Highly recommended."

Thomas R. Bransten, author of A Slight Case of Guilt and Journey to Zembeylia

———

"I read fiction all the time, and this is as good as anything I've read."

L.I., NY reader

"Thoroughly enjoyable, and I can see it as a movie, too."

Quincy, MA reader

"Anything worth doing is worth doing to excess."

Nick Friel

CHAPTER 1

For a burglar there's nothing quite like having a good friend at the local post office.

Cynthia Kincaid wasn't actually Maguire's friend, of course. Quite simply, they had an "arrangement." He paid her $100 for the name, address and dates for each person who notified the Brookline post office to suspend mail delivery.

How better to know when a home will be vacant?

Over the years Maguire had adopted certain rules: avoid occupants, burglar alarms, neighbors, video surveillance systems, and dogs. Especially dogs. As for alarms, if he heard beeps signalling a countdown, he would exit with haste and drive to a completely different neighborhood.

To enhance knowledge useful in his trade, Maguire had studied the *MIT Guide to Lock Picking* (1991) and used its guidance to advantage. A safecracker he was not. On the rare occasions where he needed access to a safe, he used cobalt bits in a half-inch drill to remove the hardened steel lock, then popped the door open. Cobalt worked best, experience had taught.

Maguire didn't ordinarily concentrate on the estate areas of Brookline and other wealthy communities. He focused on neighborhoods where the "middle class" families that politicians are always yapping about live. He worked those sections during daylight hours, usually between 10:00 AM and 4:00 PM, when owners would most likely be at work. For these expeditions he wore casual slacks, button-down shirt, and sports jacket.

In contrast, Maguire's occasional night-time excursions into rich areas warranted dark clothing. Burgling homes of the wealthy presented greater risk—the likely presence of elaborate video security systems, for example. Maguire tended to leave such dwellings for times when he wanted a bigger score.

Tonight he wanted a bigger score.

At the front door of this brick, slate-roof Queen Anne-style house, Maguire slipped on latex gloves and a Halloween face mask, inserted the blade of his electric lockpick in the keyhole, and pulled the trigger. The machine made a brief grinding sound. Then he felt the cylinder turn. The heavy door opened smoothly. No warning beeps followed.

Before stepping inside, he returned the lockpick to its holster, next to the fishnet carrier which hung from his belt. He softly closed the door behind him, listened. The tick-tock of a clock presented the only sound. The air seemed a little cool, but no cooking or other odors suggested an occupant. Moonlight streaming through the windows made the expansive foyer quite visible.

Directly in front of him a broad stairway rose to the second floor. A hall to his left led to the rear of the house. Further to the left, double pocket doors gave access to a living area: sofas, chairs, fireplace, oriental carpet.

From his earlier survey outdoors, Maguire knew that the turret typical of a Queen Anne was to his right. He expected to find the library there. And his prize.

In the turret a large, leather-topped, cherry pedestal desk stood near the windows. Behind it a chesterfield-style judge's chair upholstered in burgundy leather was placed so that the owner could swivel from the desk to gaze at the bucolic scene outside. Thick hedges screened adjoining properties from view.

The desktop was bare except for a hand-held magnifier and a cup of felt-tip pens. A quick search disclosed that the desk drawers held nothing of apparent value. Maguire turned to the built-in bookcases, crowded with leather-bound volumes. *This guy's a leather freak!*

Three boxed, three-ring binders stood out from the others. Their green, leather spines were embossed in gold with vertical lettering in Old English script proudly announcing the "Willenbrandt Collection."

Maguire withdrew the binders from their shelf and stood them upright on the desk. He quickly leafed through each. They were filled with transparent plastic pages of stamps. Stamps from all nations. In all denominations. All manner of colors, sizes, prices, even shapes.

He shook out his fishnet carrier, spread it on the desktop. Carefully he stacked the binders inside, pulled the drawstring tight, threw the net over his shoulder, started toward the door.

"Harold?" a voice uttered.

Maguire stiffened, held his breath.

"You're back early?" A woman's voice. Nearby. Elderly.

Now he heard a shuffling noise, slippers sliding across the floor. Right outside the library door.

He remained still.

The voice again. "Didn't expect you until next week." Nearer. "Nothing bad happened did it?"

A woman, late seventies or early eighties, stepped inside, saw him. She said, "Who—?"

Without warning, her right hand flew to her chest and she collapsed against him. Reflexively he reached to prevent her fall. Her body sagged, began to slip down his torso. Her head dangled. He eased her to the floor. As he did, her eyes fluttered, and her hand gripped her chest.

She said weakly, "Pills. My pills."

Maguire stood upright, started toward the front door.

In a feeble voice the woman said, "Nitro. My Nitro."

His hand touched the doorknob.

In a pleading tone she added, "Please. Please. In the kitchen. On the counter. Please."

He looked back at her. She lay on the carpet just inside the library. She looked frail, tiny, helpless.

Without conscious thought he dropped the carrier, turned and raced toward the rear of the house. He scanned the kitchen countertop, grabbed a pill bottle labeled "Nitroglycerin," hurried back to the woman, knelt beside her.

"Open it," she begged.

He pressed down on the cap, twisted it off the bottle, shook a tablet into her hand. She placed the medication under her tongue. Her "Thank you" was barely discernable.

Maguire said, "Will you be all right?"

She nodded. He rose to his feet, picked up the binders at the front door, fled from the house.

He thought: In a minute she'll be calling 911.

CHAPTER 2

It was all Simone's fault. Everything.

Mike's near disbarment. Two-year suspension from the practice of law. All Simone's fault. Everything.

A sound from behind interrupted Mike's ruminations. High heels tapping on the marble floor just inside the lounge entrance.

He turned, saw a woman standing near the entry. She quickly surveyed the barroom, then approached him, glided onto the stool next to his.

Late afternoon, Mike's mood mildly celebratory because of getting his law ticket back. He had intended to leave as soon as he finished his third drink, but that was before the fleshy redhead settled on the barstool. He didn't particularly favor redheads, but one takes what one can get. Besides, another drink for the road wouldn't hurt.

"I'm having a scotch and soda," he said to the woman. "What's yours?"

"Sidecar," she murmured throatily, with a toss of the head, hair swirling. Blue, light-weight V-neck dress cut low, double strand of pearls, pearl earrings. Remarkably pale skin, light freckles, blue eyes. A real redhead. Early thirties, he guessed. About his own age.

He ordered the drinks, sensed from Dianne's glance that the new arrival was not known to the barkeep.

Drinks served, he turned, held his glass out toward her, said, "Mike. Mike Ratigan."

Their glasses clinked.

"Florence," she said. Lips full. Kissable. Voice soft. No last name.

Florence! How can this be?—no one is named Florence these days—or for fifty years. On second thought, Florence *has* to be her real name. Nobody would pick it as a pseudonym.

She smiled, leaned toward him. The tip of her tongue penetrated the slight oval made by her lips. "I know. Isn't it awful? I've thought of changin' it. Do you think I should?"

For a moment Mike felt bad for his mean thought about her name. Could she possibly have detected this? I must've made a face. He said, "No—don't do it! Wonderful name."

"You can call me Flo," she confided, still leaning close.

"*Flo.* I like it."

A sultry smile in return. She switched subjects. "You're a lawyer, aren't you?" She spoke with confidence.

"How'd you know?"

"You look like a lawyer and you talk like a lawyer. I've known lots of lawyers. Always suited up, and they all talk the same way. Use big words all the time, tryin' to make people think they're better'n everybody else."

Momentarily Mike felt diminished. Then thought, I don't talk like other lawyers. I talk *better* than other lawyers. And I hardly said a thing—and screw the big words, which I didn't use anyway.

Flo went on. "What kind of law?"

"Trial. Mostly criminal cases now."

"Oh! Any I might've heard of?"

"Sure. How about Millicent Waterhouse, the Back Bay socialite accused of killing her husband?" He watched for her reaction.

"Oh my God!—the shotgun-on-the-stairs murder?"

"Yeah, but not murder. The jury found her not guilty."

"That was *your* case?"

He acknowledged with a simple, "Yes."

"Wow!" Flo looked at Mike with new respect. "Wow!" she repeated. "That's cool. And you got her off. How'd you do it?"

"Superior representation, but it wasn't easy. Extremely tough case. Bottom line, she wasn't guilty. The Commonwealth didn't have the evidence."

"Wait a minute!" She put her hand on his arm. "She shot him on the stairs, right? With a shotgun, right? When he was comin' up to their bedroom, right? And he wasn't dressed—he was *naked*, right?—stark naked?— just went downstairs to get a drink of pop or somethin' in the kitchen, came back upstairs and she blew him away on the staircase? How could she get away with that?"

"Thought he was a robber—burglar—coming up to—to do whatever—to kill them, rape her—God knows what."

"Their bedroom was on the third floor, right? I remember."

"You have excellent recall. That was four years ago."

Flo slid her empty glass toward the inside of the bartop.

Mike placed his glass next to hers, signalled a reorder to Dianne.

Flo resumed. "He was naked, right? That's the thing. How many robbers go around breakin' into houses with no clothes on?"

"Not too many," Mike admitted.

"So she had to know it was him. That's the amazin' thing, how you got her off. Reminded me of the OJ trial."

"Doing my job," he said, pleased that she was impressed.

"I remember now. I saw you on TV too. And there was a spread about you in *Boston* Magazine."

"Where'd you happen to see that?"

"In the shop, probably. I know I read it though." A quick smile traced the corners of her mouth.

Dianne served the new round and retreated discreetly to the other end of the bar.

"Shop?"

"Beauty parlor, where I work. Somethin' else too—you keep a gynecological examination table in your conference room."

He chuckled. "Funny what people remember. You read that whole article and the thing you remember is that GYN table."

"Not just me. The rest of the girls thought that was so *hot* too, and one of my customers said she should've had that lawyer in her divorce—*you*. She said at least she wouldn't have gotten stiffed just for the fee."

Mike smiled. "A guy never knows what's working for him. Maybe you'd like to see it."

"Maybe I would." A few moments passed while they digested this exchange. Then Flo said, "You won some other big cases too, around the same time. In the headlines every day, practically. Right?"

"Yeah."

She paused for a sip of her drink, said, "Don't I remember you got into . . . some kind of—I don't know—*some*thing . . . some problem? Somebody got pissed at you, sued you or somethin'?"

Uh-oh. Too close to dangerous territory. "Nah, nothing interesting there. What about you, Flo. What do you do at the beauty parlor?"

"Oh, nothin' much to talk about—not like with you. Just styling, and I'm a cosmetologist too."

"Cosmetologist? What's that?"

She explained the work of cosmetologists and cosmeticians. Mike felt relieved at the change in direction. Avoid perilous ground.

He eased his cellphone out of his suitcoat pocket. "You mind if I make a quick call? Don't like to when I'm with someone, but . . . ?"

Now Flo would know that he was "with" someone—herself.

"No, no, go right ahead."

He speed-dialed his office, interrupted Kaitlin's "Ratigan Law Chambers" announcement. "Listen," he said, "I'm tied up longer than I thought I'd be, and I won't be able to make it back to the office before you leave. Just lock up, okay? I'll see you tomorrow."

Kaitlin said, "Hope you get the new client."

"I'm working on it right now. Don't worry. It'll happen."

"Okay, Mike. See you in the morning."

He tapped the end button, put his phone on the bar, bent his head toward Flo. "You're a client," he disclosed with a grin.

There was no way for him to know that he was not far off the mark.

CHAPTER 3

Sheila Graham was working at the computer in her study when the telephone rang. Agnes, her cat, snoozed on the leather wing chair next to the slider, which opened to the patio. An oversized framed color photograph of the cat was displayed on the wall above the computer monitor. Sheila checked the answering machine display. It showed "Robert K. Friedlander" and a telephone number beginning with Area Code 410. She recognized neither the name nor the number, but willing to take a chance that on a Sunday afternoon it would not be a sales call, she pushed the speakerphone button. "Hello?"

"Hi," a woman answered. "Is this Professor Graham?"

Sheila did not recognize the caller's voice. "Yes."

"You probably don't remember me, but we met at Jonathan's graduation. I'm his sister Madelaine."

Jonathan? Memory came quickly. "Do you mean Jonathan Wright?"

"Yes. My brother. I'm his sister Madelaine—'Maddie' they call me—regrettably," she sighed. "I met you at his graduation. I thought you might remember?"

Late May so many years ago, the Yard pulsating with graduating seniors, along with postgraduates, family, alumni. Trees leafy green in a wet spring. Jonathan, tall and gangly, a young woman standing beside him, much shorter. "Maddie,'" he announced with a broad smile. "My little sister you've heard so much about." He had put his arm around the younger woman and pulled her toward him, all the while looking at Sheila for approval.

Sheila had not expected to see him that day, not even planned to attend graduation. She'd received her own Ph.D. the year before, and was invited to this ceremony as the last-minute guest of a foreign student whose family had not been able to attend. She accompanied the senior as an act of kindness.

In the period since that long-ago day, Sheila had forgotten Jonathan. No, not forgotten, never forgotten, but for years he had come to mind only sporadically. Their affair had been brief, intense—beyond intense.

Jonathan showed brilliance, was often hypercritical, nervous, even jumpy sometimes, moving like a deer startled on a forest path.

"You have such long fingers," she remembered having told him. "You should have been a pianist. You'd make a magnificent pianist. A concert pianist. Playing Carnegie Hall. I can see you there, bowing to a standing ovation, the orchestra behind you rising to their feet in approval, the string players tapping their bows on the instrument strings."

Jonathan had shown her how his long fingers could work a different kind of miracle, bringing her body into tune with a divine orchestra. How strange that, once so close, they had grown apart—slid apart, really.

A sound on the line brought her back to the telephone. "Yes, I do recall you. How are you—and Jonathan—how is Jonathan?"

"I'm fine, but . . . ." Silence briefly, then, "It didn't occur to me you might not've heard. Jonathan died . . . oh my God, nine years ago now."

Sheila said, "Oh, no! No! I didn't know—how could . . . ? What happened?"

"Fire. His cabin burned down. They don't know exactly how it started. He was inside. Asleep, I guess—they found him in bed."

"How horrible. It's just . . . . It's just unthinkable. I haven't heard anything about him for—well, for years, but . . . ."

"He was out West—Wyoming, in the forest, basically—working on some project of his all the time and he had become . . . . He'd become kind of eccentric—reclusive, actually, and . . . ." The caller paused, seemed to collect her thoughts. "We didn't hear from him much ourselves back here either."

"Back here is . . . ?"

"Randallstown—just outside Baltimore . . . . Anyway, the reason I called is because I know you and Jonathan were in the same area of stud—same discipline—and the last time he was here—I remember because it was the first anniversary of 9/11—and he left behind a bunch of stuff he had done. Now we're getting ready to move and I thought it might be of some use to someone, but I have no way to know, really, and you're the only one I could think of, so I kind of thought if I could send it on to you, you might take a look at it and . . . ." She slowed, continued. "I know I'm just rattling on, and it must sound silly to you."

She went on haltingly. "I don't mean to bother you or anything, but if you could use it . . . . It's just a manuscript and a computer disk—CD or DVD or something. The material doesn't mean anything to me, and it might . . . ."

"Yes. Yes, of course I'd be glad to." Sheila took a breath before resuming. "It's terribly upsetting to hear about Jonathan. He was such a fine man, and . . . ."

"I know," the caller said. "I miss him so much myself you can't begin to imagine, even though we didn't see much of him for such a long time. You never realize until . . . ." She sniffled. "He was a little bit in love with you back then, when I met you, you know. A lot in love, really, and still was when he—when he died."

Sheila's chest constricted as memories flooded her. Tears welled. She wiped her eyes.

When they concluded their conversation, Maddie confirmed Sheila's mailing address and said, "I'll send it out tomorrow. Then it'll be done and I'll feel better about it. I know Jonathan would want you to have it."

Sheila touched the speakerphone button to silence the dial tone. Random thoughts of Jonathan cascaded through her mind. Sadness overcame her as memories drifted through her consciousness; she lost sense of time.

After a while she returned to the present and her attention was drawn to the large photograph of her beloved Agnes. In late fall the cat had been playing in the leaves while Sheila was raking them. Sheila had run into the house and grabbed her camera, snapped the picture. The rich colors of the leaves melded with Agnes's coat. Sheila's love for the animal was unbounded. Perhaps some small substitute for the marriage she never had.

CHAPTER 4

Five days later Sheila Graham arrived home to find a package at her front door. She carried it into her study and cut the heavy wrapping tape with scissors. Inside were a large manila envelope containing a half-inch-thick typed manuscript and a paper CD sleeve with a plastic window.

The envelope bore the word "Dissertation" scrawled across its face in pencil. The same word appeared hand-written on the disk label. The once-familiar sight of Jonathan's writing brought a momentary chill to her.

The manuscript title read "Inhibiting the Aging Process Through Manipulation of the Telomerase Rate." Upon sight of this Sheila gasped, grew dizzy, steadied herself, then shushed Agnes away from her spot on the wing chair and sank into it.

Recovering after some moments, she read the next line on the face page of the manuscript. Light streaming through the slider illuminated the page. "Dissertation Submitted by Jonathan B. Wright." For several minutes she held the document in her lap, finally turned to the first page of text.

After skimming a few pages, Sheila rose and went to a bookcase. She withdrew a bound index from the end of a set of soft-cover journals, quickly found the page she sought, then removed one of the journals from the shelf.

She returned to the armchair, compared a few lines of text in the journal with corresponding text in the dissertation. Again she felt dizzy. "Oh my God!" she said aloud. "Oh my God!"

Too unnerved to take any immediate action, she decided to do nothing until the next day. To calm herself she went to the kitchen and brewed a pot of tea. A good night's sleep will help, she thought. Then I'll know what to do.

But little sleep came to her that night. While she lay awake, she decided upon a course of action.

CHAPTER 5

Sheila braced herself before tapping out the number. She touched the numeral pads almost tentatively, as though fearing that the call would actually go through.

"Dr. Fessenden's office," a female voice answered.

"This is Professor Graham," Sheila said. "Is he in?"

"Just a moment. I'll connect you."

The twenty second wait seemed an eternity. A brief urge to hang up was interrupted by her former mentor's voice. "Sheila, what a pleasure to hear from you. How've you been?"

"Fine, Dr. Fessenden. Fine." She hesitated. "I need to see you about something urgent. Is there any chance you could be available this afternoon?"

"My, this sounds serious. What's it about?"

"I'd rather not get into it over the telephone. It's too—too . . . . Could you see me this afternoon?"

"I'm sure I can free up some time for you. Would 3:00 o'clock be all right?"

"Thanks. I'll see you then."

Sheila replaced the handset on its base and sat for a time staring out through the slider. Usually, viewing the flowers which surrounded the small reflective pool calmed her, but on this day relaxation did not come. She felt as though she had already been through a great ordeal, rather than preparing to face one yet to come. The muscles at the base of her neck tightened; she rolled her shoulders to loosen them.

Agnes appeared from behind a pot on the patio and ambled toward the door. Sheila hastened to let the cat in before it began to cry. Seated once again, she signalled for the cat to take its place in her lap. Disdaining the offer, Agnes instead sauntered to her bowl in the kitchen. Speaking to the photograph on the wall, Sheila said, "How can you be so persnickety when your mother really needs your affection so much?"

* * *

Sheila dressed carefully for the meeting. Powder blue suit with matching shoes, a beige silk blouse, no necklace or earrings; she always disdained cosmetics, decided to forgo hose as well.

She gave grudging approval to her image in the mirror, while regretting the few pounds added during the last decade. They show in my face—and on my waist . . . . But not too bad.

Sheila made a copy of the journal article and slipped it into a file folder along with a copy of Jonathan's dissertation. She left the house when the clock neared quarter past the hour, even though the drive to Dr. Fessenden's office at the university was less than one-half hour. She did not want to chance being late.

She parked in a "No Parking" zone behind the ivy-covered red-brick building, shut off the engine, leaned back against the headrest, took a deep breath. The dashboard clock registered 2:46. She waited ten minutes before climbing the stairs to the professor's second-floor corner office.

The silver-haired secretary in the outer office greeted her without rising. "You can go right in. He's expecting you."

The door to the inner office was open. Books stuffed every crevice of bookcases lining the office walls. Piles of books were stacked on the desk and floor. Still more books lined the windowsills, partially blocking the view of the quadrangle that Sheila had crossed and recrossed during those semesters so many years ago. A large wide-screen computer monitor, keyboard, and mouse rested on a wheeled table next to the professor's desk.

Dr. Fessenden had been her dissertation advisor when she was pursuing her doctorate. She had never been close to him, nor did she know anyone else who had. His manner was always distant, somewhat cool, although ever polite and courteous.

She had last seen him at a symposium three years earlier. He looked then—and did still—just about as he had during her student years. Head crowned by a full shock of graying hair. A couple of inches short of six feet, posture fully erect. Frame wiry but strong from daily walks. Van Dyke beard, pursed lips, wire-rimmed eye-glasses. Gray pinstripe suit with a vest. Subdued tie in a Windsor knot; a pocket square matched his tie.

As she entered the office, Dr. Fessenden stood, walked around his desk, greeted her with a firm hand-shake. "You look well," he said. "It's quite a while. How long now?"

Anxious to get to the point, Sheila nevertheless tried to conceal the strain she felt. She said, "I heard you speak in Atlanta. That must be about three years ago?"

"Yes, that's right." He waved her to an armchair, closed the door to the anteroom, returned to his seat, placing the desk as a barrier between them. "How've you been?"

This was no time for small talk. Sheila said, "Dr. Fessenden, as I indicated to you over the telephone, there's a very serious matter we need to discuss."

She accepted his nod as permission to continue. "I'd like you to look at two documents. They seem to me to be virtually identical, and I want your comments." She opened the file folder and placed the two copies on his desk directly in front of him. She watched carefully as he picked them up.

He scanned the first page of each paper, turned briefly to the second page, then placed the documents back on his desk. He gazed at Sheila, but did not speak.

"They appear the same to me," she repeated. "Do they to you?"

"Yes, no question about it, except for the name. May I have a minute?" He removed his eyeglasses and began to clean them with his pocket square. He kept his gaze focused on his glasses, did not look up at her.

Sheila waited.

Dr. Fessenden put his spectacles back on and looked at her directly. His eyes seemed watery. He kept the handkerchief in his hand.

"You may not believe this," he said, "but you come at an opportune time. I want you to know I've been thinking about this entire matter a great deal of late. It's been on my mind constantly, disturbing me—you have no idea how much." His forehead glistened. He wiped it with the handkerchief.

Sheila exhaled. She did not realize that she had been holding her breath. To speak now might ruin everything.

"What do you want me to do?" he asked.

"There is only one right thing to do, isn't there?"

"Of course. You want me to acknowledge it was Jonathan's work."

She could no longer restrain her anger. "The work you passed off as your own! The work you received the Balzan Prize for—" her voice rose "—for *Jonathan's* work!"

She waited for a reaction but none came. She went on. "You'll have to issue a press release. And send a formal letter to the Journal of Cellular Biology. And write to the prize committee asking—*demanding*—that it rescind the award."

"You've thought of everything. Typical. You were such a good student."

"Never of Jonathan's caliber."

Dr. Fessenden fell silent, finally ventured an explanation. "It was the pressure of needing to publish. Combined with the demands of this office. Once I became head of the department, there simply wasn't time—"

Sheila interrupted. "When can we get this done?"

He sighed. "This is Tuesday. How about Friday? Will that be soon enough?"

"That'll be fine." She considered whether to say anything more, decided to be kind. "I'm sure you realize I hated to have to come here under these circumstances. I'm glad you're facing up to it. I know it must be terribly difficult for you—even though I don't really understand how you could have done it, and don't expect I ever will."

Dr. Fessenden said, "In a way I'm grateful to you for bringing this to a head. This is something I'll have to deal with—live with—for the rest of my life. But that's as it should be. A dark cloud has been hanging over me for a very long time. Now it's going to pass away." In an offhand manner, he added, "Incidentally, I'm curious. How did you find out?"

"I'd rather not go into that. Will you be good enough to email or fax me a copy of your statements in advance?"

He gave his consent, adding, "Actually, I'd like your approval, if you wouldn't mind looking at them before I send them out. Would that be all right?"

Although reluctant to be further involved, Sheila nodded. The request seemed reasonable.

Dr. Fessenden then said, "Would you mind keeping it just between us until I send out the press release? I'd feel much better if everyone heard it directly from me. Can you respect that?"

"I'll grant you that courtesy." Sheila rose, placed her card on the desk next to the manuscript copies which she had put there earlier. "My email address is on there."

She left without offering to shake his hand.

On the drive home Sheila played the scene over and over in her mind. She had expected a firestorm, never thinking that it would be this easy. But there was a reason it was easy. There's always a reason. He had been worrying about it himself, he told her. A matter of conscience. He was grateful to her, he said.

After a brief time passed, suspicion began to gnaw. Perhaps it had been *too* easy. I'd better cover myself, she concluded.

She stopped at a hardware store not far from her house and purchased a tube of epoxy glue. Thus did she begin her preparations.

* * *

That evening she received a telephone call from Dr. Fessenden. He said, "I'm so upset about this . . . . I really don't want to wait until Friday to make my announcement. I'd like to work on it tonight and release it tomorrow. Is there a chance you could come to my office tomorrow morning around eleven? That way you could be assured . . . ."

Sheila had no desire to see him ever again, but this was such a monumental step, so important to the scientific community, to Jonathan's memory—to the *world*. "Eleven o'clock," she agreed. "At your office. I'll be there."

CHAPTER 6

He wore a purple-colored turtleneck pullover, dark-brown slacks, and a black windbreaker that fell below his belt line. The panelled front entrance door was made of wood, painted dark green. It had no peephole, nor sidelights through which he could be seen. He pressed the bell button. Muffled chimes sounded from within. In a moment the door opened and Sheila stood in the entry. She stared at him in astonishment.

"Dr. Fessenden—what are you doing here? Our meeting isn't until eleven. At your—"

"I know it's early," he spoke hurriedly, "but I've been up all night." His unshaven face bore witness. "I didn't sleep at all, working on these." He held up a CD. "Letters and the press release on here. I need you to look at them—approve them. I'd really like to get them out quick—this morning—not wait. I need to get this whole thing behind me. You'll help me, won't you?"

It was early Wednesday morning, the day following their meeting. Sheila looked at him; he was seeming to gauge her. He offered the disc to her. "At least look at them, won't you?" he pleaded. "I put them on disc so we can change them any way you want." He pressed the CD toward her.

She hesitated, then took the disc and slowly opened the door for him.

"I appreciate it," he said. "It won't take long. I just need to do this. Once and for all." A moment went by. "I'm not intruding —am I?—you don't have company?"

She shook her head, stepped aside to admit him, closed the door. He followed her down the hall to her home office. The computer screen showed a document open.

Sheila motioned for him to sit in the wing chair.

He said, "No, no, that's all right. I'm too excited to sit." He pointed to the CD. "Just look at this. Please!"

She sat, bent to insert the CD. The drive whirred. She began to read the document which opened. It was captioned "Press Release" in large letters in bold type, but contained only gibberish as text. She said, "But this is—"

Standing behind her, he said sharply, "That's all right."

He swung with brutal force. The blow with a sand-filled, tightly woven sock caught her at the base of the skull. She slumped forward. Quickly he grabbed her upper body, preventing her from crashing into the desk. No bruises. The fewer external signs of injury, the better. He eased her back in the seat.

Rolling her eyelids up, he could see only the whites of her eyes. Her breathing sounded shallow. He checked her pulse; weak, but steady.

He withdrew a pair of latex examination gloves from his windbreaker pocket and pulled them on. Deciding to risk leaving her alone, he sped through the house to imprint its layout in his mind—and to make certain no one else was present.

First floor living room, office, kitchen/dining/family room, and a half-bath. Three bedrooms and two full baths on the second. No visitors.

The master bath was what he sought. This room, entered from the master bedroom, was airy, spacious, with ceramic tile, twin-bowl vanity and up-scale fixtures, including a bidet. A faint floral scent lingered. The whirlpool tub, set atop a mahogany base, was eighteen inches deep. Concern about adequate depth had been needless.

He returned to the office. Sheila still lay back in her seat, eyes closed. He knelt, eased her body across his shoulders and slowly rose to his feet, supporting her in a fireman's carry. Her sandals fell to the floor, making gentle plopping sounds. He struggled with her weight. She was heavier than expected.

He shuffled down the hall with his load, climbed the stairs slowly. At the landing he stopped to rest, leaned against the stair rail. When he resumed, her body seemed to have grown even heavier. Once he reached the second floor, the going grew easier. He passed through the master bedroom to the bathroom. At the side of the tub he knelt and carefully eased Sheila to the tile floor.

The professor stripped her. First came the slacks. They slid off easily, as did her panties. Pale flesh. A thicket of coarse, dark hairs intertwined. Next he rolled her upper body back and forth in order to remove her sweater gradually without tearing it. He unfastened her bra, pulled the straps off her arms. Padded cups. Breasts smaller than expected. Plums. He checked her eyes. Still shut. Her chest moved up and down slowly.

He closed the drain, turned the faucets on, adjusted the temperature to mildly hot. Water too hot or cold might shock her awake. He checked his watch. Only fourteen minutes since entering the house. Good. Very good. He would stay no longer than absolutely necessary.

Minutes passed before the tub filled. He turned off the water. Now came the most difficult part. Sheila lay on the floor, had to be lifted. He knelt behind her head and raised her arms. Her head flopped to one side. He lifted her torso and eased it to the side of the tub. There he got purchase, forced her arms over the edge, getting part of her weight in the tub. Next he pushed the whole body into the tub, careful not to splash any water on the floor. She started to slide into the water sideways. He caught her and held her so that she would not bang against the hard surface, create bruises. Finally he positioned her to lie face up. She did not awaken.

The water level was high enough. He needed only to push her head down slightly. Her knees bent and rose above the water line. Her head dipped below it.

He had been worried that she might struggle. She did not. He must have hit her harder than he thought. No need to contend with scratches, pulled hair, contusions. Just the kind of good fortune he needed.

Imagine, the stupid bitch actually thought that she would destroy *me*!

In seven minutes he was fully satisfied that it was over. Really, it's her parents' fault she's dead. She died from politeness. Never should have let me in the house.

He emptied the sock into the toilet and flushed, flushed again, waiting to be sure that all of the sand was gone. Still wearing the latex gloves, he gathered her clothing, carried the garments into the bedroom.

A flood of questions came to him. What would Sheila have done with her clothes after removing them for a bath? Would she have left them on the bed? Hung them in the closet? Put her underwear in a hamper? He had not planned this part, and did not have the luxury of time to resolve these questions at leisure. It would have been impossible to know anyway. He must act.

In the walk-in closet he found a clothing basket and deposited Sheila's panties there. He hung the slacks on a hanger and rapidly opened and closed dresser drawers until he found one containing sweaters. He took care to study the way in which the sweaters were folded. Carefully, he arranged the one removed from her body in the same fashion. The bra he left on the bed, as perhaps she might have done.

Once back in Sheila's office, he noticed her sandals where they had fallen near the desk. He would deal with them in a few minutes. Next he took inventory of the desktop.

Computer monitor, keyboard, and a mouse resting on a pad imprinted with a cat's image. An oversized inkjet printer sitting at the rear, with yet another cat photograph lodged in the ejection bin. Next to the printer, a telephone answering machine with a speakerphone function and a portable handset. Empty pencil holder. An easel with nothing on it, and a stack of papers, on top of which lay an issue of the Journal of Cellular Biology.

He picked up the journal, recognized the issue which contained his article. He crossed to the bookcase and returned it to its place.

The stack of papers yielded an unbound copy of Jonathan Wright's draft. The only one? Would she have made a copy? He had to know. The thin latex gloves made it easy to thumb through the remaining papers. Nothing else of interest.

He sat at the desk chair and opened the drawers one by one. Plain paper. Letterhead stationery. A box of paper clips. Rubber bands. Felt-tip pens, only two colors, blue and red. First-class postage stamps along with some two-cent ones. A pair of scissors. Box of staples. Nothing here.

In the bottom drawer he found the original disc which Maddie had sent. Ah! Good. Looks like Sheila wasn't taking any special precautions. He stuffed the disc into his jacket pocket.

He moved the mouse. The screen popped to life, revealing a Word document titled "ReadMe.doc." From the first sentence he confirmed this to be related to the Wright draft. The computer was running Windows. To see where the document was stored, he clicked on the "File," "Save As" dropdown box option. Sheila had placed the file in a "Jonathan" subdirectory under "My Documents."

He opened Windows Explorer to see what else was stored in that subdirectory. Along with the Wright draft and the backup copy Word had made automatically, the subdirectory contained two other files.

All right. That's a plus. Now let's see if the sneaky bitch sent any emails—or kept her promise. Outlook, her email program, was already open. Nothing in the inbox alluded to him—or to the Wright draft—in any way. The Outlook calendar showed their appointment scheduled for 11:00 this morning. He opened the appointment and changed the time to 9:00. Then he clicked on "Sent Messages" and reviewed the messages she had transmitted over the past two weeks. The usual female drivel. No message dealt with his problem or contained any attachment.

A review of deleted items produced the same result. Finally, he looked in the junk mail folder. Perhaps she had hidden something there. She had not.

He returned to Word and closed the program without saving the document. In Windows Explorer he deleted all of the document and the Jonathan subdirectory from the My Documents directory. He followed this step by opening the Windows Recycle Bin and deleting every document that it contained. While he waited for this process to complete, the telephone rang, startling him.

He listened. Four rings. "Please leave a message," Sheila's voice said, "and I'll get back to you as soon as I can."

A man's voice followed immediately. "You're cat's at it again! If you don't get that little bastid out of here within ten minutes, I'm gonna call the cops again. I toldja I've had it! This is the last time—I toldja!" The caller's handset crashed onto its cradle.

Dr. Fessenden swung the chair around and stood. Have to leave right away. Not finished, but can't risk staying for even part of the ten minutes before this nut calls the police.

At that moment a cat appeared on the other side of the patio slider. The professor slid the door aside, said, "Here kitty. Come on in, kitty. Come on in." He was about to bend over and offer further encouragement when the cat decided on its own. It ambled in, jumped onto the wing chair and settled there, resting its head on its front paws, eyes on the interloper. A reprieve.

Relieved, the professor closed the slider, blocking exit, and returned to the keyboard. No rush, now that the "kitty" situation was resolved.

He checked the computer's system information to make sure that there was no additional hard drive where copies could be kept. None shown. He searched for any file which contained the word "Wright." None. Next came a search for all documents created within the past two weeks. This would show any which Sheila had hidden. He set wild card parameters and clicked to start the search.

While the computer was performing the search, he went into the kitchen and made a call from his cellphone to Sheila's residence telephone. No feedback wanted when the message later played on the answering machine.

The house telephone rang. When the greeting ended and the record tone signalled, he said, "Sheila, this is Dr. Fessenden. I'm waiting for you. Where are you? Did you forget? Call me. Let me know you're all right."

He ended the call, returned to the office, set his cellphone on the desk, and sat down at the computer to complete his search. Then he pressed the eject button on the CD drive. The drive opened and he removed his phony disc, stuffed it into his jacket pocket next to the Maddie copy. Just as he did, door chimes sounded.

"Shit!" He stiffened. His heart raced. Did that guy call the police anyway? The chimes rang again. A long minute passed and he heard the front door open.

"Hello? Hello?" Male voice, but not the caller. "Anybody home?"

The door closed. Footsteps sounded near the front entrance.

Dr. Fessenden quickly aborted the computer search, grabbed the Wright draft, hurried outside through the slider, closed it behind him. Swiftly he made his way across the yard, removed the latex gloves and stuffed them in his pocket.

He worried that he had not been able to complete his computer tasks. And the sandals! He had left them on the floor! But maybe that was all right. A woman might have done that herself before going upstairs to bathe.

He reached his car, which he had parked out of view one street away. He drove toward the university at moderate speed. Most important of all the "yet-to-do" steps, he had not made the intended *second* telephone call, the call from Sheila's house to his cellphone, the call which would show her to be alive at a definite time, if ever need be.

But wait! An ugly thought abruptly intruded. Where's my phone? He tapped his jacket pockets, felt the CDs, but the familiar cellphone bulge was not there. Alarm gripped him. He rubbed his hand against the jacket material. Nothing. Where is it? Suddenly, he realized: he had left his cellphone on the desk!

He jammed his foot on the brake pedal. The car swerved to the curb. His mind froze, cleared gradually. Must go back. No choice.

He was surprised to see two squad cars parked in front of the house. He thought of driving away, decided against it. He would brazen his way through. Somehow. He must get his phone.

The front door stood open. In the hallway the professor encountered a uniformed policeman. The officer saw him approach, raised his hand, barring the way. "Who're you?"

"I'm Dr. Fessenden."

"You got here awful fast!" The cop shook his head with sadness. "I'm afraid you're too late, doctor. She's already dead."

"No!" Picking up on the policeman's belief that he was a medical doctor called to render assistance, the professor said, "That's so sad."

CHAPTER 7

The call came in early afternoon.

"I need a lawyer right now," a male voice said. "My girl gave me your name. Said you're tops."

"I am," Mike said. "She knows what she's talking about. What's your name?"

"Maguire. Frankie Maguire."

"Where're you calling from?"

"Jail."

"Which one?"

"Colchester."

Colchester, a town of around 20,000 people, was situated about twelve miles northwest of Boston, a roughly twenty minute drive from Mike's Somerville office in light traffic.

"I'll be there in half an hour. Don't talk to anybody—don't say anything to *anybody*—until I get there. Then you talk to me. Only me. Got that?"

"Got it."

* * *

By the time he was thirty-two, Mike Ratigan had already reached the top of his game. Within barely sixteen months he won three murder acquittals and got a hung jury in defending an arson case. Two of the murder trials were especially high profile. All over local TV, newspapers. *Boston Globe, Boston Herald.* Cover photo on *Boston Magazine.* One case—the Back Bay socialite—even made national news. Saturated CNN for a week. Mike had then felt confident that he could glide with ease through the next two or three decades—that is, if he even decided to continue practicing law that long.

He would make oodles of dough, live high. Eventually retire, maybe. After piling up a huge investment portfolio, of course. The Mediterranean coast. South of France, Spain, Italy—not Greece. Or maybe one of those islands where there are always lots of "good rides." What else does a guy really need? After these victories his phones would never stop ringing. He could name his own price. It would last forever. Why not?

Well, an institution called the Massachusetts Board of Bar Overseers. That's why not. On the basis of allegations by Simone's husband—by then Mike's *ex* law partner—the Board had conducted a full investigation. Ultimately Mike admitted to the facts. No sense in contesting the matter, his counsel—tremendously expensive counsel—advised. Would only make the outcome worse.

Mike Ratigan's name now showed up in the disciplinary reports: *In the Matter of Michael T. Ratigan.* Followed by a two-year suspension from the practice of law. Destroyed his practice. Had to withdraw from all his cases, arrange for other lawyers to take them over, send certified mail, return-receipt-requested notices informing every client of his suspension and withdrawal from representing them, file an affidavit with the Massachusetts Supreme Judicial Court—the state's highest—stating that he had done so. The ultimate embarrassment.

Exile from his profession ended just three weeks ago. Those two years had been oppressive. Slid from high earner to "no earner." From a deluge of choice cases to no cases at all. Severance from his source of income. Funds exhausted.

Now starting over. Reinstated but broke, waiting for the telephone to ring. Waiting. Waiting.

*   *   *

Finally, reinstated, Mike had his ticket back. A "license to steal," Simone had called it. Simone, his former partner's wife. Mike's downfall.

Two weeks ago Mike had hired Kaitlin as his multitasking sole employee: receptionist, secretary, bookkeeper, paralegal—and law-associate-to-be upon her forthcoming passage of the bar exam and swearing in. A third-year student at Suffolk University Law School's night and weekend J.D. program, Kaitlin had come with a near-perfect grade-point average, highly recommended, impressed Mike on interview, and had shown promise in the short time since. Now all he needed was a client. Or rather, *clients.*

The call from Maguire had come just in time.

CHAPTER 8

The jail was located in the Colchester police station. Mike was well known there, having served as an Assistant District Attorney (ADA) in Middlesex County for several years after his stint as a Suffolk County ADA upon graduation from law school. He picked up a copy of the arrest report and met Francis Maguire in a six-by-eight interrogation room which doubled as a conference room for attorneys and their jailhouse clients. The space was so tight that there was barely room to pull chairs away from the table to sit down.

After handshakes and introductions, Mike said, "Did you say anything to the police after you spoke with me?"

"No. Not a word."

"Good. Keep it that way." Satisfied, he said, "I'm going to record this." He placed a pocket mini-recorder on the table and switched it on. "My name is attorney Michael Ratigan." He nodded at Maguire. "Your name is . . . ?"

"Maguire. Francis Maguire." He paused, leaned toward Mike, whispered, "You sure it's okay to talk here? They pro'bly have the place bugged."

"Don't worry. It's okay."

Mike glanced at the arrest report. "Any middle initial?"

"X."

Mike stated the date and said, "Do you willfully consent to the recording of our conversation here today at the Colchester, Massachusetts, jail?"

"I do."

"Want to check the background information first, okay?"

"Sure."

Mike read from the arrest report. "Says you're twenty-eight. Is that right?"

"Yes."

"Citizen?"

"Sure am."

"You live in Watertown." Mike recited the street address.

"That's right."

"Own or rent?"

"Own."

"That a condo?"

"Two family. My sister lives on the first floor."

"Tell me about your record."

"Record?"

Is he stupid? "Your arrests, convictions, time in jail . . . ."

"Zero. I've never been arrested."

Mike switched direction. "How long've you been doing this?"

"A while."

"How long's 'a while'?"

"Quite a while."

Impatient, Mike snapped, "You want me on your side or not? How long?"

"Eight, nine years."

"All right. From when you were a kid. Now: how many times have you been arrested?"

"Never. I already told you I've never been arrested."

"You've been doing this for all these years and never been caught?"

"That's right."

Mike looked dumbfounded. He said, "Amazing." Unbelievable, actually. But anything's possible. Now to the guts. "Tell me what happened."

Mike expected a lie. All his clients lie.

Maguire grabbed Mike's jacket sleeve, looked at him straight on, said, "I didn't do it. I'm a burglar, for chrissake, not a killer."

Frankie Maguire looked quite ordinary. About five feet eight inches tall, slim build, skin clear but freckled, he wore dark brown slacks, a darker shirt, and a checkered brown sport jacket. No tie. Blue eyes dominated his expression. His easy, lop-sided grin and curly carrot-top added to the overall impression of a typical Irish guy whose worst offense was hanging out at the neighborhood saloon too late, catching hell from his wife when he drags himself in at 3:00 o'clock in the morning.

"Tell me what happened," Mike said again.

"The cops showed up almost as soon as I got in the house."

"What house?"

Hesitation. "The house I was in. I don't know—some house."

"What were you doing there?"

Maguire spoke with exasperation. "For chrissake! You know!"

"I don't know unless you tell me. What were you doing there?"

"All right, to steal, for chrissake."

Ruffled. Doesn't like being pushed. "How did you get in?"

"Key."

"Where did you get the key?"

Maguire smiled. "They almost always leave an extra one someplace near the front door. This one was stuck to the bottom of the mailbox with one of them magnetic key holders."

"So you went in?"

Maguire nodded.

"That's a 'yes'?"

"Yes."

"Tell me everything that happened, starting with the beginning, when you were at the front door. And I mean *everything*."

"Rang the bell. After a little incident in Brookline I always ring the bell."

Mike decided not to inquire about the "little incident." He said, "Go ahead."

Maguire spread his arms. "Somebody answers, I show them my clipboard, tell them I'm there to do the floor plans. They tell me I got the wrong house, and off I go. And if nobody answers, then . . . ."

"Ah, your clipboard. The police have it, I understand."

He nodded. "Right. A bunch of sample floor plans on there too. Got business cards to go with 'em."

"What did you do next?"

"Put on my gloves, checked—"

"Gloves? What kind?"

"Latex. You know, like the doctors wear. Didn't want to leave any prints."

"So no prints."

"No prints."

Obviously proud of his subterfuge, Maguire went on. "I opened the door, went inside, hollered 'Anybody home?' a coupla times. When nobody answered, I closed the door and started to have a look around. Ordinary place, but done up. Coat closet right near the front door. Livin' room on the right, a hall leadin' straight ahead."

"Okay. What did you do next?"

"Checked out the coat closet to see how many people might be livin' there. Looked like only one—a woman. Then went down the hall—kind of open, actually, not really a hall."

"Keep going."

"After the livin' room was a little sort of office like. I just kinda looked in there. Nothin' 'cept a computer, some writin' on the screen. Anyways, I don't fool with that electronic stuff. Too heavy and not worth much any more. There's a little bath off the hall. Went in the kitchen—nothin' there—then upstairs."

"Did you see anybody, hear anything?"

Maguire shook his head.

"For the recorder, you've got to answer out loud."

Headshake again, then "No."

"Okay. Keep going—" Mike glanced at the arrest report. "No, wait a minute. Go back. Says here there were a pair of women's sandals on the floor in that office. Near the computer. Did you see them?"

"Jeez, I don't remember seein' 'em." Shakes his head. "Just don't remember that at all."

"Okay, go on then."

"Went upstairs. Three bedrooms and a bath off the hallway. Two of 'em had beds and stuff but didn't look used, so I just headed straight for the master bedroom. That's where the stuff would be anyways. Saw a wallet and keychain on the bureau, knew right away I had to get outta there pronto." He stopped again.

"Because you figured somebody had to be in the house?"

"Women don't go out and leave their keys and wallet."

"But you still didn't see anybody?"

"No way."

"So what did you do then?"

"Grabbed the cards and cash outta the wallet, coupla pieces of jewelry off the bureau, ran downstairs."

"How much cash?"

"Four hundred, round numbers."

"You didn't see her?"

Maguire reached out, gripped Mike's arm, squeezed. "Honest shit; I never seen her. I heard them say she was in the bathroom—that's what the cops said. I didn't go in there. You never find nothin' in the bathroom. That's why I don't go in there. I swear, honest to Christ, I never seen her."

Too defensive. "So you never saw her at all?"

"That's right." Maguire leaned forward. "You gotta believe me. I had nothin' to do with it."

"Okay. I believe you." Sure. "After you found the stuff in the bedroom, you left?"

"Lit right out of there. In and out is my system anyways." Proud of his methodology.

"And that's when the police caught you?"

"Yeah, goin' out the side door. Damn cat was tryin' to get in and I was tryin' to get out without lettin' him in. I was afraid if he got in they'd get in a fight, raise all hell. I had to push him away with my foot."

"They?"

"Yeah, him'n the other cat, the one was already in there."

"The *other* one? You didn't mention any cat."

"In that room, the room where the computer was. An office, like. The cat was there when I went in. Sittin' in a chair. Layin' down, actually. Lookin' at me."

"Well, that's probably not important, but you have to tell me everything you saw, everything you noticed. It's impossible to know whether even a small detail might prove valuable later on."

"Well that's where I saw it—the cat, I mean. And that computer was on, 'cause I saw stuff on the screen—words."

"Okay. How come you were going out through that door instead of the way you came in?"

" 'Cause somebody was at the front door."

Surprise registered on Mike's face. "How did you know that?"

"I heard the bell ring."

Mike rolled his eyes. "You didn't mention that before. I need you to tell me everything, even if it doesn't seem important to you."

"Okay. I heard the bell ring—chimes, sort of—so I went out the side door."

"And that's when you saw the cop."

"Yeah."

"Did you say anything to him?"

Maguire looked at the table.

"Did you say anything to him?"

"I guess I did."

"What did you say?"

"I guess I said, 'Alarm?' Somethin' like that."

Mike could not avoid smiling. "That was a little bit of a tipoff, wasn't it?"

Maguire stared at him, added nothing.

"What happened next?"

"They asked what I was doin' in the house."

"They?"

"Another cop was there too."

"What did you say?"

"Nothin'."

"Was that your answer to the police, or did you simply not say anything?"

"I didn't say anythin'."

"Good. Anything else?"

"Well, they read me my rights, and when we got to the station they made me empty my pockets out, and naturally they saw the stuff."

"What stuff?"

"Coupla trinkets. Necklace, diamond earrings, I guess — though they could be fake. It's hard to tell nowadays," he confided, shaking his head at the duplicity of man. "They took my gloves, and the key, too."

"The house key?"

Maguire nodded, added, "My own ones too."

Mike glanced at the arrest report. "You had all this stuff in your jacket pocket?"

"Why I only take the small stuff."

"Okay, start when you were in the bedroom. When did you first see Sheila Graham—the dead woman?"

Maguire leaned forward, his face taut. "I told you—I never saw her at all—*ever*. That's the God's honest truth. You have to believe me!"

Okay, not working. Mike changed path. "Did you have any conversation with the police about those items in your pocket?"

"They just asked me where I got 'em."

"And what did you say?"

"I didn't say nothin'. I just shut my mouth."

"Good. The arrest report says you had some credit cards too. Did you look at any of the cards to see whose name was on them?"

Maguire shook his head vigorously. "No. Didn't. Didn't want to take the time. Wouldn't matter anyway."

"Let's go back a bit. You say you never saw the woman."

"Jesus Christ, I swear I didn't see no woman." He raised his hand, palm forward. "The only livin' thing I saw in the whole house was that cat—and the other one—outside."

Living thing.

"Okay. Let's go back to the woman. The arrest report says she was found in the tub. You never went in the bathroom?"

"Oh, Jesus Christ no! How many times do I have to tell you? I swear it on my life!" His fist pounded the table top. "I had no reason to go in the bathroom. There's never any stuff in there. Never!" He struck the table again.

"Okay, when you did get outside, that's when you ran into the police?"

Maguire nodded, added a "Yes."

"You asked if there was an alarm. Did you say anything else to them?"

"They asked me if I lived there—if I was the owner. I didn't say nothin'."

"Good. Were you carrying your clipboard?"

"Yeah. They grabbed it, looked at the samples, asked if I'd mind waitin' while one of 'em checked out things inside. That's when he found the . . . the body, I guess."

Maguire placed his hands on the table, rose slightly, again leaned toward Mike. "You've got to believe me! I may be a burglar, but I never had nothin' to do with no murder. That's not my game, and anybody who knows me'll tell you."

Mike liked the "*may be* a burglar" part. No one admits responsibility for anything. But the man's denial did have the ring of truth.

Mike said, "So far, there's no proof that the woman didn't simply have an accident in her own bathroom. Things like that happen all the time. People have a heart attack, drown. Or trip and fall, bang their head. Or do drugs and pass out. Look at all those movie stars. Whatever you can think up, it's happened."

"Yeah." Maguire frowned. "Look, somethin' I've gotta say to you, somethin' you've gotta unnerstand. I can't stay in this place. You've gotta get me out."

Mike shook his head. "That'll be tough. There's a good chance I could get you admitted to bail on the burglary charge, but there's a dead woman on the scene. You can bet the DA'll bring an indictment for murder against you and ask the court to keep you incarcerated."

"Murder!" The man seemed genuinely shocked. "Murder! That's crazy."

"Crazy or not, we'll have to deal with it."

"I'll kill myself rather than stay in this shithole. I can't stand to be locked up."

Mike thought of suggesting, "You may have to kill yourself then," but decided against it. Such an offering would at the very least carry a distinct possibility of interfering with collection of his fee. "We're going to try to get you out on bail, but it'll be tricky. Anyway, you can't testify at the bail hearing."

"Why not?"

"You'd just hurt your case."

Maguire shot him a disbelieving look.

Mike said, "Let me tell you how it would go, okay?"

Maguire nodded.

"The Assistant DA cross-examines you. He says, 'Do you have a regular day job?' "

Maguire listened.

Mike said, "Okay. Now you answer."

"No."

"You file a tax return last year?"

Headshake.

"That's a 'No.' Where'd you get the money to buy your house?"

Maguire waved his hands.

"Where do you work?"

Maguire opened his mouth, but no words came out.

"Who is your employer?"

Blank face; no response.

"What are your hours of employment?"

His client-to-be slouched.

"Do you get a W-2 every January?"

No answer.

"How many years have you spent breaking into homes?"

Silence.

A rapid-fire series of questions now. "What's your business address?" "Where did you get the money to buy your car?" "Why do you carry a business card for a non-existent business?" "How did you get into the Graham house?" "Was Sheila Graham on the downstairs level when you first saw her?" "How many women have you killed?"

Finally Mike stopped. "Have I made my point?"

They spent the next hour going over the details of Maguire's observations during his time in the house.

Eventually Mike turned to the most important subject. "We have the matter of a fee to discuss. I need $40,000 to defend the burglary and larceny charges, but that's not going to do it. I'm sure the DA will waive the preliminary hearing and go directly to the grand jury with a murder charge. I can guarantee you're going to have to defend a murder indictment. That costs more—a lot more."

Maguire didn't ask the obvious question. He asked another: "What does that mean, waive somethin'?"

"If there's a preliminary hearing, witnesses have to testify. So they're committed to the record and we can use it against them later, at the trial. Plus we get to cross-examine them at the preliminary inquiry."

He continued. "The DA doesn't like that, so he'll take the case into the grand jury, where everything's secret—but we do get a copy of that transcript. That's what waiving the preliminary hearing means."

"Oh."

"So it'll cost you 200K. That's for the murder trial, and believe me, that's a good price. And it doesn't include any appeal. Do you have that kind of money?"

"I thought you said forty."

"That was for burglary, and I threw in the larceny charges. The two hundred is for murder; it includes burglary and whatnot."

"Jesus! I didn't murder anybody. I didn't even *see* her."

Yeah, sure you didn't. "So do you have it?"

"I can get you fifty quick. And I think I got somethin' maybe worth the other—a lot more, pro'bly—but I ain't sure yet."

"Can you get the fifty to me right away? That'll at least get you started." Fifty thousand dollars would carry Mike through the next few months.

"Yeah. I'll have my girl bring it to you."

"What about the rest?"

"I'll have her bring you a sample of that stuff too, and you can find out what it's worth."

"What is it?"

"Stamps. Rare stamps."

"Humph. When?"

"Tomorrow afternoon. I'll have her bring everything to you tomorrow afternoon."

"Another thing," Mike said. "I always want to know who recommended me to take on a case. Where did you get my name?"

"My girl gave it to me. A friend of hers knows you—or knows *about* you."

"What's his name?"

"Forget. And it's not a him—it's 'her.' She's a hairdresser, does my girl's hair."

"Okay. Thanks. I'll ask your girl when I meet her."

Mike and his new client both stood, shook hands. Mike turned toward the door.

"Wait a minute," Maguire said. "I remember. Her name's Florence, like that place in Italy." He grinned at Mike, obviously proud of his recall. "Name association, you know?"

Mike smiled. Flo. You never know. "Thanks. I'll mention my appreciation to her."

He pressed the buzzer to announce his intention to leave. A uniformed officer approached to unlock the door.

*   *   *

Mike drove back to his office, parked. Outside the front door of his building he stopped, leaned over and groped for the brass hook, partially hidden beneath a floorboard at the side of the porch. He unhooked the key and pocketed it.

When he entered the office, Kaitlin was typing at her keyboard. He said, "I've been thinking about this for a while and decided not to leave our 'emergency' key by the front entrance any more. Somebody might spot it and break in. We'll just have to make sure not to lock ourselves out."

"No problem, Mike. I always reset the lock even if I'm just stepping outside for a minute. Anyway, I always take my key. How'd it go with the new client?"

"Okay, but it's going to be a tough case."

"Well, that's the kind you like. What's it about?"

"Right now it's burglary, but it'll be murder before the week's out."

"Murder! Sounds exciting."

* * *

In a post-hiring conversation, Mike had called Kaitlin's law school adviser, thanked him for his recommendation.

Harvey Katz taught criminal law and evidence at Suffolk. "Glad to help," he had said. "Any time."

"I'm genuinely grateful for your thoughts."

"So you owe me," Harvey said. "I'm curious to know. Did she tell you about the bonds?"

"Bonds? What bonds?"

"Ah, she didn't tell you. That's like her." He elaborated. "A few months ago she hailed a taxi and found an envelope on the seat. She looked inside and discovered bearer bonds. Ten of them, $100,000 each. She took the cab right to police headquarters. They were able to find out who had most recently been a passenger, and returned the bonds to the owner."

"God, that's quite a story. Not many people would do that. *Bearer* bonds. She could've sold them and pocketed the money, walked away. She must be super honest."

"She is."

"She get any reward?"

"Don't think so."

"Jesus, you'd think the owner would've given her something handsome."

"I guess her reward is her clear conscience."

"Yeah. Well, thanks again for recommending her. I feel confident she'll work out."

In the brief time since her hiring, Kaitlin had shown intelligence and strong motivation. On her first day she had fully explored the office to become familiar with its layout, equipment, and other resources. Later she had spent considerable time studying the Charles Bragg lithographic prints mounted on the reception-area walls.

"These are fabulous," she said to Mike. "It seems odd, though, that two quite different ones have the same title."

"Yes. You mean *Cross Examination*—with no hyphen. It's my favorite."

"Which one?"

"Oh, the one with no jurors—just the judge, the interrogating attorney, and the witness."

"I like that one best too. The witness is so pompous, confident, self-assured—complacent, even."

"Until you look at his hands."

"Yes. Crunching the witness box, the wood crushed—cracking and splintering from his powerful grip."

"Right. That's every trial attorney's dream."

She frowned. "I can believe it, but does it ever really happen?"

"Not like you see on TV and in the movies, but sometimes. Although rarely." He called her attention to the print's emphasis of the witness's posture. "Do you notice that he's standing uncommonly erect?"

"Yes. Looks like a Very Important Person. Don't most witnesses sit? I see that the witness in the other Cross Examination print is sitting. He looks terrified—but he has good reason. Both the judge and the lawyer have horns."

"Not too different from real life," Mike said. "But to answer your question, in this state most witnesses sit while giving testimony. Often, witnesses who insist on standing tend to be arrogant, slippery—tricky. Very difficult to cross-examine. And they almost never give even an inch."

Kaitlin said, "I'd love to get a print of the one crunching the witness stand."

"I'm pretty sure you can order one on line. Just search Charles Bragg and the title. In fact, I wouldn't be surprised if Bragg has a site himself. He seems to be very successful."

Mike had no means to know that before long he would be cross-examining a witness who would crunch the witness box.

* * *

It was all Simone's fault. Everything.

Sometimes Mike's head still ached from her husband's kicks. Vicious kicks. The neurologist had told Mike it would probably hurt off and on for at least several months. Perhaps even years. "Prolonged, dull pain"—the doctor's words. Accurate.

Mike had known the affair shouldn't—couldn't—go on. Never should have started, actually. That's why he had stopped it. He had told her flat out, "No more! No more! It's over!" It was plain to him, had to be to her too, that something bad would necessarily come of it.

Dick Johnson, Mike's law partner—Simone's husband—was not a numbskull. Eventually he would see what was going on. Everybody else in the office knew.

One night—the night of the vicious kicks—Dick finally caught on.

It was the gynecological examination table that did it, Mike sometimes felt. Simone loved that stirruped table, the spot where they eventually would have wound up that night his partner found them, his wife's thighs splayed for maximum access. A shock to all—Dick was supposed to be in San Antonio taking depositions. Mike later learned that the case had been settled. His partner returned home early.

In truth Mike's "library" wasn't much of one. The former first-floor bedroom also doubled as his conference room. Bookcases strung along the inside wall, the wheeled examination table jammed into an outside corner. Six serviceable chairs on casters surrounded the mahogany conference table, all picked up second-hand.

Mike could do his legal research on line, but kept some law books mostly for show: the black set of the *Massachusetts General Laws Annotated*, a few volumes of the *Massachusetts Practice Series*, along with a treatise on cross-examination techniques in criminal defense cases. Clients are reassured when they see that their lawyer maintains a law library. They think he's actually read the books.

Mike had inherited the examination stand along with numerous other medical artifacts when he bought the house from a retiring OB/GYN specialist who kept an office there. Mike had considered discarding the special-use item; his decision to keep it was basically whimsical. Who knew to what good uses it might be put, he had thought at the time.

"Irishmen are the most underrated lovers in the world," he had explained to Simone, and demonstrated what he meant.

She agreed, with one caveat: "You have to find the right Irishman, and I did."

His two-year suspension resulted from Dick Johnson's complaint to the Board of Bar Overseers charging Mike with making false representations to the court about his inability to obtain the appearance of a witness at trial, when Mike had in fact procured the witness's absence.

Now Mike's law firm was gone, dissolved, and he was back practicing law alone after the two-year hiatus courtesy of the Board of Bar Overseers. He had moved back upstairs to the second floor of the two-family at 71 College Avenue he had bought six years ago with proceeds from the Tucker settlement.

The building was in a desirable location close to Davis Square, and about a mile from Tufts University. What had been second-floor offices in his firm were once again Mike's apartment, just as when he purchased the building.

Kaitlin's desk sat right inside the reception area entrance, originally the first-floor living room of the two-family house. Besides the reception desk and chair, the furniture consisted of an oriental rug, tan leather sofa with two matching leather-upholstered chairs, curtains and two table lamps. The several Charles Bragg prints provided decoration.

At the reception room's far end stood a fireplace with no screen, the chimney visible above the mantel. The brickwork had been painted, a crime which Mike felt ought to be punishable by sentence in hell. Beyond the fireplace was a sunroom, unused.

Two wide, multi-pane French doors opened to Mike's office. The doors were usually left open, but when in conference they were closed and the Venetian blinds adjusted to afford privacy. The remaining rooms on the first floor consisted of the kitchen—still kept as a kitchen—two bedrooms, and a full bathroom. The front bedroom was now Mike's library and conference room, while the rear bedroom served as a spare office and file room.

At his desk Mike loaded the digital recording of his jailhouse interview with Maguire onto his computer, ran the speech recognition program, and dictated additional notes of his conversation with Maguire. The program converted his input to text, did a good job of recognizing words despite not having been trained to his client's voice. Later Kaitlin would clean up the transcription, and he would do a final edit.

Somehow, antiseptic jailhouse odors seemed to linger in his nostrils. He decided to shower before meeting Anne for dinner in the Back Bay.

CHAPTER 9

Mike arrived at Steve's a few minutes early. Steve's, a small Greek-American restaurant in the Back Bay section of Boston, sat right across from the Boston Architectural Center, a concrete monolith. Over the years Steve's had won several "Best of Boston" awards. It was a congenial place, informal, having no more than twenty tables, the food good and not pricey. The restaurant held a special place in Mike and Anne's memories because they had gone there on their first date. Anne Carlson was the only woman with whom Mike had maintained a friendship after their affair ended.

He took a window table. He and Anne both favored this particular spot because it was so much fun to watch the parade of people on the sidewalks. All ages and dress mixtures crowded the streets this day, many of them college students of a variety of ethnic backgrounds. Anne popped in a few minutes later, waved with a smile and hurried to the seat opposite Mike. He stood, adjusted her chair, slid it in as she sat. He bent and kissed her cheek.

She said, "You order yet?"

"Just got here."

"Good. I'm starving." Foregoing the menu, she glanced at the specials on the blackboard posted near the far entrance. "I'm going to have the grape leaves special: stuffed with ground lamb and rice topped with egg-lemon sauce."

"Sounds yummy. I've decided on the moussaka."

When the waitress took their order, Anne added, "And a glass of your house wine."

"A Heineken for me," Mike said, "with the moussaka." The eggplant casserole, stuffed with lamb, was far too rich for him, but what the hell. Once in a while is okay.

Anne's dark hair, with a natural wave, was worn off the shoulder. Her skin tone was light, except that her prominent cheekbones always seemed to look as though just moments earlier they had been burnished with blush. Of slender figure, her legs were such that Mike used to tease her about how "those sticks" could possibly support her. Hands and feet finely sculpted, wrists narrow, features delicate without fragility.

She was a playful and cheery woman, always ready to laugh, make fun, and have a good time—odd characteristics for a psychologist, Mike thought. Sometimes he regretted their breakup, but he knew that they could not have continued. His fault, no doubt at all. It would have ended in disaster, just as had his marriage. Much better that he and Anne stay friends.

"There's something you might be able to help me with," she said. "Let me ask you while we're waiting. You know computers, right?"

"Well, I took a couple of computer science courses, but that was quite a while ago." His look told her to go on.

"In my advanced psych class I have eight seniors—all boys—who've been scoring much higher on tests than they should. I'm sure they're cheating, but I can't figure out how they're doing it."

"What makes you so sure? Couldn't it just be that they're studying harder?"

"Not these boys. They never even open a book unless they absolutely have to."

"What kind of grades are they getting?"

"A's. Straight A's on the last four tests."

"Let's see if we can work out a solution. Somehow they must be getting the answers in advance of the test. How do you prepare the tests? On your computer?"

She nodded.

"And you create them yourself—they're not standardized tests, or taken off the Web or something?"

She adopted an indignant look. "Really, Mike!"

"All right. Sorry. What computer do you use?"

"My laptop."

"What kind of test is it? Essay, multiple choice, true-fal—"

"Multiple choice. Twenty questions. Five choices of answer for each question."

"So once they have the answers, all they need is a crib sheet, right?"

She nodded. "1c, 2e, 3a, and so on—pretty simple."

"Actually, they don't even need the numbers. Just the answer letter. They could make up a sentence using the first letter of each word as the answer. Like in your example: Copy Every Answer . . . . C. E. A. Easy as one two three."

"Mike, it sounds to me as though you might've been pretty good at cheating."

"On my oath, *never*! Wait!—Once! One time! Same kind of test as yours. I didn't know the answer to one question and looked at the paper of the guy sitting next to me. He was a dummy and I figured he'd get it wrong, so I picked one of the other four answers."

"Did you get it right?"

"I don't remember, but I got an A in the course."

The waitress served their dishes. Mike tasted the moussaka. "Delicious."

"Mmmm," Anne said. "The lamb is out of this world."

Mike looked at her dish. The stuffed grape leaves seemed particularly inviting. Maybe he should have ordered that. Anne saw his glance, cut off a portion of her serving and deposited it on his plate.

He tasted it and said, "You're right, but the moussa-ka's great too. You want a taste?"

She shook her head. "No, this is fine. I've got to watch my figure."

This falsehood he ignored. "Tell me how you develop the test, what you do with it from beginning to end."

"I put it together on my laptop, at home. Then, on test day I print the copies at school."

"Where do you keep the tests until you pass them out?"

"In my desk at school." She anticipated his next question. "It's locked, and I have the only key."

"That you know of."

"Yes, but they couldn't get it that way because I'm almost always in my room after I print the tests."

"We'll say your desk is secure, then. That leaves two possible weak points. One is your laptop itself. The other is the department's computer network."

"Unless somebody's got a tap on my brain."

"You psychologists are all alike."

"Don't kid yourself. That'll be coming next."

"It wouldn't surprise me . . . . When you print the test at school, how do you do it? Do you send it from your lap-top to some other location on the network, or . . . ? Is there a wireless network, or Ethernet, or —"

"I have a connector at my desk. One of those things you plug into, like a telephone jack only it's bigger."

"Ethernet. But your laptop must have WiFi too. Where's your desk in relation to the printer?"

"Just down the hall. A few doors."

"In a room by itself?"

"No, there are other things in there too. Desktop com-puters for us to use, a fax machine, projection viewers, stuff like that."

"How long between when you send the file to the printer and you pick up the output?"

"Hardly any time at all. I go right down and get it."

"Is there usually anyone in the room?"

"Sometimes. It depends. But when someone is there it'd only be one of the teachers, and I can't imagine them being involved in this."

"No, wouldn't seem like it. So it's not likely one of the students could have been waiting there, picked up the test, made a quick copy, then put it back again, right?"

"Not a chance. Anyway, how would he know when I was going to print it? He wouldn't."

"True. So we can exclude that possibility—but they could plug into the network, or maybe pick off your laptop's wireless signal. What about your laptop? I don't suppose you have it with you every minute."

"No, but when I don't, I shut it down and lock it in my desk, or take it home. I had one stolen once and it took me forever to recreate my files."

"I had two hard drives fail in law school, so I know what you went through." He turned to a new aspect. "What about backups?"

"I store my files on a flash drive at home."

They decided to let the matter percolate for a while and return to it later. When they finished the main course, both passed on dessert and lingered over decaf.

Mike said, "I think I see a way to catch them, and we don't even have to know where the leak is."

Anne leaned toward him. "Tell me."

Mike described his plan.

"I love it!" Anne giggled. "Let's hope it works."

"It will. When's the next test?"

"Friday."

"When can I get a copy of it?"

"I'll email it to you tonight as soon as I get home."

* * *

Anne's message read, "Here's the next quiz, along with the key to the correct answers." Attached to the message was a twenty-question quiz. Mike raced through the test, bothered that he did not know the answer to even a single question, although he did guess four correctly. Four out of twenty: only twenty percent. Pretty abysmal.

The test dealt with color blindness. The first question read:

> (1) Photoreceptors in the retina of the eye, called cones, contain these photosensitive pigments:
>
> (a) red
> (b) green
> (c) blue
> (d) all of the above
> (e) none of the above.

Because he knew that television sets and computer monitors use an RGB color system, Mike correctly guessed (d).

He stumbled on the next one:

> (2) The most common form of color blindness involves difficulty in perceiving
>
> (a) red and green
> (b) blue and green
> (c) blue and yellow
> (d) green and yellow
> (e) red and yellow.

He guessed blue and green. The key showed (a) to be the right answer.

Mike missed the next question too:

(3) The most common form of color blindness is

(a) inherited
(b) found in 8% of males
(c) found in only 0.4% of females
(d) all of the above
(e) none of the above.

Surprisingly, (d) was correct.

After completing the quiz he rearranged the question subsections and created a new key. When finished, he called Anne at home. "I've got this done, but I forgot to ask you something."
"That was quick."
"How many kids will be taking this quiz?"
"Twenty-nine."
"Okay, I'll print thirty—an extra one for you."
"Wait a minute. Can't you just e-mail it back to me and I'll print it?"
"That would give them another chance to get it."
"Yes, I see. You're right."
"I'll print these and get them to you."

* * *

Anne was already seated when Mike arrived at the café on Walnut Street—another favored spot when they had been dating. She had taken a corner table near the front window, and already ordered. Before her sat two large, heavy, earthenware cups, brimming with chocolate café latte topped with whipped cream.
He placed the stack of printouts on the table and took a seat opposite her. Today she wore a celery-colored suit with a mauve blouse, colors which Mike thought would not blend but in fact went well together. Her face appeared clear, lips full.

"You look great," he said. Sometimes he wondered if he had made a mistake when . . . .

"Thanks."

Mike sipped his latte. "Rich flavor. It's nice to be a hedonist." He relished another sip, rolled his tongue around the inside of his mouth before addressing the test. "I found the questions quite interesting. Felt a little guilty I didn't know any of the answers. Should've known some, at least. I was especially surprised to learn color blindness mostly affects males."

"It's passed through the mother, you know. Probably Nature's way of giving a little bit of payback."

Why do women always say stuff like this, Mike thought. Must be some kind of perpetual grievance, an eternal sense of feminine disadvantage.

He said, "Seriously, to think that almost one out of every ten guys I know is color blind—that's quite something."

" 'Color blind' is a misnomer. Most people we call color blind are actually suffering from a color deficit. The red-green form of color blindness, which is most common, permits people to see other colors. They just have trouble with red and green. It's not that they can't *see* what's there; they can—they're not blind. They simply see things in shades of gray."

"I'd think that could be a major problem. Not seeing a stop light, for instance."

"Well, they learn to adjust. In that situation, of course, they can tell from the position of the lights. Red on top, and so on."

"Sure, but all the same, I think it would be difficult."

"Probably is, but I wouldn't know because I'm a woman, and the eight percent of the men I know who statistics say are color blind are afraid to admit it. It's like asking for directions. They have to keep up a front of invincibility."

Mike felt that she was only partly joking. To get off this new slant, he tapped the stack of printouts and explained the changes he had made, showing her the revised tests, describing what she should do.

"You need to send your original quiz to the printer just as you normally would, and print the twenty-nine copies—thirty if you want one for yourself. Pick them up and take them to your classroom. But when you get there, and you're ready to administer the test, pull my printouts out of your briefcase and distribute them instead of the ones you just printed. Then we'll see what happens."

Anne grinned. "I like it. I think we're going to catch some cheaters."

"I do too. What time's the test?"

"My first afternoon class. A little after one."

"Let me know."

"I'll call you."

They left the café and she headed up the street away from him, toward the high school. For a moment Mike watched her legs flash beneath her skirt. Remembering. Then he shook his head and returned to his car. On the way back to Somerville he detoured to the Colchester Police Station and got the key to the Graham house.

He stopped at a nearby hardware store on Main Street and had a duplicate key made. Now he could have access to the house any time he wished. The DA didn't need to know the details of his comings and goings. Tomorrow morning he would pay his first visit to the crime scene.

On his return to the office Mike called Monument Video and arranged to meet a videographer at the Graham house the next day. Then he reread the arrest report. The initial incident complaint had come from a neighbor named Ralph Burgoyne, identified as a retired police officer. Mike figured that a former cop would be unwilling to cooperate with him, but better to find out for sure how the ground lies rather than get ambushed in a courtroom.

Only one telephone listing appeared for a Ralph Burgoyne, this at 74 Brandywine Road, right next door to the Graham house. Mike tapped out the numbers. A woman answered on the second ring. From her voice Mike guessed that she was in her late forties or early fifties.

Mike said, "Is Mr. Burgoyne home? I'd like to speak with him."

"He's always home. Who's this?"

Mike explained who he was and the purpose of his call. She said, "Just a minute."

Soon a man said, "This is Ralph. You're callin' about the Graham woman? Terrible thing. Terrible. You can believe me that."

"Yes, it was." Mike waited a suitable moment, then said, "I'd like to come by and chat with you if you don't mind. I won't take much of your time."

"It's not *time* I mind. Got plenty of that."

They arranged to meet the following day, an hour before Mike's appointment with the videographer.

CHAPTER 10

In order to have time to scout Sheila Graham's neighborhood, Mike arrived fifteen minutes early for his Burgoyne appointment. "Remington Arms," a large sign announced at the entrance to the moderately upscale complex. Mike speculated that the name might represent the developer's idea of a mild joke at the expense of the firearms manufacturer.

The houses were all similar in design, two to four attached townhomes, each with at least one wall shared with a neighbor. Neatly groomed shrubbery dotted the landscape. Grass freshly mown. No potholes in the streets. The entire complex well tended.

Yellow crime scene tape no longer cordoned off the Graham house. The Burgoyne house was similar to Sheila Graham's, but basically a mirror image. The two attached homes shared a wall, but held no property jointly with any other house.

Viewed from the street, the Graham house was on the right, Burgoyne's on the left. The garages were underneath the houses, apparently taking up about one-third of the rear part of the cellar.

At exactly 11:00 AM Mike rang the Burgoyne's doorbell. A short, stocky woman wearing a neatly pressed blue house-dress and wooden clogs answered the door.

"You Mr. Ratigan?"

Mike nodded, offered his card. She said, "You're right on time. That's what I like. Come on in."

She escorted him into the living room and introduced her husband. "This is Ralph."

A husky, gray-haired man wearing a heavy cotton bathrobe sat sunken into a black vinyl recliner. A large-screen rear-projection television set in the opposite corner was tuned to a game show, sound turned high.

He clicked a button on the remote control, muting the sound, then half rose from his chair, bracing one leg against the base, leaned toward Mike, held out his hand. The man's eyeglasses slid to the end of his nose; he pushed them back up. Favoring one leg, he seemed to totter in place.

"Pleased to meet you, Mr. Burgoyne."

"Ralph. Call me Ralph. Have a seat." He waved in the general direction of an overstuffed easy chair next to his own, then plopped back into the recliner. Mike sat on the edge of the easy chair.

"Terrible thing," Burgoyne said. "I still can't believe it happened. Can't believe it." He made a clucking noise with his tongue. "She was a nice enough girl, in spite of the trouble we had. Wasn't her fault, really, I'd have to say that."

"Yes," Mike agreed, wondering what kind of trouble Burgoyne was referring to. "As I indicated on the phone, I'm representing the defendant—the man the police have charged with burglary. We want to get statements—"

"Burglary! What about murder? I thought it was murder."

"All we know at this point is the woman apparently drowned in her bathtub. So far as I'm aware, no one has any reason to believe it was anything other than a natural death. She might have had a heart attack or stroke—or anything."

Burgoyne nodded.

"So, what I'm trying to do is get statements from everybody who might know something about what went on. I understand you're the one who called the police. It would be useful to know what caused you to make that call."

Burgoyne looked at Mike steadily for a moment before responding. "I'm an ex-cop, you know. Patrolman fourteen years. Out on disability. They only gave me a seventy percent though, and I'm a hundred percent disabled. Bastids—I have to fight with 'em for every fuckin' nickel."

He caught himself and looked toward the kitchen. "Goin' up 'fore the review board again next month. You can't believe how cheap them sonsabitches are. A nasty bunch of penny pinchers, the whole lot of 'em."

He halted and peered at Mike through thick lenses before going on. "You ever have a government job?" He pronounced it "gummint."

Mike shook his head.

Ralph nodded with satisfaction. "Lucky. You don't know what it's like, then. If you're smart you won't ever find out. You can believe me that. They try and screw you at every turn." Suddenly he said, "Whadda you want to know?"

"You called the police, right?"

"Sure did."

Burgoyne didn't immediately go into his story, so Mike asked the question. "What made you do that?"

He took no notes; experience had taught that witnesses tend to be less forthcoming if he did. He would record his recollections later, as soon as he returned to the office. If he developed a rapport with Burgoyne, he would record the man's statement later.

"It was that goddamn cat—great big thing. Big as a mountain lion. She knew it was drivin' me crazy. Screeched so loud you'd think one of the neighborhood girls was gettin' raped. I don't know how many times I'd told her to keep the goddamn cat in, and this wasn't the first time I had to call the station."

Ralph's eye strayed to the television screen for a second, then he looked back toward Mike and spoke in a conspiratorial tone.

"I have trouble sleepin'. Take all kindsa meds. It's my back. Constant pain. That's why I'm out on disability. Lotsa times have to sleep durin' the day too. Anyhow, that cat of hers sits right outside my bedroom window and meows—no, screeches—for hours. I used to call the Graham woman and she'd get the cat in, but I got so pissed off the last coupla times I called the station and a coupla the boys came over and took care of the situation.

"I figured that'd be the end of it and she wouldn't let the cat out no more, but when it happened again that day, I got really pissed and called the station right up. I wasn't gonna put up with that shit no more, you know what I mean? I've suffered enough. A man's gotta get his sleep."

His eyes flicked back to the screen, but a new thought quickly intruded. He glanced at Mike and said, "I've got a lawyer—Caccavaro—over in Cambridge—Central Square—you know him?—anyways he's all right but he only got me seventy percent and I'm a hundred percent if you ever saw one. You know him?"

Mike shook his head.

"Not a bad guy, but—You ever get involved in comp work?" Burgoyne held up his hand before Mike could reply. "Helpin' guys injured on the job with their disability claims?"

Mike admitted that he had no such experience. "Sorry, like to help you, but I just do criminal work now." He steered the discussion back to the reason for his visit. "Did you know the Graham woman well?"

"Naw, never saw too much of her. I don't get out hardly at all. I'm pretty much tied to this chair and my bed, though I can get 'round if I have to. Did that day, when all the ruckus started next door."

"Ruckus?"

"You know, the police comin'. I had to go over and check out what was goin' on."

He stopped and went back to the original question. "Besides, her garage is on the other side and she almost always drives— drove—right in there, so we didn't get to see her unless she happened to be outside lookin' after her flowers or somethin' like that. She worked a lot of hours at the school, but I know she told Mame she had an office in her house."

"Mame?"

He nodded toward the kitchen. "Mame—my wife. Real name's Catherine, but nobody calls her that."

"So you didn't notice anything unusual about your neighbor recently?"

The ex-cop shook his head. " 'Cause I didn't see her."

"And your wife—Mame?"

Burgoyne hollered to the kitchen, "Mame, you seen Miss Graham lately—in the last coupla weeks?"

Mrs. Burgoyne clogged to the entry and stood in the doorway. "Nope, didn't see her at all. She's never 'round much. Always at that school. Works all the time."

"Sorry," Ralph said. "Guess we're not much help."

"Not true at all," Mike responded. "You've been a great deal of help already. Let me ask you a couple of questions about some other things though. Do you know if Ms. Graham had a boyfriend—or a male friend—who visited regularly—" Mike interrupted himself. "Strike the 'regularly.' Did she have a boyfriend or anyone like that you know of?"

"Nope. Not that I know of."

"What about friends or other visitors?"

"Nope. Same thing there. Sister came once in a while, that's all. Like I said, we talked only on accounta that cat."

"What about people hanging around the neighbor-hood? You notice any strangers lately, cars that don't be-long here?"

"Don't get out, so you'd have to ask Mame 'bout that." He hollered toward the kitchen again and his wife once more appeared in the entryway. Mike repeated the ques-tions and she denied having knowledge of anything un-usual.

Mike said to both of them, "What about break-ins? Any trouble like that around here?"

"Naw," Ralph answered, "this part of town's pretty safe." His wife nodded agreement while he went on. "You can ask down at the station house, but I bet we haven't had a burglary in this development since I've been here, and that's goin' on eight years now. Except for your cli-ent—Mr. what's-his-name— he's the first one."

"Maguire," Mike said, and felt obliged to point out, "He hasn't been convicted yet."

"True," Burgoyne acknowledged, "but from what the boys told me, it looks pretty bad for him. Anyways, he came right out and admitted it, didn't he?"

"I haven't seen the file yet, and we don't know what the evidence will be."

Mike stood, thanked Burgoyne for his time. The re-tired officer started to get up in that awkward way of his, but Mike said, "No, no. Stay right there. I can let myself out."

Mame went to the door with Mike and closed it be-hind him.

Once outside, Mike checked his watch. The video ap-pointment wasn't for another twenty minutes. Good. This would allow him time to survey the premises at leisure. He ambled next door and prepared to let himself in. His cellphone rang. The screen showed "Ratigan Law Cham-bers." His office calling.

Kaitlin said, "There's a Mr. Beaulieu here. He says he's a client of yours and he's going up to Montreal; he wants to leave a couple of cases here—attaché cases. He said it would be all right with you, but I thought I'd better make sure. I did check the client list and saw he's on there."

"Pierre. Yes, it's okay. Is he still there? Put him on."

Pierre Beaulieu, a counterfeiter who with Mike's help had twice managed to escape conviction, came on the line. A deep French accent ladened his speech.

"Allo, Mike. I knew it would be all right, but your beautiful young lady here . . . . Of course she did the right thing. What happened to Daisy—and the rest of your office?"

"Long story, Pierre. We had a little breakup, so now I'm back on my own. You're heading up north?"

"Few months this time. I figured you wouldn't mind holding onto my stuff for me. I'll pick it up when I get back."

"No problem. I assume it's the usual."

"Of course."

Mike wished Pierre well and asked him to put Kaitlin back on the line. No need for her to know.

"The cases are full of fake money. Pierre's a producer and uses the currency as a prop in movies and stage plays. Just pop it in the hall closet."

At the entrance to the Graham house he inserted the key in the lock, turned.

CHAPTER 11

The air smelled stale from the house being closed for days, so Mike left the front door ajar. Ample windows let enough light in to brighten the rooms; he opened a couple to let in fresh air.

The interior was essentially as Maguire had described, but the finish was superior to what the neighborhood suggested. In the entrance hall he found flooring of white marble striated with gray. Quartersawn maple floors in other rooms, glazed tile floors in kitchen and bath. Marble again on the master bath floor and part way up the walls. In the dining room a hand-painted mural—a fresco, actually—of a bucolic scene in which a country estate stood in the far distance. Sheila Graham must have had money.

Three 16 X 20 inch framed photographs of a tortoise-shell cat were mounted on the walls of the first-floor office, and in the kitchen, magnetic frames on the refrigerator held smaller snapshots of the pet. All showed full, rich colors reminding of fallen leaves in New England's peak foliage season. One photo showed Sheila Graham, a handsome woman, cuddling the cat in her arms—the animal hardly the "monster" Burgoyne had described. The victim's smile reflected a level of adoration most people reserve for fellow humans.

Mike wondered where the feline was now. No sign of its presence remained in the house, no food bowl or water dish. Someone must have taken custody of the animal and its paraphernalia.

En suite with the main bedroom, the master bathroom drew Mike's particular interest. The room was at least eight by twelve, with a half-walled area concealing a toilet and bidet. The tub, raised about two feet off the floor and surrounded by a mahogany base, was an oversized freestanding cast-iron Kohler whirlpool bath, porcelain enamelled in teal. Carpeted mahogany steps led up to the tub.

All of the fixtures had heavy brass faucets ornate in design. Like the tub, the dual lavatories, toilet, and bidet were finished in teal. The six-foot base cabinet holding the washbasins was mahogany, like the tub enclosure. Dual, mirrored medicine cabinets were inset in the wall above the sinks.

Unaccountably, the tub reminded Mike of one of the "Rumpole" episodes on public television where the story revolved around whether the husband—a judge—or wife suffered to sit next to the tap while bathing together.

Mike wondered whether Sheila Graham ever bathed with a man in this tub, and if so who sat next to the tap. Mike suddenly felt sad about the loss of this woman whom he had never known.

While waiting for the videographer, Mike returned to the first-floor office and took a seat at the computer. Green LED's (light emitting diodes) shone on the computer case and the monitor too. It struck him as odd that the computer and monitor were both still turned on, but he guessed that they had been on when Sheila Graham died and no one had ever thought to shut them down.

The mouse pad bore the face of the same cat whose image appeared in photographs displayed throughout the house. A large inkjet printer sat at the rear of the desk. A photograph of a cat rested in the ejection tray: same cat. Next to the printer, a telephone answering machine's red LED blinked the numeral 2.

Mike pushed the PLAY button and listened to the messages. In the first, he recognized Burgoyne's voice. "You're cat's at it again! If you don't get that little bastid out of here within ten minutes, I'm gonna call the cops. I've had it! I toldja! This is the last time—I toldja!" This was followed by the sound of a handset crashing onto its cradle. In a pleasant female voice, the timestamp on this message announced, "Thursday, May 18, 8:49 AM."

In the next message a male voice said, "Sheila, this is Dr. Fessenden. I'm waiting for you. Where are you? Did you forget? Call me. Let me know you're all right." The timestamp read fourteen minutes later, Thursday, May 18, 9:03 AM.

Mike picked up the handset and paced through the recent calls on the LCD display. The screen confirmed the times of the last two calls and showed the calling numbers, but not the callers' names. Prior calls were also shown. He dictated this information to the recorder on his cellphone. His computer program would transcribe it later.

Mike moved the computer mouse. The hard drive and fans whirred as they came up to speed. The screen popped to life, showing a list of files in the C:\ drive. When he started to read the first file name, a melodious voice called from the front door, "Hello! Anyone here?"

"Be right with you." Mike had expected a man, but was surprised to see an attractive young woman, blonde hair pulled back, gathered behind her neck. She wore a tan skirt, a light-brown sweater, and brown flats.

She was carrying a large video camera and a light mounted on a light stand. "Hi," she greeted with a ready smile.

He introduced himself. She set the light stand down and they shook hands.

"Jeri," she said. "Jeri Thompson."

Mike fished a card out of his card case and handed it to her. "You have one?"

She reached into a skirt pocket and passed one to him. His hand brushed hers briefly. The card confirmed her name and company, Monument Video, with an address in Charlestown.

"If it's okay with you," Jeri said, "I'll start upstairs, work my way back down. Just give me a minute to set up these lights and I'll get going."

Mike grasped the light stand. "Let me take this for you."

"Careful."

He followed her, carrying the light stand. "How long do you think you'll be?"

"Probably about forty minutes or so on the inside, then the outside'll take maybe another ten minutes."

As Jeri went from room to room, Mike trailed her, keeping out of the way. He learned that a couple of years ago she graduated from Emerson College, where she majored in film and video.

"So taping crime scenes helps you in your career?"

"Not at all. Just helps pay expenses while I wait for my 'big break.' This stuff is about as basic as you can get. We do it in 'high def,' though, so you'll really appreciate it if you project it in court, or have an HD monitor."

"Both."

While she was recording, Jeri told him that she had been involved in filming a half-dozen local independent movies, all of which failed to get distribution. She had also been a second-tier videographer in a documentary done in Providence. Final production was under way.

She grew animated describing her involvement in the productions, the contributions made by other members of the filming crews, the actors, the film editors—even the gofers. It seemed that everyone pitched in to do whatever job was necessary. Mike envied this sense of camaraderie. He had that once—until his partnership broke up.

She videoed the rooms and hallways, but spent extra time in the master bedroom and the bathroom where the body was found. She finished by videoing each first-floor room. After the final series of shots, she said, "I'm done in here now. I'll do the outside and that'll wrap it up."

"I want you to get something else too. In the den." Mike led Jeri there and pointed to the answering machine. "There are a couple of messages on here. I need them too."

He waited until she set up her tripod and camera before he pressed the PLAY button. With her lens trained on the answerer, the videographer recorded the Burgoyne message and the following one as well.

"Probably won't need them," Mike said, "but you never know."

He decided to check the answering machine's time against that displayed on his cellphone, which he knew to be extremely accurate.

He pressed the "Anno" button. The metallic voice said, "Friday, May 20, 12:43." The machine's internal clock was accurate.

When she went outside to videotape the exterior, Mike returned to the den. He moved the computer mouse, and the screen came to life. The time in the lower right-hand corner was accurate. He shut the computer down. Before leaving, he went to the side entrance to ensure that the slider was locked. He left through the front door and double locked it.

He found Jeri at the back of the building.

She said, "I'm just about finished. I'll be out of here in a couple of minutes. You don't need to stay if you don't want to."

"That's okay. I like the view."

She smiled faintly at this indirect compliment. In another minute she was ready to go.

Mike said, "Maybe you'd like to get a coffee or something."

She shook her head. "Can't; I've got to be in Weston in half an hour. I'm already running late."

With mild disappointment, he noted that she had not suggested another time. "A rain check then?"

"Yep, sure, a rain check." She smiled, extended her hand, and Mike shook it, unsure if she was confirming their hoped-for appointment, or simply being polite. Either way, he liked her firm grip and the smoothness of her hand. Especially the smoothness of her hand.

Jeri drove off. Mike had just started his car when his cellphone rang. The screen showed his office calling.

Kaitlin said, "A woman called—Elaine Fowler—and said you expect her to come in today. She'll be in around two. I figured you'd better know, in case . . . ."

"Thanks. I'm coming back now."

Maguire's girl. Fowler—what a name!—worse even than "Florence." Coming in with the fifty thousand. What would she bring with her worth the other one hundred fifty? It had better be good.

CHAPTER 12

Kaitlin tapped on the door, leaned around it. "Elaine Fowler's here to see you." She stepped aside, and the woman behind her glided into the room. She carried an oversized manila envelope.

Something saucy about her step. Height about five-three, he judged.

She wore black. All black. Black pointy-toe, over-the-ankle boots with three-and-one-half-inch stiletto heels. Just-above-the-knee black leather skirt. Semi-sheer black blouse (silk?) tucked in at the waist but worn loose, the hint of a black brassiere visible beneath. Black earrings, glistening teardrops. A large pocketbook, black leather, slung below the hip, inch-wide strap worn over the shoulder. Clear nail polish. No lipstick.

Late twenties, he guessed. Maybe thirty. Brunette. Fine facial bones, no lines, high cheeks, flesh tones buttermilk-creamy-rose, lips full (all the better to suck on you, the ruby mouth whispered). Curves that don't stop. Bust not oversized, but somehow pronounced in a provocative way, projecting as though her breasts sought to thrust themselves into his hands without warning. Tips obvious; does she use nipple enhancers? Despite this, her carriage and mien bespoke of a woman accustomed to receiving respect.

He rose from his seat and walked around his desk to meet her, extended his hand. She took it. Grip firm.

Standing right next to her, looking into her eyes, an urge to be deep inside her seized him—an overriding impulse.

"Mike Ratigan," he said. "Pleased to meet you." I'd love to fuck you right this second. Throw you on top of my GYN table and pound away for an hour. Two hours!

"Elaine Fowler." Her voice held the huskiness of a smoker.

"Have a seat." He closed the French doors and waved to a chair in front of his desk. God!—no woman had ever overwhelmed him so quickly. What is happening? Danger—a call for wariness, caution.

She sat down, knees together, giving no indication that she had any inkling of his reaction to her. Mike hoped that she would cross her legs, but she didn't. She leaned forward. Her breasts strained against the fabric. She has to know how she looks!—must have planned it this way. Why?

She placed the envelope on the desk and opened her handbag, withdrew a thick stack of hundred dollar bills held together by rubber bands at each end.

She offered the wrapped currency to him, slowly wet her lips with her tongue. "I didn't know he had this."

Seems disgruntled. Good. "Oh?"

"He hid it from me."

A wise man. What to say? Better nothing. He riffled the pile. "Do I need to count?" Of course he would. Kaitlin too. But not now.

Elaine shook her head. "I did. Fifty thousand." She pursed her lips. "You'd think he would've told me." Again the pink tip of her tongue circled her mouth.

I'd've told you. *I*'d've given you the whole fifty grand for one pop. Well, a thousand anyway. Caution quickly interceded—he didn't have his fee yet. In another moment he mentally adjusted the price to five hundred.

He said, "That covers the deposit. What about the rest—the other $150,000?"

"That's an awful lot of money. You're very expensive."

She waited.

I bet you're expensive too. "A modest fee for defending the extremely serious charges we're going to have here. A bargain, actually." He paused. "The rest?"

She pushed the manila envelope toward him. "He told me to bring this sample." The tip of her tongue circuited her lips once more, wetting them so they glistened lightly.

The envelope was not sealed. Mike opened it and withdrew an eight-and one-half by eleven inch, three-hole-punched, heavyweight transparent plastic sheet. Attached to its face were three polyethylene envelopes of two different sizes. The smaller envelope contained one postage stamp. The larger two envelopes held a block of four stamps each.

"What're these?"

Elaine shrugged. "It's what he told me to bring you. I didn't know he had these either."

"He thinks these are worth $150,000?"

Another shrug.

Tread cautiously. Don't ask where Maguire got the stamps. "I have a client who's in the stamp business. I'll ask him to take a look at these, tell me what they're worth."

Without prelude she slid her chair back and stood. "Let me know. Frankie is very concerned." She turned toward the door, showing a curvaceous rump. Built-in swivel. Mmmm. Calves tightened with each step. A dancer's legs. Easy for Mike to imagine them wrapped around him.

He stood. "Wait a minute. I don't know how to reach you."

She turned back.

He continued. "And I want to thank you for recommending me. I understand you heard of me through—"

"Florence. Yes. My cosmetician. She speaks highly of you." A hesitation, hint of a smile at the corner of her lips. "You're quite good friends, apparently."

Mike did not know how to react, how much to disclose. The less, the better. He nodded.

Elaine produced a card from her pocketbook. It read "Elaine Fowler, Photographer," with an address on Huron Avenue in Cambridge and a telephone number. At the bottom of the card appeared website and email addresses, along with the words "Portrait, Fashion, Wedding, Erotica."

"I'll be sure to call and let you know," he said, opened the door for her. "I'll walk you out." From behind. With pleasure.

After Elaine Fowler left, Mike keyed her telephone number and other data into his contacts list, then synchronized his cellular telephone with the computer. A step forward—toward what?

* * *

Later his cellphone rang. Anne said, "The boys got zeroes, Mike. Every one of them—the whole eight!"

"Jesus, that's wonderful. What're you going to do?"

"I don't know. It's up to the principal; they may get expelled. Cheating is grounds for expulsion."

"That's what they deserve, the little bastards."

"Might be too harsh."

"Jesus Christ, Anne, if that's the way you feel, you should've thought of it before we did this." Bleeding heart!

"Don't get huffy, Mike. How about dinner tonight—you have time?"

Peacemaking. "Sounds good. Locke-Ober?"

"Okay. Dutch, agreed?"

"No, no, I'm springing." Newfound solvency demanded expression.

"Dutch or no date."

"Okay, okay. Dutch."

CHAPTER 13

Mike found the listing for David Rosen in the Massa-chusetts Lawyers Diary. He tapped out the number, and after exchanging pleasantries said, "Dave, I remember hearing a month or so ago you were representing a client charged with—I don't know, some kind of fraud having to do with stamps—selling bogus collectible stamps to collec-tors. Have I got it right?"

"Yeah, almost. But that was more like a year ago, not a month. It's up on appeal now. You got one too?"

"Sort of in that line, but a little different. I was won-dering if you'd mind if I talked to your guy. He might be able to give me something in the way of background, is all." No sense in telling Rosen stuff he doesn't need to know.

"No problem. He's out on bail pending appeal, still running his shop. Only thing is, you've got to make sure there's no talk about his own 'situation,' okay?"

"Promise."

"Okay. I'll clear it with the client so he'll expect to hear from you. Otherwise you'd be completely out in the cold—he wouldn't tell you shit."

Rosen gave Mike the contact information and they hung up. Mike made two color copies of the stamp pages and placed the copies in a file folder in his desk drawer.

He drove into downtown Boston, parked in the Pi Al-ley garage, on Washington Street close to the city's business center. Cost for one-half hour to one hour: $18.00. Cost for two hours: $35.00. Robbery. Pretty soon they'll be charging as high as lawyers' rates.

His destination was less than two blocks away. Israel Weissman's shop was located on Bromfield Street in an early-Twentieth Century stone-faced six-story building just off Washington.

A slow, shuddering elevator ride brought Mike to the third floor. The Bromfield Coin & Stamp Emporium occupied space in the front of the building, overlooking the street. Mike had to be buzzed in to enter, the electronic lock clicking to release the latch.

The shop was orderly and well lighted. Obvious video lenses high in the corners. Glass cabinets displayed the collections, those for numismatists on the left and center, for philatelists on the right.

A gray-haired man stood behind the counter, the only person in the shop. Late fifties or early sixties, slightly stooped, thin mustache stained yellow from tobacco; he wore an unbuttoned vest over a long-sleeved shirt with the sleeves rolled up. The odor of cigar smoke hung thick in the air. Mike's nose twitched.

"Mr. Weissman?" Mike asked. He placed his card on the glass countertop. "I called earlier."

The counter man glanced at the card, nodded. "You bring it?" His voice sounded scratchy, like a phonograph record from the Twenties.

Mike handed the manila envelope across the counter. The dealer withdrew the transparent sheets and peered closer. From a drawer behind him he retrieved a set of delicate plastic tongs and a jeweler's loupe, swivelled a countertop ultra-violet lamp over the first sheet and switched it on. With the tongs he extracted the single stamp from its miniature envelope. The plastic made a crinkling sound. The dealer bent over the stamp and scrutinized it. His breath rattled.

After a brief time Weissman looked up at Mike. "This one's a perforate Scott Catalog 12, an 1858 Jefferson 5¢ red. Appears mint. And the others . . . ." His gaze bore in at Mike. "I think I know where these came from. Brookline, right?" He held his hand up, palm forward. "You don't need to answer."

"How much are they worth?"

The dealer seemed to change his mind. "Don't you watch the news? Brookline? The Willenbrandt Collection? It was all over TV and the papers a few months ago."

Mike shook his head. "Didn't see it. How much are they worth?"

"This Jefferson retails about twenty-five thousand." His gaze fixed on Mike. "Brookline, right?" The man immediately interrupted himself. "Never mind." He bent, removed the blocks of four stamps and examined them critically. When finished, he again looked up at Mike. "Where's the rest?"

"The rest?"

"This is only a small part of the collection. Just a teaser."

"I don't know anything about that." Mike pointed to the first block of four stamps. "How much are these other ones worth?"

"Look," Weissman said, "these have to be separated. They can't be sold together. They're hot, don't you understand, mister? Most I could give you is five cents on the dollar."

"Five cents on the dollar! Jesus—that's robbery."

Weissman made no comment about the irony, confirming that sometimes no argument is the best argument.

Mike again pointed to one of the blocks of four. "How much're the other ones worth?"

"You want to sell these or not?"

Mike nodded.

The dealer gestured toward the second block of stamps he had removed from its envelope. "I really don't have to study these." But once more he peered at them through the loupe. "I know they're genuine, but it doesn't hurt to be sure."

He continued to examine the stamps. In a few moments he stood back from the counter, looked up at Mike. "These are exceptionally rare. Catalog value of over three hundred thousand. That's what a dealer would get at retail for stamps with an impeccable provenance—not what he'd *pay* for them. You understand?"

He rubbed his chin, looked closely at Mike. "I could only give you fifteen thousand, and at that I'd be taking a helluva risk. There aren't too many of this set out there." He stopped, seemingly weighing his thoughts, eventually added, "Any way you can get the rest of the collection?"

Mike said, "I don't know. This came to me sort of by . . . ."

"Yeah, I figured. But if you could get the whole thing, it's worth . . . well, twenty to thirty million dollars—that's at auction, of course. You'd never get anything like that in a private sale—and that's what I'd have to do. You could never auction these. Every serious collector would know where they came from. I'd have to . . . well, ease them out into the right collectors, men who aren't so fussy about all the niceties—men who really care about their collections."

Calculation was easy. Screw five percent. Mike felt confident that he could negotiate the old guy up. Ten percent of thirty million dollars equals three million dollars. If Weissman won't come up, I'll sell them somewhere else. My problem is how to get the remainder of the collection. Does Elaine know where it is?

Mike bargained with the dealer and they settled on payment of $46,000 for the stamps he brought with him that day. Mike signed a bill of sale in his own name as "Trustee."

He agreed to call Weissman in a few days to discuss the rest of the collection. The dealer could use the profits from their anticipated resale to pay the legal costs of his appeal.

Counting the $50,000 in cash already received, Maguire was $104,000 short on his fee. Tomorrow Mike would put his client to the test.

He would call Elaine Fowler to tell her of the shortfall. And that the stamps she had given him were just a "teaser." She would become his ally.

And more.

CHAPTER 14

For the trip into Boston that evening Mike decided to take the rapid transit system rather than drive and face traffic. One convenience of his location on College Avenue was the five-minute walk from his office to the "T" station in Davis Square. The day was warm and bright, fluffy clouds dotting the sky.

He boarded the Red Line train to Park Street Station, at the north end of the Boston Common. On the ride he noticed a woman who wore a tight black skirt. Immediately his thoughts turned to Elaine Fowler and he drifted into a richly textured fantasy surrounding their forthcoming meeting.

From Park Street Mike strolled to Locke-Ober, an Old World-style restaurant situated in Winter Place, a byway near Downtown Crossing, once the focus of Boston's shopping. Jordan Marsh, Filene's, Filene's Basement, R.H. White, Gilchrist's, Raymond's: multi-story department stores with street-level display windows showing coveted merchandise—stores all gone now. Macy's, a late-comer through acquisitions, the only major store remaining.

Locke-Ober, founded in the 1850's and expanded in the 1870's, had long been noted for two things: its French cuisine, and for many years refusing admittance to women— as well as any male Hollywood star who sought to enter without wearing the requisite jacket and tie. All changed now. Women, tieless men welcome.

Mike got there early and waited in the anteroom adjacent to the main dining room on the first floor. From prior visits he knew that the restaurant offered private rooms on the third floor, the JFK suite being the most sought-after.

Anne arrived right on time and the maître d' seated them at a table for four in the center of the room. White linen tablecloth and napkins, heavy silverware.

The room was sizeable, with high ceilings; huge plate glass mirrors hung on the walls, and painted leaves, flowers and mythical animals decorated the ceiling, lighted by ornate chandeliers. Carved mahogany bar. Six capacious silver tureens. A bronze sculpture known as *Gloria Victis*, still one of Boston's most notable hat racks. All of the other tables but one were occupied, most by men, a few women sprinkled among them.

Anne started with clams casino, followed by wiener schnitzel à la Holstein with a side of creamed spinach as her entrée. "No wine for me tonight," she said.

Mike chose to begin with JFK's lobster stew, followed with a main course of calves liver and bacon smothered in onions, accompanied by mashed potatoes and a side of broccoli. "I saw in the paper broccoli's good for you," he explained. For wine the waiter suggested a Pierre Amiot burgundy, Clos de la Roche 1998. Mike acceded. "Sure you won't change your mind?"

Anne said, "You talked me into it."

While waiting for their appetizers, Mike said, "What happened with our trap? Did the boys fess up?"

"I made all eight stay after class, and told them I knew they all had cheated. Every one of them denied it, but I said I knew better, and told them we were going straight to the principal."

"Did you?"

"Yes. I told her what had gone on and showed her the evidence. She said she would review the matter and decide on punishment—that it might include expulsion."

"What was their reaction?"

"Oh, they all started yelling, jumping around, saying they were being railroaded, that it was all just accidental, and so on, but she wasn't having any of it. She told them to leave school right then and she would be in touch with their parents. That's the only time they seemed scared— when she mentioned their parents.

"After they left, I told her there was one boy in particular I thought might be the best to approach: Bobby Friedman. So we had him come back by himself, and he did prove to be the weak link, admitted everything."

"How did they do it?"

"One of the boy's brothers is sort of a computer nerd, and he was able to use his laptop to intercept the signal somehow. I think it might even have been from my house—when my computer was at home, I mean."

"So are they going to be expelled?"

"I don't know. That's pretty harsh, but maybe they deserve it. It'll all be decided by the school board now. The parents are going to be up in arms over their precious little darlings being disciplined."

" 'Precious little darlings!' That's a laugh. They're all jocks aren't they? Seniors? Football players?"

Anne smiled. "Right. Funny, though, you're not sounding very much like a defense lawyer. Where's your sympathy for the poor accused? Maybe if they're expelled, this would be a good case for you. That would be ironic."

"I've got enough headaches right now with the Maguire case."

"Speaking of which, how's that going?"

"The arraignment's tomorrow, but I bet the prosecution's going to tell the judge that the grand jury has indicted Maguire for murder, and ask for a continuance and no bail. They'll get it too."

"I suppose if he's guilty of mur—"

"He's not guilty of anything yet," Mike said with a touch of anger. "Don't forget, he's only charged with burglary at the moment, and that's a bailable offense."

Anne held up her hand. "Take it easy, Mike. I was just—"

"That's the problem! People are always 'just' thinking somebody's guilty when they haven't even heard any evidence. And you especially ought to know better, what with all the time we spent together. You know how the system works, all the ins and outs. How many clients have I got 'Not Guilties' for, when everybody thought they were?"

"Sorry, Mike, you're right. Ease up. Let's not spoil this."

"I agree." He reached for her hand and touched it gently. "May I be forgiven?"

The waiter arrived, served the clams casino and lobster stew. They both partook of their dishes.

"Succulent," Anne said. "You want one?" A peace offering.

"No, I'm okay."

After finishing her appetizer, Anne started to speak, halted, then said, "I thought I should tell you, I met someone. He's nice, and I like him."

Mike felt a momentary twinge of jealousy. So far as he was aware, Anne had not been involved in a romantic relationship since their parting more than two years earlier. Immediately he suppressed his reaction. He and Anne were friends now, always would be. "Where did you meet him?"

"At the gym. He comes in—"

Mike could not resist. "Ah! A hunk!"

"—sometimes when I'm there, and one day we just got chatting . . . ."

"What does he do?" Always this question.

"He's an architect. Works for a small firm downtown. Designs commercial buildings mostly."

"That's great, Anne. How long've you been seeing him?" Why didn't she mention this the other day?

"Just a few weeks. I don't know if it'll go anywhere, but . . . ."

"You don't have to know. What's important is that you have some fun now. You deserve it. "

"I guess you're right."

"You know I'm right." After a moment Mike added, "I hope he's not the jealous type. If he is, this might be our last dinner together. I wouldn't like that."

"Don't worry, Mike. That'll never happen."

The waiter arrived bearing a tray containing their main course dishes. He served, poured dinner wine, and removed himself to the far end of the room. Mike sliced a piece of the liver, spread some onion over it, and tasted it.

"Scrumptious," he said. "Out of this world." He took another bite, this one topped by a piece of crisp bacon. "How's yours?"

"Couldn't be better." Anne punctured the egg with her fork; yolk began to run over the wiener schnitzel.

"A lot of people can't stand the egg part," Mike said. "My wife was like that. She loved the veal, but couldn't tolerate eggs of any sort. Made her face break out."

Anne continued eating for a bit before speaking. "Your wife. I always wondered about her. You never wanted to talk about her. Do you ever see her these days? Think of her?"

Mike stiffened. Dangerous territory. "No. I don't. Think about her. That whole thing was a disaster, as you know. I told you about it."

"No you didn't. All you told me was that you had been married. That's it. Sum total." He frowned, and she tried to add a note of levity. "And you never mentioned egg yolks."

"Ha! Ha! Big joke."

Mike's irritation was palpable, but Anne did not give way. "All right, forget your wife. But have you thought any more about getting serious—maybe even getting married again?"

What's she asking this kind of shit for? "No, I haven't. You know that. I learned a lesson, and I'm not making that mistake again."

"But the lesson you learned is the wrong one, Mike. On some level you must know it."

"Jesus, Anne!"

"I'm sorry, but I'm just thinking of you. I understand why you broke up with me, but that doesn't mean you'll never find someone who's right for you. I don't think you should give up. In fact, I still think you should try some kind of therapy. That whole business with your parents was just too much for anyone to handle."

Mike pounded his fist on the table, making the silverware jump, startling diners at nearby tables. Their waiter looked in their direction but did not approach. "Goddamn it, you promised not to do this any more—ever again. You know I can't stand this pop-psych crap. Just because you're a psychologist . . . ."

She leaned toward him and put her hand over his. "It's not 'crap,' but you're right. I did promise. I beg forgiveness. My desire to help you . . . ." She smiled. "Forgive me? Please?"

His anger already subsiding, he turned his palm up and clasped her hand, squeezed gently, nodded.

* * *

When Mike was three his father "disappeared" and his mother dropped him on his Aunt Julia's doorstep, telling her sister, "I'll be back to get him in a week or so. I just need a few days till I get my head straight."

Fourteen months later she showed up unannounced, accompanied by a mustachioed string bean with long sideburns. His name was Ed. Ed grinned a lot and sucked air between wide-spaced teeth. He and Mike's mother were both stumbling drunk. They giggled and sang while Mike's aunt looked at Uncle Fred in hopeless perplexity.

"I can't take him with me now," Mike's mother said when she and Ed were leaving, "but don't worry. I'll be back to get him."

Mike never saw her again. A postcard now and then with no return address. A year or two apart at first, then growing to three, four, finally nothing at all.

As for his father, Mike once heard a rumor that he was a dealer in an Atlantic City casino, but never pursued the lead. Why bother?

*　*　*

"It would never work," Mike had told Anne on their final night as a "couple." After having gone to the Comedy Connection, they were having a nightcap at Anne's Newton condominium.

She had raised the issue of marriage, albeit through indirection. "We could live together as a trial, see how it goes. I know it would be fine."

He hated to disappoint her. But he knew.

"Why wouldn't it?" she said. "I love you, and you love me—at least you say you do."

"You know I do. But you also know why it wouldn't work."

"We respect each other, enjoy one another, laugh, have fun together . . . ."

"Love isn't enough, Anne. I can't give you what you need. You need fidelity, and I understand that. You have a right to expect it. Maybe every woman—everybody—does. But I know myself well enough to realize that I'm never going to be faithful to any one woman. It hasn't got anything to do with you. That's just the way I am—my nature—that's all."

"But that's because of your childhood, being abandoned. Counseling would help you work through that."

"Jesus Christ, Anne! We've been over this a thousand times. I happen to think that I'm as normal as it gets. Every married guy I know is out screwing around, chasing something on the side. That's the way the male is built. That's the natural course of conduct for men, not the unrealistic restrictions imposed by society. And even if this is not so, it's the way *I'm* built, so that's the way I have to live—not a lie."

Anne shook her head vigorously. "I just don't believe you! Not every man is the same way, and you don't have to be if you don't want to. You're just too spoiled, too self-centered."

* * *

Anne passed on dessert, but Mike ordered a strawberry-topped cheesecake, wondering why he did; he already felt stuffed. They both had coffee.

When dinner finished they ambled toward the subway station, sat on a park bench in the Boston Common, chatted for a while. When they parted at Park Street Station, Anne offered her cheek for a kiss, said goodbye, and took the Green Line to Newton. Mike descended the stairs to the Red Line and waited for a train.

On the ride back to Davis Square he thought about what the coming day would bring: first, Maguire's arraignment, and later—more important—his next meeting with Elaine Fowler, who would show up with Frankie Maguire's treasure trove.

Worth millions.

Maybe.

CHAPTER 15

Mike researched defenses to felony murder, dictated a brief memorandum on issues, then sat back with his feet up on his desk, idly reviewing facts in the Maguire case. Unfocused, he gazed at the tree outside his window. Without warning, his computer's monitor screen fell dark. Mike blinked at the blank screen. A stray thought clicked in his mind. That's it! That's it!

Maguire had told him that *he saw writing on the screen*. But Sheila Graham's computer screen had been *dark* when Mike went to the house, even though the power was on. The screen was also blank when he left the house. So a screensaver feature was active, and a blank screen was the default screensaver.

This meant that someone had been using the computer not long before his client arrived at the house. The real killer, surely! And even if not, this would provide evidence sufficient to create doubt. For the first time, Mike began to embrace the idea that his client might not be guilty of murder.

To check his memory, he retrieved his original notes from his first meeting with Maguire. He skimmed them until he came to the part where Maguire had described his visit. He said that he had seen "some writing on the screen" in Sheila Graham's office. Mike then checked the digital recording which he had made. "And that computer was on, 'cause I saw stuff on the screen—words," Maguire had said.

To establish a defense, Mike would have to find out the exact time lapse before the screensaver kicked in. That should be easy. He could do it right from Sheila Graham's desktop. He would also try to find out what this unknown person was doing with the computer.

It was a good bet that the *real* murderer had been using the computer for some truly important purpose. Killers don't hang around a crime scene unless they have to. There had to be something critical on that computer.

Mike drove to the house and unlocked the front door. The air still seemed stuffy. In the office he turned on the lights and opened the slider, sat down and booted Sheila Graham's computer. The Windows logo came on. When the system loaded, the screen displayed a host of icons on a background showing a picture of her cat. The computer was not password protected.

He right-clicked in a clear space on the desktop. This brought up a menu. He clicked through to the screen saver feature. "Blank" had been selected, confirming what he had surmised. The figure "20" appeared in the "Wait" box. The time lapse was set to twenty minutes before the screen blanked.

Mike decided to stop, make no input, and see what happens. In twenty minutes the screen went dark. This confirmed that someone had been using the computer within twenty minutes of Maguire's arrival.

Next he clicked the Recycle Bin icon. The directory showed that the Recycle Bin held no entries at all. Someone had erased all of the "deleted" files.

Unlikely that the Graham woman would have emptied the Recycle Bin just prior to drowning in her own bathtub. More probable, the person using the computer just before Maguire came upon the scene was the "someone" who had emptied the bin.

The feeling that his client might not be guilty of murder began to solidify in Mike's mind.

On his way to the Colchester jail Mike began to consider potential attacks based on this newfound evidence. Who could testify about the screensaver timeout? Mike could hire an expert to examine the computer and testify, but that evidence would be subject to serious assault. No one could state what condition existed on the date of the victim's death. Anyone—including Mike and his client—could later have changed the timeout.

Further, only Maguire himself could testify as to what he saw on the screen. A jury would likely disbelieve this as inherently self-serving—wholly aside from the fact that it would doubtless be against Maguire's interest to take the witness stand.

So what could Mike do with this knowledge—perhaps proof of innocence?

CHAPTER 16

"Got the deposit," Mike said to his client at their next meeting. "Your girl tells me you have a way to come up with the rest."

"Yeah. She told me you met her. Wha'ja think?"

"Very nice lady. You're a lucky guy."

"Till I got in here."

Best to get off the Elaine subject. Mike said, "When I was here that first time, you mentioned that you had gone into the den and looked at the computer."

"Not 'looked'—just noticed it, is all. Saw the cat too, like I said."

"But you saw the monitor—the screen—something on it."

Maguire swept his hair back from his forehead, answered. "Yeah, somethin'. Not much. Just some words."

"Do you mean text?"

"Yeah, like that." He paused. "Maybe a list of stuff."

"List?"

"Yeah. You know, typin'—typewritten stuff."

"What was behind it—the list on the screen? Background? Any graphics? Anything?"

"Nothin'."

"No pictures?"

Frankie shook his head.

"Do you have a computer at home?"

"Yeah, but I never used one. Elaine does that kind of stuff for me anytime I need it."

"This could be important."

His client shrugged, waited for an explanation.

"The computer uses a screensaver where the screen goes dark."

Maguire looked puzzled.

Mike explained. "A screensaver like this one produces a blank screen when the computer isn't used for a while. But when you were there, the screen wasn't blank—you saw something on the screen, so someone had to have been using that computer within twenty minutes before you got to the house."

His client clapped his hands, grinned. "See! I told you it was somebody else! I didn't have nothin' to do with it . . . . And you even know the time—twenty minutes?"

Mike nodded.

"Somebody else had to be there. I knew it!"

"My job is to find out who. That's the only way we're going to get you off."

Frankie grinned broadly. "I'm so glad I hired you!"

CHAPTER 17

The Woburn (pronounced "Woo-bern") District Court held jurisdiction over crimes committed in Colchester and surrounding towns. A suburb about ten miles northwest of Boston, Woburn was a city with a population close to 40,000. The two-story brick courthouse, located in Woburn Square, sat next to Woburn City Hall. With tall, narrow windows, the building appeared more like a fortress than a place to dispense justice.

The court had scheduled a probable cause hearing, but experience had taught Mike that no such hearing would actually occur. The Commonwealth would get a continuance, avoid early disclosure of its evidence, secure a grand jury indictment for murder, and proceed anew in the Superior Court.

Mike waved his lawyer's bar card at the entrance guard, who merely glanced at it and nodded, recognizing him from many past visits. Mike stepped around the metal detector rather than pass through it, climbed the stairs to the second floor, where criminal sessions were held.

The bulletin board adjacent to the second session listed *Commonwealth v. Maguire*, captioned by the official name of the court, The Fourth District Court of Eastern Middlesex, Hon. Martin Becker presiding. *Maguire* was seventh on the list. Mike would have a moderate wait while earlier cases were called.

The courtroom was partly filled, with lawyers, accused persons, their relatives and friends, and members of the curious public scattered around the room. The clerk had not yet entered, but the bailiff—a uniformed officer of the Massachusetts Trial Court—had taken his position at a raised stand on the right side of the room. A few lawyers sat on the front benches nearest the bar. Mike joined them and greeted two he knew.

The judge entered promptly at 9:00. In his late forties, Judge Becker was regarded by the trial bar as both learned and fair. The first few cases called were routine driving-under-the-influence arrests, plus one shoplifting charge. Because the matters were contested, all were placed on "second call."

When the Maguire case was called, Mike strode past the bar and took a seat at the table on the right. A Colchester police officer escorted a handcuffed Maguire to the defense table. The officer stood guard behind him.

Maguire surveyed the courtroom, leaned toward Mike and whispered, "I wish Elaine was here."

"Don't worry. You'll be all right."

A slender, wavy-haired attorney not more than a year or two out of law school took his place at the prosecution table, representing the Commonwealth. The DA could safely rely on a junior attorney today, secure in the knowledge that nothing was going to happen.

The Commonwealth would request a dangerousness hearing, the court would grant the request, bail would be denied, and a probable cause hearing would never be held.

Mike rose to address the court. "Your Honor, Michael Ratigan appearing for the defendant, Francis Maguire. We are here also for Mr. Maguire's motion to admit him to bail. I understand that the Commonwealth opposes the bail motion."

The Assistant DA stood. "Richard Thornton, Your Honor, representing the Commonwealth. May it please the court, the Commonwealth does indeed oppose the bail motion. In fact, we request a dangerousness hearing. I have the motion here." The young lawyer furnished a copy to Mike, handed the original to the clerk, who passed it up to the judge.

The prospect that Mike could successfully combat the request for a dangerousness hearing fell between none and zero. By the time set for the hearing, the grand jury would already have returned indictments, the case would be transferred to the Superior Court, and because of the murder charge, higher standards would govern Maguire's request for bail.

The judge glanced at the motion, turned to Mike. "All right. There's no sense in having a bail hearing under these circumstances. The Commonwealth is entitled to a dangerousness hearing. I'll set it down for—" he glanced at his calendar "—next Tuesday at 9:00 o'clock. How does that sound?" He did not wait for a reply, pronounced, "Motion for bail remittance denied. The Commonwealth's motion for a dangerousness hearing is allowed."

Maguire turned to Mike. "What happened?"

"The judge said you have to stay in jail for a while— like I told you would happen. I'll see what I can do, but nothing is going to happen until next week." Mike put his arm around Maguire's shoulders. "In the meantime, indictments will be returned against you and we'll have more serious charges to deal with."

His client mumbled, "Shit!"

Mike said, "I'm doing everything possible for you. Just because you're going to be charged doesn't mean the state has an easy case to prove." He gripped his client's bicep.

Maguire nodded, looked glum.

* * *

When Mike returned to the office, Kaitlin asked for details. After listening to his account, she said, "He must've been pretty disappointed."

"Yeah, but I had already told him not to get his hopes up."

"You think that makes a difference?"

"No, but you do what you can."

"By the way, that Fowler woman called and said she'd be here later this afternoon. Around 4:00 o'clock or so."

A slight note of disapproval? "Thanks." He started toward his office.

Before Mike took two steps, Kaitlin said, "How could a lawyer be so stupid?"

Mike stopped. "What's that?"

"Charles Broadhurst. Read it in the *Globe*. Did you see this?" She held up the newspaper which she had been reading.

Mike shook his head.

"You know him?—Broadhurst—practices in Boston?"

"Never heard of him. What'd he do?"

"Criminal lawyer. He had this client who left some paintings with him for safekeeping. A few months later the client was found dead—shot. Well, the lawyer kept the paintings in his attic for a few years.

"Eventually he pulled them out and had them appraised. Turns out they were stolen, worth millions. He figured no one knew they didn't belong to him, tried to sell them at auction. But somebody informed the auction house they were stolen, and now he's in big trouble. Federal indictments for everything. Interstate transportation of stolen goods, conspiracy, larceny, you name it."

"Sounds bad. How did they find out about it?"

"There's some kind of international stolen art registry, and these paintings all showed up in it."

"Talk about bad luck."

"I'm not so sure it's only luck. Plain old stupidity. I wonder what he'll get?"

"Has he been convicted yet?" The defense attorney speaking.

"No, but . . . ."

Her unfinished sentence said everything.

* * *

At his desk Mike pondered his own situation. Suppose there's some kind of registry for stolen stamp collections too? Maybe selling the stamps to Weissman isn't worth the risk.

He tapped out the number of the Bromfield Coin & Stamp Emporium. The telephone rang and rang. No answer. What kind of business is this, where they don't answer the phone, don't even have an answering machine or voicemail? Hope the guy's not back in jail—or had a heart attack. Or *anything*!

Mike made several more calls to the shop; still no answer. Between calls he did a Web search to find articles about the Brookline stamp collection burglary. Both the *Globe* and the *Herald* had run stories. "Burglary Nets Multi-Million Dollar Stamp Collection," one headline trumpeted:

> Yesterday evening Brookline resident Benjamin Willenbrandt arrived home after a vacation to find his personal stamp collection missing. The collection, which Mr. Willenbrandt had assembled over the course of more than three decades, was valued at an amount exceeding $30,000,000, according to sources.
>
> The owner had left the collection in the library of his brick mansion, located in an exclusive section of the upscale town. "I'll get them back," the collector said, confident that many of the stamps in his collection are so rare that they cannot be sold. Any dealer or serious collector would know that the stamps were stolen, he affirmed, because they'll show up in the stolen artwork registry.

Several follow-up articles appeared in both newspapers, but the story died in a couple of weeks. Most interesting to Mike were references to a $50,000 reward for information leading to the arrest and conviction of the perpetrators and, of greater import, a reward of $700,000 for return of the stolen property. *That* was a sum worth considering.

* * *

Elaine was late. Mike wondered what had caused her to be held up. He had been thinking of her all day, had grown extremely anxious. Where is she? Is she coming? Has something happened? Does she have the stamps? Did she do something with them? Can't she find them?

In an attempt to unwind, he went to his library to research cases on the charges which he expected to be forthcoming. There are few defenses to murder: (1) The accused didn't do it; this includes alibi ("He wasn't there; he was with me."); (2) self defense (inapplicable here); and (3) insanity (ditto).

Mike also needed to bone up on lesser included offenses. "Lesser included offenses" are those of which a defendant can be found guilty even though charged with another, "higher" offense. An example is where a defendant charged with murder is convicted of manslaughter. These lesser included offenses usually play a significant role in plea bargaining, and Mike wanted to be prepared.

In mid-afternoon Kaitlin told Mike that she would be leaving a few minutes early today. "I've got an exam in Legal Ethics tonight," she explained. "Any advice?"

"Yeah. Put not your trust in courts—especially in judges."

They both chuckled.

"But seriously," Mike added, "the best thing you can do the night before an exam is not cram, but relax in some way. Go to a club, read a mystery, watch a good movie."

"That's what we always do—my roommate and I. Watch a movie. I love noir flicks, especially those made in the Forties."

"Humphrey Bogart?"

She nodded. "In *The Maltese Falcon*, for instance. Love it. And the ones with Lauren Bacall, like *The Big Sleep*."

"And what about some of those great characters who crop up all the time? Sidney Greenstreet, Peter Lorre . . . ."

"Wonderful villains."

"Have you picked out one for tonight?"

She nodded. "*Out of the Past*."

"Robert Mitchum."

"Oh, you know it."

"One of his best roles."

"I agree."

Just before 5:00 o'clock, Kaitlin announced over the intercom that Elaine Fowler had arrived.

"Show her in," Mike said from the conference room. His heart beat faster.

CHAPTER 18

Mike rose when Elaine entered the room. Today she wore a markedly different outfit. This one too made no effort to conceal her femininity. But no leather. A plum-colored skirt without pleats. Beige blouse with three buttons open at the collar, showing a single strand of pearls and remarkable cleavage. High heels again, but this time in stylish, pointed-toe shoes matching the color of her blouse. No hose. Stunning. He caught his breath.

"Sorry to be late," she said, but offered no excuse. That throaty voice again.

Elaine held three large, green, leather-bound binders to her chest. Each folder was more than two inches thick.

"Let me have them," Mike said. She held them out toward him, revealing even more of her ample cleavage. He took the binders and set them on the table, waved her to a chair.

She sat opposite him, glanced at the GYN table in the corner. No visible reaction.

"Are these the rest?" he asked.

"That's what I found." The tip of her tongue wet her lips. Arousal time.

"You have any idea how much they're worth?"

"I didn't even know he had them." Again a hint of displeasure?

"We've got to devise a new tactic. What I was first thinking of won't work. It's too risky—might come back on Frankie." Or me.

"How's that?"

"My client in the stamp business told me there's a registry of stolen collections. Any buyer of a collection of this magnitude is sure to be aware they're stolen. So they could probably trace it back to Frankie."

"Trace it back to *you*, you mean."

Ha! "To any of us."

"So what's your new plan? What're you going to do? And how much will we get out of it?"

Mike took notice of the "we." Elaine is in for the ride. Good!

"I don't know. I'm not sure. I think I'm going to go the insurer route. The insurance company would be much better off paying a small percentage to recover the stamps than to pay the value of the entire loss."

Kaitlin's voice came over the intercom. "I'm getting ready to close up. You need anything before I leave?"

Mike answered, "No thanks, I'm all set. Have a good evening."

"Okay, you too. See you in the morning. I'll lock up."

Elaine said, "Noticeably attractive."

Mike deflects. "Very capable."

"You mentioned the insurance company will only pay a percentage. How much is a 'percentage'?"

"Ten percent, I'd guess from what I saw on the Internet, although the company is only offering $700,000. So far."

"That's a lot better. You'd only get five percent from the dealer, didn't you say?"

"Right, but he'd probably go up."

"Any idea what the whole bundle is worth?"

"As much as thirty million. Maybe more."

"Wow! At ten percent that's three million dollars."

"I see you're good at math."

"I get better as the numbers get larger."

She leaned back in the chair, crossed her legs, offering Mike a view. His heart seemed to begin pumping harder.

Elaine said,"Speaking of staying out of jail, how is Frankie's case coming along? What're his chances?"

Mike explained that he expected murder indictments to issue. "It's not going to be easy. Tough, in fact. There's a pile of evidence against him, not the least of which is a dead body. And he *was* in the house."

Elaine bent forward. "Frankie's no killer." She seemed to speak with genuine earnestness.

Mike could not take his eyes off her cleavage, creamy mounds now displayed more prominently as she leaned toward him. "Maybe that's so, but we have to prove it."

"I thought the state has to prove its case."

"Technically that's correct, but in reality *we* have to prove he's *innocent*. I know it's not supposed to be that way . . . ." He shifted direction, deciding to get matters on smoother ground. "Would you like a drink while we talk?"

She rolled her tongue around her lips. "I'd prefer a toke if you happen to have one someplace handy. You look like the kind of guy who just might."

"I can rummage around a bit, see what I come up with." He stood. "Be back in a minute."

He went into his office, removed a pre-made joint and a book of matches from his desk, returned to the library. Elaine was standing next to the examination table. An appealing perfume surrounded her.

Mike handed the smoke to her, opened a drawer in the conference table, pulled out a battered metal ashtray and placed it on the table. Elaine put the reefer in her mouth and waited for him to light it. She drew deeply, held the smoke for more than a minute, gradually exhaled. He reached out to take it, but she took another long drag before handing the smoldering weed back to him.

Mike took a deep pull. Elaine leaned against the examination table and began to run her fingers slowly along the curve of the chrome-plated stirrup. Back and forth. Back and forth. After long seconds, she said, "An interesting choice of furnishing for a law office." Her eyes seemed to have clouded. "Flo told me about it."

"Flo. Yes, Flo."

"A friend of yours, I heard."

He did not respond.

"She been here?"

His senses were overloaded by her presence. Now he was beginning to feel the power of the weed as well. He felt slightly awkward standing so close to her but not touching her, ready to touch her—but not yet ready to risk. She continued to stroke the stirrup with a slow, almost sensual caress. With her other hand she retrieved the weed from Mike and again dragged at length.

"You're not answering," Elaine went on. "She try out the table?"

He felt disoriented, did not speak.

"Do I make you nervous?" she added. "You seem tense."

"Tense?" He had never felt more anxious. "I'm not tense at all."

She removed her hand from the stirrup, stroked his forehead. "Look at you. You're all tightened up."

"I'll show you." He removed the joint from her lips and kissed her. Her mouth opened; their tongues quickly found each other. Mike pressed her to him, backing her against the examination table. He put the cigarette on the edge of the ashtray, returned to his mission.

The buttons of her blouse came undone with ease and he toyed with her breasts through the brassiere's material, a task he often found more appealing than cupping and caressing the bare treasures themselves. So many failed to fulfill the promise made richer by padding and wire supports. Elaine responded by undoing the clasp.

Her breasts sprang into view, standing proudly, pink-tipped nipples as hard as pencil erasers, the areolae no larger than a dime.

He licked, sucked, prodded her breasts with his tongue, nibbled, finally pressed the heel of his hand into her crotch. She offered no resistance, instead rocked against him. He lifted her skirt and pushed aside light cloth to reach her core, surprised to feel a prickly thistle against his palm. He rubbed gently before entering the valley, encountered thick moisture, easing passage of his finger. Elaine unzipped his trousers and removed his throbbing cock, held it firmly, with authority. A mild pout followed by successive squeezes showed her approval. Mike moved against her, seeking entry.

"Wait!" she urged. "Let me get up here." She kicked off her shoes and stepped on the platform, eased herself onto the table. She placed her feet in the stirrups, slid her buttocks forward. Mike stepped onto the platform, pushed aside the crotch of her panties and quickly entered her. The lubricious passage welcomed his movement.

In a moment he felt as though he was gripped by a magical velvet-gloved fist saturated in hot oil, clasping, releasing, clasping, releasing, clasping, releasing. With only a few thrusts he exploded within her. He did not immediately withdraw, could not permit himself to abandon this miraculous port, wherein lies the key to all the mysteries of the universe.

A minute later he said, "I'm sorry. I couldn't hold it. Next time'll be better."

Elaine drew him to her. "Don't worry. That always happens the first time."

"Let's go upstairs. We can resume there." Illogically he wondered how many men had enjoyed a "first time" with her. The thought prickled.

"For a second session?"

"And a third. And a fourth. I guarantee it."

Elaine gathered her shoes and pocketbook and pre-ceded him up the stairs.

CHAPTER 19

Mike did not awaken until nearly 10:00 o'clock the next morning. Elaine had left. He brewed coffee and ate a doughnut before showering, shaving, dressing and going downstairs.

"Rough night?" Kaitlin asked, arching her eyebrows.

Mike shrugged. He checked the conference room. The stamp collection still rested on the table. He sighed, went to his desk and tapped out the number for Weissman's store. Again no answer.

Son of a bitch! I've got to get those stamps back.

Kaitlin's voice came over the intercom. "I noticed those stamp binders on the table. They look like they might be valuable. Where do you want me to put them?"

"In the supplies cabinet."

"You sure?" She sounded doubtful. "Maybe I should put your client's cases in there too, you think?—M. Beaulieu's?"

"Sure. Go ahead." He hesitated, added, "While you're at it, you might as well have a look at them."

At the hall closet Kaitlin removed the Beaulieu attaché cases, aluminum shells with faux-leather exterior, and carried them to the file room. Mike joined her to see her reaction. She set the cases on a table and released the clasps, raised the lids. "Omigod!" Her breath caught. The cases were stuffed with banded stacks of crisp $100 bills, arranged in neat rows. Each band bore the imprint $10,000.

She looked at Mike. "There must be—how much is here?—hundreds of thousands of dollars."

"Not to worry. It's not real. But you're right: put it in the cabinet so nobody'll be likely to steal it."

Kaitlin picked up one of the bundles and examined it closely. "Looks real to me."

"That's the idea."

*   *   *

Concerned about the potential risks of seeking a ransom for the stamp collection, Mike did a Web search. He found that, as a rule, most insurance companies deny that they pay "ransom" for stolen artworks. At most they sometimes admit to payment of "rewards" for information leading to the return of the stolen items. In one case involving a Titian painting, a "middleman" received £100,000 sterling, the equivalent of approximately $150,000 at the time. The private detective in the case stated that the middleman was not involved in the painting's theft. "You cannot pay a ransom," the detective had declared with solemnity.

One of the most notorious incidents concerned a 2003 art theft from the Austrian Art History Museum in Vienna. A solid-gold Benvenuto Cellini sculpture known as the "Saliera," or "Saltcellar," had been stolen from the venerable museum. By letter the thief demanded €5,000,000 (roughly $7,000,000) for return of the statue, which had an estimated value of €50,000,000. (He later increased his demand to €10,000,000—then equivalent to around $14,000,000.)

The thief had made his demands to the insurance company through text messages which he sent on a cellular telephone purchased expressly for the purpose. Through signals intrinsic to that particular telephone, the police were able to identify the store which sold it. In one of those accidents of fortune, the store happened to have a mounted surveillance camera and it had recorded the sale. The clerk who sold the telephone identified the purchaser from his photograph. The police posted the photo on television news, and within minutes several viewers who knew the thief came forward to identify him. Authorities arrested the thief and recovered the statue.

One case of *admitted* ransom involved a 1994 theft of three famous paintings from the Kunsthalle Schirn, a Frankfurt art gallery. The stolen paintings were *Light and Colour* and *Shade and Darkness*, by J. M. W. Turner, on loan from London's Tate Gallery, and *Nebelschwaden*, by Caspar David Friedrich, on loan from the Kunsthalle Hamburg. Two of the thieves were apprehended quickly, but they refused to disclose who ordered the theft, and police were unable to obtain the paintings.

The insurer paid the Tate Gallery £24,000,000 to cover the loss. However, four years after the theft, the Tate paid £8,000,000 (near $13,000,000) to the insurance company in return for ownership of the paintings, should they ever reappear. A Tate director, with the knowledge of the police, negotiated with the Mafia through attorney Edgar Liebrucks for return of the paintings. The two sides agreed on a purchase price of 5,000,000 DM (~$2,500,000) per painting. The thieves increased the demanded advance payment from one to two million marks, and Liebrucks took out a personal loan to cover this payment. The deal for the first painting went through, Liebrucks received about €320,000 (~$352,000) as compensation from Tate, and *Shade and Darkness* returned to London in 2000. Further negotiations then halted.

In the fall of 2002 two men contacted attorney Liebrucks and indicated that they held the remaining paintings. The Tate Gallery then bought the stolen Turner for €2,000,000 (~$2,000,000—the Euro having declined by then). Consequently it received more from the insurers than it paid to the thieves, profiting by about €20,000,000 (~$20,000,000). A Tate spokesperson insisted that all payments were cleared ahead of time with German and British authorities, and that millions were not paid to criminals as ransom, but for *information* leading to recovery of the paintings.

Following this, the Kunsthalle Hamburg authorized Liebrucks to recover the Friedrich painting. The attorney negotiated the price from €1,500,000 (~$1,500,000) down to €250,000, and secured return of the artwork by using his own money. He delivered the work to the Kunsthalle, which thereupon refused to reimburse him or to pay any fee. Liebrucks instituted litigation against the museum and recovered his €250,000 (~$250,000) out-of-pocket plus a fee of €20,000. This result especially pleased Mike. It could be done!

Armed with knowledge of a way to proceed, as well as hazards to avoid, Mike began to formulate a plan—a way to advance his own interests along with those of his client, Maguire. Or Elaine. Before pursuing it, to make sure, he would initially undertake further investigative groundwork.

But first to speed-dial Elaine and arrange to meet.

"I'm psyched," she said. "I can hardly wait."

"Me neither."

"I've got a confession to make," she said. "I keep thinking, 'Thy rod and thy staff, they comfort me.'"

Mike smiled. "You turned religious all of a sudden."

"Extremely. Extremely religious."

CHAPTER 20

Mike tapped out the numbers. The telephone rang eight times before answer.

"Hello," a woman said, her tone subdued. She sounded old enough to be Sheila Graham's mother.

"This is Mike Ratigan calling. I'm defending—"

"I know who you are." The phone smashed to the cradle.

Well, who could blame her?

It was too early for the probate inventory to be filed. He decided to approach the law firm representing the estate, which would by now have taken inventory of its assets. A telephone call to the District Attorney's office revealed that Highsmith & Drinkwater represented the estate.

Mike called the firm and asked to be connected with the attorney handling the matter. Immediately he was put through to a young woman. "Mr. Talbot's desk. This is Roberta Spang speaking."

"I'm attorney Ratigan. I'd like to speak with Mr. Talbot."

"I'm afraid he's not in right now," she said. "Can I help you?"

Mike explained who he was and what he wanted.

"I can't give out any information myself, but if you like, I'll leave a note for him to call you back, or you can go into his voicemail."

He left a voicemail. Talbot returned his call late in the afternoon.

Mike said, "As you may know, I'm defending Frank Maguire. I'd like to have a look at the estate inventory."

Talbot said, "Actually, everything is passing through a trust, so there won't be an inventory. Inasmuch as the trust is a wholly private matter, I wouldn't feel at liberty to disclose anything to you." He hesitated, then added, "Under the circumstances, I rather suspect that the beneficiary would not be inclined to cooperate with you, so I don't think it's even worthwhile asking."

"My client hasn't been proven guilty—indeed, he's presumed to be innocent. I'd genuinely appreciate your forwarding my request to the beneficiary. I'm sure the beneficiary wants to see justice done here."

"I'll think about it."

Mike didn't want to leave the matter hanging. "When can I expect to hear?"

"A week," the other attorney said, his tone begrudging. "Give me a week."

Talbot never called. Mike telephoned his office, could not get past his assistant.

"I'm sorry," Ms. Spang said with finality, "but Mr. Talbot says that he is unable to provide any information to you."

*   *   *

Later that Tuesday Mike drove to the Graham house. A large "For Sale" sign was staked in the front lawn by ASAP Realty. A SUV was backed into the driveway and a fortyish woman with a stocky figure was loading a sizeable cardboard box into the car.

Mike pulled to the side of the road and parked, got out, walked to where she was standing. Her face had reddened from straining with the load. He recognized her from photos he had seen on the refrigerator.

"Can I help?" he asked. "You look like you're having quite a struggle here."

For a moment she looked at him without answering, and he figured he should offer an explanation.

"I didn't just happen by," he said. "I'm one of the lawyers working on the case—the murder case—and I was going back into the house to check out some details."

She smiled. "Oh, sorry. I'm Pamela Stevens, Sheila's sister. Pleased to meet you." She offered her hand and Mike took it. "I thought I would handle it all myself, but I could use a little help. There're a couple more boxes. If you could . . . ."

"Sure." Apparently she assumed that he represented the prosecution; he was not going to disturb this impression. They went inside through the sliding glass door where Maguire had been caught. All of the furnishings, books and papers had been removed from the office. Mike followed her to the kitchen. The refrigerator still stood in the same place, but without photographs. The table and chairs were gone, the walls and countertop bare except for two cartons resting on the island countertop. Three drawers stood open near the sink, and a shallow box sat on the counter above them. The drawers contained cooking utensils and silverware.

"Just taking care of some last-minute cleanup," she said. "What are you looking for?"

"Oh, something I wanted to check on the computer—you know, the one that was in the office down the hall. I didn't realize it was gone."

"I gave it to Dr. Fessenden—do you know him? He was Sheila's mentor at Harvard, and they were working on a project together when she was . . . at the time she . . . when she died. He's such a nice man. He'd do anything for her. So I gave him the computer and her books and things. He offered to pay, but I wouldn't take anything. It seemed like the right thing to do. Don't you agree?"

"Yes, exactly. The right thing."

"Maybe he'll let you look at it in his office."

"A good idea. I'll try that."

She started to move the box towards the edge of the island and he stepped forward. "Here. Let me take that for you."

"All right. Thanks. I really appreciate it. While you're doing that I'll clean out these last couple of drawers."

Mike carried the package to the car, shoved the carton forward to make room for the final box. When he got back in the kitchen, Pamela was emptying the silverware drawer.

Tears brimmed her eyes. She pulled a tissue from her pocket and wiped her nose. "I'm sorry to act like this," she said. "It's just that it's so sad. I gave her this set when she graduated from college. It's only stainless steel and she could have got a lot better one but she always kept it."

Suddenly she was sobbing and Mike felt helpless. He hesitated a moment, put his arms around her. She rested her head on his shoulder, heaved against his chest, eventually stood back, wiped her eyes.

"Don't be embarrassed," he said. "It's only natural to be upset."

"I know that, but I don't know you, or anything . . . ."

"Don't worry about it. I understand perfectly."

Pamela returned to finish the job of emptying the drawer. She held up something he couldn't see, and said, "I don't know what this is. I suppose it has something to do with cooking, but it's funny it's in the cutlery drawer."

She turned toward him; he saw that she was holding a USB flash memory drive. The black-cased thumb drive was about two inches long, maybe three-quarters of an inch wide, less than half an inch thick. It might possibly contain some bit of useful information about who was in the house right before Maguire. Unlikely, but possible.

"Probably recipes," he said. "A lot of people do that."
How can I get it? This could be an answer—how can I get
it?

She turned the case around in her hand. "I don't
think I've ever seen one of these before. I'm not really
. . . . They're awfully small, aren't they?"

"Yes, they definitely are." He thought for a moment
and said, "My fiancée's a great cook. If you're not going to
use it yourself, I'd be happy to buy it from you."

Pamela held out the flash drive. "Here, take it; it's
yours."

Mike felt a twinge of guilt. "Oh, no, you don't need to
do that. I'd like to pay you for it."

"No, I couldn't hear of it. You've been so kind, helping
me here, listening to me, and . . . ." When she saw his reluctance she said, "I'll tell you what. I'll make a deal with
you. If your fiancée finds a really good recipe on there,
you promise to let me have it."

Mike nodded agreement. Pamela scribbled her name
and email address on a piece of scrap paper, pressed the
note and USB drive into his hand.

"Thank you," he mumbled. "I'm sure my fiancée'll be
so happy to get it—and she'll use it wisely."

* * *

In his office Mike slid the thumb drive into the USB
port. A popup box on the screen showed the contents. Recipes! A sample of the files:

Amy's chowder.txt.
Baked ham (glazed).doc
Clams Casino.txt.
Megan's Apple crisp.doc.
Oysters Rockefeller—from Jenny.pdf.
Ursula's double chocolate brownies.txt.
And so on. He had hoped for much. He found nothing.

On the off-chance that the file contents were not what the names suggested, he opened several at random. All indeed were recipes.

Sheila Graham's sister had also presented another avenue of approach. He now pursued it.

*   *   *

She had given the computer and some other property to Dr. Fessenden. The arrest report had shown that a Dr. Fessenden had arrived at Sheila Graham's house shortly after the police themselves. A detective had taken a brief statement from him to the effect that he and the decedent were colleagues working on a project together, that they had an appointment that morning and, out of concern when she did not arrive for their meeting, the doctor called her home. Unable to reach her, he had driven to the house.

A Web search quickly disclosed that Dr. Fessenden was renowned in his discipline, cellular biology. He had received several prizes, including the distinguished Japanese International Prize for Biology. He had also been awarded the Balzan Prize and the Crafoord Prize. Never having heard of these, Mike checked them and was surprised to learn that they were considered the "triple crown" of biology. The monetary awards totalled several million dollars.

A bibliography showed that the professor had written numerous monographs on cellular biology, and had authored two texts widely used in post-secondary school education. According to synopses of his writings, his area of specialization dealt with telomeres. Having never studied biology, Mike grew interested in the account of Professor Fessenden's research.

He learned that telomeres are DNA sequences required for cell reproduction. Without them the body cannot generate new cells, and humans would quickly die.

Telomeres are located at the very ends of DNA strands. Each time a cell is replicated, genes near the end of chromosomes are lost. Cells can replicate themselves only about fifty times.

Eventually the cell can no longer divide, and protein instructions required for continued life are unavailable. Ultimately the organism ages and dies. But there is a kicker, and that is where Professor Fessenden's research led.

Scientists had long sought ways to slow the aging process and extend life. For some time biologists had recognized that telomeres are *not* present in the DNA of a fertilized egg. Instead, during early development they are added by a substance called telomerase. Yet telomerase disappears from the body after its work is done.

Professor Fessenden had found in experimenting with mice—genetically similar to humans—that adding telomerase to the immune cells of animals suffering from esophageal cancer led to a remission of symptoms. Further, the destruction of telomerase activity in cancerous cells prevented their replication, eradicating the disease in the experimental subjects.

A follow-up Web search showed that these developments had generated popular press announcements that the quest made famous by Ponce de León had finally achieved its objective. "Harvard Prof Discovers Legendary Fountain of Youth," the front page of the *New York Post* trumpeted. Other tabloids echoed. "Secret Elixir Promises Eternal Life," one announced. "President Gets First Dose," a popular blog proclaimed, resulting in caustic witticisms on numerous talk shows. Even such newspapers as the *New York Times* and the *Wall Street Journal* acknowledged the development in glowing terms. "Bio-Research Yields Potential Nucleotide Extensions," appeared just below the fold in a *Times* front page.

Mike called Dr. Fessenden and identified himself as the attorney for Francis Maguire in the Graham murder case.

The academic promptly granted Mike's request for an appointment. "I can squeeze you in Thursday at noon. I can give you a half hour. Is that enough?"

CHAPTER 21

The police reports had proved valuable to Mike mostly because they corroborated what Maguire had told him.
The medical examiner's report was more revealing. Dr.
Philip Atwater, an Assistant Medical Examiner, attended
the death scene at 12:32 PM, somewhat more than three
hours after the initial call reporting a disturbance had
been placed to the Colchester Police Department. The ME
found the victim in the master bathroom tub fully submerged face-up in bathwater. He observed pink froth
around the nose and mouth.

Indications of the onset of both rigor mortis and livor
mortis were evident. Rigor mortis was found in the muscles of the face and neck, but had not yet extended lower,
indicating that death had probably taken place within
two to four hours prior to initial observation.

The ME wrote that it is well accepted that increased
temperature hastens rigor, and noted the determination
of approximate time of death as inexact because of ambient temperatures, both room and bathwater.

Ambient room thermal reading was measured at 76°F
within one hour of discovery of the body. The bathwater
temperature, at 81°F, was 5°F higher than the ambient
room condition. The victim's body temperature, measured
rectally, was found to be 93.2°F. "Normal" is assumed to
be 98.6°F, but this varies widely, the ME's report stated.
The discrepancy between the victim's temperature and

normal reading was attributed to (a) her death, and (b) the unknown heat of the bathwater in which the deceased was found.

Crime scene photographs showed the victim lying submerged in a whirlpool tub. From appearances there was no gross distortion of features, such as would exist if she had remained in the water for a long time. This was confirmed by the medical examiner's report, which estimated that she had been in the water for not more than a few hours. The ME had noted, however, that this estimate was subject to modification because of uncertainty about the temperature of the bath water during the victim's time in it.

The medical examiner found no evidence of bathwater or room temperature at the time the victim originally entered the tub. Hence the data did not provide any way to reasonably estimate the rate of change in body condition, and by extension, time of death. For these reasons, the decedent's body temperature at the time of examination was not considered to be a particularly useful indicator. Dr. Atwater remarked that, because of unknown constants, body temperature is often a notoriously unreliable means of fixing time of death anyway.

His interim report stated in addition that there was no apparent evidence of sexual assault, or recent sexual activity at all. No semen was found in any orifice, or on or near the body, but final conclusions would await autopsy. Determination of both cause and manner of death could not be made until autopsy, toxicology, and collateral findings were completed. He ruled tentatively that the cause of death was asphyxiation by drowning.

* * *

The secretary ushered Mike into Dr. Fessenden's office. An oversized widescreen computer monitor beside his desk displayed two pages of text side by side.

The professor rose to greet his visitor, offered his hand. "Pleased to meet you." He waved to a chair in front of his desk. "Have a seat."

The man looked remarkably similar to his photographs on the Web. Perhaps a couple of inches short of six feet tall. Graying hair. Single-breasted brown tweed suit with a vest, buttoned. Gray eyes behind wire-rimmed eyeglasses. Particularly noticeable were his clipped beard and mustache.

When Mike was seated, Dr. Fessenden said, "I've read something about your case in the newspapers. Looks like you have impossibly high hurdles to surmount."

"Not an easy case. But you know what Yogi said."

" 'It ain't over 'til it's over'?"

"Right. We have a long way to go, and the prosecution by no means has an open and shut case."

"I see." The professor paused briefly. "I'm sorry, but I have a small favor to ask. There's a call going to come in I have to take. I don't usually take calls when someone's here, but . . . ."

"No problem at all. I understand. I appreciate your seeing me on such short notice."

"Glad to do it. How can I help?"

"I understand from Sheila Graham's sister that you obtained some of her things—her computer in particular—"

Dr. Fessenden nodded, stroked his beard.

Mike continued. "I'm hoping that you'll agree to let me have a look at her computer files."

Dr. Fessenden leaned back in his chair, seemed to relax slightly. "I'd be perfectly glad to, except for the fact that I donated the computer to a charitable organization, so it is out of my hands. Completely."

Mike saw a way out. The professor had not shut the gap entirely. "That's not a problem, Dr. Fessenden. If you just let me know where you donated it, I may be able to track it down without too much trouble."

The other man's face seemed to twitch for the briefest moment before he spoke again. "That won't help you, I'm afraid. I had the hard drive removed and destroyed. I didn't need to look at any of the files on it, because I knew what they were, and I didn't want to take any chance on their being publicly disclosed. And none of the files you might be interested in would be on it anyway."

He saw Mike's puzzlement and went on. "Please understand. Sheila and I were working on a very important scientific research project together. She had the project files on her computer and I have them on mine too. The files are wholly confidential. I could not permit any possibility to arise where they might fall into the hands of someone who might use them for an impermissible purpose. Of course I'm not suggesting that you—"

"I understand," Mike said, "but—"

The telephone rang and Dr. Fessenden picked up a portable handset, pressed a key, listened for a moment before saying, "Where are you?" After a brief pause he added, "We're to meet at 1:00 o'clock. Can you be here by then?"

He listened briefly, said, "I don't know. There's someone here who might know. Let me ask him." He turned to Mike. "I'm sorry to burden you with this, but I don't know a thing about the public transportation system. There's a man who's going to be in our graduate program—he's at Logan Airport right now and needs to come here on the subway. Is there any way you could help him?"

"Sure; it's easy." Mike gestured toward the computer monitors. "Just bring up MBTA.com, click on 'Schedules & Maps,' then 'Subway' in the drop-down menu. That'll show the route. They're all color coded—blue, red, green lines, and so on."

The professor did this and Mike continued. "See the Blue Line near Logan? It's called 'Airport.' Just tell him to catch a shuttle bus to Airport Station, then take the Blue Line to Government Center, where the Blue Line crosses the Orange Line, and then goes to the Green Line?" Mike pointed. "See? Then change to the Green Line, go to Park Street, which is the next stop—and change to the Red Line, then—"

The professor looked befuddled. He handed the portable handset to Mike and said, "Do me a favor, will you? Just tell him."

Mike took the receiver and explained to the man, who spoke with a German accent. "You got it?" Mike asked.

"I think so."

"If you have a problem . . . . Do you have access to the Internet on your phone?"

"Yes."

Mike told him how to access the "T" system route map, handed the receiver back to the professor, who hung up and apologized for the interruption.

Mike said, "No problem at all. Glad to help. Let's see, we were talking about . . . ?"

"The computer files."

"Oh, yes. Well, as I said, your concerns are certainly understandable. I guess I should ask if you got anything that, say, was different than what you expected? I mean, anything unusual? Suspicious?"

"I'm sorry to say that I didn't even look at her materials. I knew I already had copies of everything relevant in her possession, so again, I was principally interested in ensuring that they did not fall into the wrong hands. I had the drive destroyed by a professional so that wouldn't be a possibility."

"I see." By now it had become clear that Mike would get nothing of use here. He stood and said, "Well, I appreciate your taking time out of your busy schedule to see me. If you think of anything . . . ."

"Of course. And thank you for helping with my grad student."

"Glad to do it."

The professor stood and said, "If you have any other questions, just call me. My cell's on here." The professor handed his card to Mike. "That's the best number to use. And you're right: I am interested in fairness, so I have no hesitation in helping your client. Call me if you can think of anything—any way I can help at all."

When leaving the building, Mike had a nagging feeling that he had just been bested in a contest before taking the field of play—or even knowing that a battle was in progress.

A question lingered. If the professor had destroyed the drive, as he claimed, why did he not say so immediately? In retrospect his reference to donating the computer to a charity seemed misleading. Perhaps deliberately misleading.

In his car Mike called the Bromfield Coin & Stamp Emporium. No answer.

CHAPTER 22

The grand jury handed down indictments against Francis X. Maguire on the afternoon of the last Friday in May. The charges began with breaking and entering a dwelling house with intent therein to commit larceny of goods of the value over two hundred and fifty dollars (a felony). Next they proceeded to larceny, went up the scale to conclude with murder. Arraignment was scheduled for Monday morning at 10:00 AM.

The indictments were served on Maguire at the Colchester jail, where he remained confined. Immediately he telephoned Mike. "Jesus! It's for murder!" His voice choked on the words.

Over the years Mike had learned that in such situations the actual words he used made little difference, so long as they were supportive. "It's okay," he said. "We expected it. Just stay calm and we'll forge ahead with our original plan. I'll see if I can get the judge to hear our bail motion right at the arraignment—although I don't want to give you false hope. I have to tell you candidly that I don't think he's likely to grant bail. But I'm going to try damned hard."

"Jesus, I hope he will. I've gotta get outta here!"

"Hold on there, Frankie. I'm not promising anything. You know—I told you—you just have to hang in there." An unfortunate choice of words, Mike quickly realized.

"Yeah," Maguire said, his usual timbre flattened.

Mike did not notice. At this moment he had but one quest, a venture doubtless not in his client's interest.

* * *

With two days before the arraignment and nothing to do by way of preparation, Mike planned to spend the weekend in bed with Elaine. At times he felt that he could devour her. Quite simply, he could not get enough of her. They fit together perfectly. Never in his experience had he so enjoyed the act of intercourse, but beyond that, the pleasure of being in the company of a woman with whom he felt conjoined in some inexplicable way, sharing body and spirit.

During interludes he admired her features: eyes clear and deep; flesh smooth and glowing; earlobes delicate; nose straight, clean lined; hair naturally thick without any sense of brittleness; limbs long, flowing; teeth shining brightly with each smile.

Mike marveled at not only her beauty, but her intelligence and gift for quick repartee. He most admired her unflagging physical responses to his continued onslaughts.

Elaine came back from the bathroom and said, "I love that Jacuzzi—it looks wonderful. We'll have to try it soon."

Mike said, "It isn't a Jacuzzi; that's a brand name. It's a Kohler whirlpool tub."

"Ever the lawyer."

"You're right. Can't help it. Professional disability."

The bathroom was the only significant improvement he had made to the second-floor apartment after his firm dissolved. He had gutted the room to the studs, incorporated an adjacent closet, spending entirely too much money. Recessed ceiling lights, ceramic tile floor, marble-topped cabinet with an oval, inlaid porcelain sink, theatrical-style lighting above and on each side of the mirror, separate glass-enclosed shower, and the most beneficial feature, this whirlpool tub.

On many evenings Mike had relaxed there, adjusting the nozzles to direct the streams to points where most needed. At times he had fallen asleep, lulled by the gentle throbbing of the pump and the constant waves against his skin.

Returning to a subject of more immediate interest than the tub, he said, "Making love with you is like being in paradise. I never knew I could enjoy heaven right here on earth. If there is a heaven, it can't be any better than this."

"You sure know how to sweet-talk a gal, I'll say that for you."

On Saturday morning they had slept late, lay in bed and talked, got up slowly. In the kitchen he brewed coffee while frying bacon until crisp, then dropped bagels into the four-slice toaster. Without asking, he followed with fried eggs sunny side up.

"I never eat like this," Elaine said. "If I did, I'd look like a blimp."

"Once won't hurt."

She commanded a serious look. "If this is anything like your other behavior, it won't be once, it'll be multiple, multiple times—practically nonstop."

He smiled. "What do you mean, my 'other behavior'?"

Grinning, she said, "I suspect you know what I mean."

Elaine sat at one end of the maple table, rectangular with drop leaves. A matching chair had been placed at the other end of the table; two others, unused, were positioned against the wall. The kitchen, not large, had been used as a secretarial area before the firm breakup.

The morning sun shone brightly through the windows, illuminating decades-old faded floral wallpaper and a vinyl tile floor of a washed-out lemony color. Fifteen-year-old refrigerator, gas stove, dishwasher. The cabinets were white. Mike felt slightly ashamed that the kitchen looked so tired, out of date. Hardly the way to impress a captivating woman.

The bagels popped at the same time the eggs were done. The odor of bacon fat hung heavy in the air as it sizzled in the pan.

Mike served two eggs and several strips of bacon to Elaine, more for himself, with three eggs. He poured mugs of coffee and placed the bagels on a plate. "You want jam or jelly?"

"God, no, this is more than enough." Despite her earlier protestations, she ate heartily, left nothing on her plate.

When working on a coffee refill, Elaine said, "What are we going to do?"

Surprising her, he said, "I'll get the paper. It's downstairs. We'll take a quick look, rest up a bit."

"No, that's not what I meant. I meant what are we going to *do*."

He shrugged. "Why do we have to do anything right now? He's in jail."

"It's not that easy." She explained that she should not have stayed with him last night. "Frankie and I live in a Watertown two-family house Frankie owns. His sister Joanne and her family live on the first floor. She'll be sure to tell him I wasn't there, and he'll be quizzing me."

"So what? You're a free woman. You can do whatever you want."

"Sure, but are you looking to lose a client? And the money?"

A pause. "Maybe I *was* a little hasty there."

"Something else too. Frankie's got some pretty nasty friends."

"The kind I wouldn't want to meet in a dark alley?"

"You got it."

"Hmm." With his finger he made a check sign in the air. "Another point."

* * *

In mid-afternoon Elaine's cellphone rang. She glanced at the screen. "It's him—the jail number." She clicked the receive button and said, "I hate to ask you how you're doing, because I know you can't be doing too great in that place—but how're you doing?"

She listened, then said, "I'm sorry I missed it. I didn't hear it ring."

Later, "I'll see you in a couple of days. I've been awful busy with—"

Following another pause, "I know, I know. Tomorrow then. I promise. Don't worry, everything's going to be all right."

More listening; finally, "Yes, me too. Me too." She tapped the end call button.

Mike did not ask.

* * *

Eventually he led her into the bathroom and waved at the oversized whirlpool tub. "Hop in. You're going for a ride."

Elaine said, "I think I know what kind of ride you have in mind."

"Climb in."

While resting on his bed afterwards, Elaine said, "I'm beginning to feel like Marilyn Chambers."

"The Ivory Snow girl."

"Right."

"The eighteen orgasms?"

"Oh, you know about it."

"I do. Read her interview. Kind of a sad case, actually. She thought it would help her cross over to mainstream."

She snuggled against him. "Speaking of *stream* . . . ."

He said, "You want to shoot for the record?"

"*Shoot* is the correct word . . . . I'm certainly willing to try." Later, she said, stroking his semi-flaccid cock and offering a gentle squeeze, "If I had something as beautiful as this, I wouldn't ever put it inside anything with teeth."

Mike shuddered at the image her comment evoked. "That's something to think about, for sure. I'll keep it in mind."

"I bet it won't change the way you do anything."

"I suspect you're right about that." He added, "Or you either."

"You're right," she squeezed, formed her lips to an inviting oval.

* * *

Lying in bed later, Mike said, "When you speak, I detect a slight accent, but can't quite place it. Where are you from originally?"

"Nashville. Inglewood, actually; it's part of Nashville, a neighborhood."

"How long did you live there?"

"Always, until my sister died. Then I couldn't stay there any more. I had to leave—it was too full of memories."

"Oh!—I didn't know. How did it happen?"

"Her boyfriend killed her."

"God, how awful! How . . . ?"

"He was crazy. They were both crazy—on drugs. He had a knife. He stabbed her in our house. I came home . . . ." Tears welled up in Elaine's eyes, and Mike put his arm around her shoulders and drew her to him.

"That's okay," he said. "You don't have to talk about it."

"No," she said. "I want to. It will help. It's . . . ."

"You sure?"

"They were fighting about something—I don't know what. They were always fighting. They were into drugs really big time, and . . . . I don't know. Meridee was so beautiful, and such a wonderful girl, full of fun—until she got mixed up with Rod." Elaine took a tissue and blew her nose, wiped her eyes. "I was sick for a long time afterwards. I missed her so much; we were so close. You can't imagine what it's like to lose your twin sister unless it happens to you.

"I'll never forget it as long as I live. She was in the kitchen. I had been out; the lights were off when I came in. I didn't see her, tripped over her and fell in something terribly slippery. I put my hands out to catch myself, and I touched her. At first I didn't know what it was. I felt with my hands, and didn't realize . . . ." Elaine's face tightened. "I got up and turned the lights on. There was blood all over Meridee, the floor; my hands, everything. I saw her and started to scream. I'll never forget it. The knife was still sticking out of her. It's the worst thing I ever saw."

Mike held her tightly. In a few minutes she seemed to calm, and continued. "After she died, I felt guilty because I'd always been jealous of her. She was so beautiful. I envied her for that. I was jealous of her name too. Can you imagine being named Elaine when your twin sister has a beautiful name like Meridee? I was soooo jealous."

"What's wrong with 'Elaine'? And as to looks, you certainly don't have to take a back seat to anyone in that department."

"Thanks, but I didn't look this way then. I kind of grew into it later. Besides, sometimes you just don't know these things about yourself."

"Well, I'm glad you do now. What about your parents? They must've been terribly distraught. What did they do when it happened?"

"My dad was a pharmacist, and my mother a secretary in a big company. They were . . . torn apart. My mother took a few months off and my dad stayed home for quite a while too. They never really got over it."

"I can imagine . . . . What happened to the guy—your sister's boyfriend?"

"He's in prison. Life sentence. Should've got the death penalty."

"*Life* may be worse . . . ." Mike sat in silence for a few moments. Wishing to lighten the mood, he said, "What brought you to Boston?"

"I wanted to play the guitar and be a singer. I enrolled at Berklee, started classes, but dropped out during the second semester. It was plain to me I didn't have what it takes to be a singer."

"I can't agree: you have a mellifluous voice. What kind of singer? What type of songs?"

"You'll think it's silly. I had a dream of being a folk singer, a balladeer."

"That's not silly at all. I bet you would've made a wonderful folk singer."

She squeezed his arm. "Anyway, I dropped out and took a job waitressing in a restaurant, went on from there, various waitressing jobs. Eventually I studied photography and got into doing portraits."

"How did that happen?"

"Accident, I guess. Just did it." She leaned on her elbow and looked down at him. "Thanks for listening. I appreciate it." She hesitated, wiped her fingers across his hair. "You're a very handsome man, you know that?"

"Ha!" He pinched his waist. "See this?"

"That's nothing. You look great."

"I used to ride a bike several times a week, tried to keep in some kind of decent shape, but I got away from it, and now . . . ."

"You don't have anything to worry about—I bet you get all the women chasing you."

"No way!"

In a moment she said, "It's funny when you think about it. We wouldn't even be here if Frankie weren't in jail."

Mike wasn't sure whether she meant they wouldn't be together because they would not have known one another, or because she would be with Maguire, or . . . . It didn't matter. He wanted Elaine for more than a weekend.

"Frankie doesn't *own* you."

"No, we live together, but . . . ."

"He doesn't need to know anything about us. We'll keep it quiet."

"Can't do that forever."

"Why not?"

"Like I told you, I won't be able to stay here, and you won't be able to stay with me—or even visit—because of his sister."

"We'll work something out."

"Another thing too. What if you *do* get him out on bail? Or he's found not guilty."

"That's not in the cards."

Enough of this, he decided. He wrapped his arms around her and clasped her body to him. His hand crept to the sacred place where her thighs met. She sounded a deep throaty laugh and tumbled back against the pillow. "I think we're going to break the record this time."

Later they relaxed in the living room, sipping wine. Elaine returned to the subject of Francis Maguire. "What're we going to do if he *is* found not guilty? He'll be out of jail then."

"The evidence of burglary is pretty powerful—irrefutable, in fact. Frankie's likely going to be facing some hard time even if I do get him off on the murder charge."

"So he won't get out?"

"Probably not . . . . But instead of just ignoring our situation and waiting for something to happen, couldn't you—can't you—just ask him—tell him—now? Ease out of it? You don't have to mention me, necessarily." Ah, the coward's way.

She sipped from her glass. Her answer came slowly, deliberately. "He'd find out anyway. I just know it. Seriously, we have to keep this quiet, Mike. Like I said, Frankie knows some bad people. I—you—wouldn't want to mix with them."

"Do you think he'd harm you?"

Elaine hesitated.

Mike gripped her arm. "Do you think he'd hurt you?"

"You! I think he'd hurt *you*."

* * *

That evening Mike said, "I've been thinking about the reward. I've got to make sure they don't trip us up when we go after it. I've got something worked out that I think will involve less risk."

"I'm listening," Elaine said.

"I've got to have everything set up by the time I contact the insurance company. There's a good chance the police, or—*someone*—will have surveillance on me once they know who I am—when they know I'm the guy who can get the goods."

"You really think so?"

He nodded. "Don't forget, I used to work in the DA's office. I saw this kind of stuff all the time. You can't trust anyone."

"So what's your plan?"

Mike explained what he intended to do.

When he finished, Elaine said, "Why don't you just hand the stamps over here, after you make a deal?"

"The police might be watching this house. I wouldn't want it to look like you were delivering them."

"That makes sense. Do you think it'll work?"

"I hope so."

CHAPTER 23

On Monday morning Mike arrived shortly before 10:00 o'clock for Maguire's arraignment in the Woburn Superior Court, as he had anticipated would occur.

The Woburn Superior Court was located in a privately owned modern office building converted to court use.

The courtroom, on the sixth floor, was generously lit by both natural and artificial light. The judge's bench was situated at the front of the courtroom on a dais, bookcases to its rear stuffed with case decisions and statutes. "Old Glory" and the Commonwealth's flag were placed prominently at either end of the bookcases. The clerk's bench was at floor level. On the right side of the room stood the jury box and the witness stand. A small desk for the stenotypist was placed in front of the witness stand. The court officer occupied a railed enclosure within the bar.

A giant projection screen was mounted opposite the jury box. At trial the judge, the clerk and each counsel table would have computer monitors to observe the display separately should they choose, and five more were mounted in the front of the first row of the jury box. Each monitor was connected to a central distribution console.

In addition, the court and counsel could independently access the Internet on their personal laptop computers. This would give them the opportunity to search case citations and other material instantly.

Perhaps equally important, all exhibits on the agreed list would be available in digital format, ready for projection at the tap of a few keys.

Upon arrival at the arraignment, Mike conferred briefly with his client in the holding cell near the prisoner elevator.

"It'll be quick," Mike said. He gripped Frankie's arm and leaned toward him. "I'll do all the talking. You don't say anything. *Anything*."

"What about my bail? Can't you do something?"

"Like I told you before, you can pretty much take it for granted that you're going to be stuck in here at least until the trial's over, and you won't get out even then unless we get a not guilty on the murder charge. Let's keep our focus on that, okay?"

"Jesus!"

"Yeah, but all I can do is what I can do. I'm not a miracle worker."

Mike turned to leave for the courtroom, but Maguire stopped him and said, "I haven't heard from Elaine hardly at all." He leaned toward his lawyer and whispered, "She bring the stuff to you?"

Mike lowered his voice in return. "Yeah, she did, and I'm working to see how much I can turn it over for. I'll let you know as soon as I find out."

Maguire seemed to relax a bit. "At least *some* good news."

Mike opened the door, said, "Don't forget, let me do the talking."

This courtroom was much larger, more modern, than the one in the Woburn District Court. Here Justice Martin Abel presided. At thirty-eight he was young for the Superior Court bench, which he had joined less than a year earlier.

In his law practice the judge had specialized in labor law. Since donning the robe he had not presided over any criminal trials. Mike knew this and felt it might be of some advantage to his client. On the other hand, the judge might feel constrained to show how tough he is.

When the case was called, Mike stood and said, "Michael Ratigan, Your Honor, representing the defendant, Francis X. Maguire. The defendant waives the reading of the indictment, and asks that the clerk enter a plea of not guilty on each charge."

"Thank you, counselor," the judge said. "Let the record reflect that the defendant has waived the reading of the indictment, and pleas of not guilty will be entered on all charges. The clerk will so indicate." The judge glanced at the papers before him and said, "I believe we have the matter of bail before us?"

"Yes, Your Honor," Mike said. "The defendant has an application for bail pending, but I understand that the Commonwealth seeks a dangerousness hearing. The judge in the Woburn District Court scheduled a hearing, but he knew the case would almost certainly be transferred to this court. The defendant is prepared to proceed on both matters at this time, if it please the court. That is, the dangerousness hearing and the bail application."

Mike knew that the judge should simply deny bail and schedule the dangerousness hearing. Yet there was a chance that this particular judge's inexperience might provide an opportunity to obtain Maguire's release. For him to see Elaine? Mike shuddered at the thought.

Judge Abel said, "Since it's the defendant's motion, I'll hear from him now."

Mike addressed the court. "Your Honor, the facts of this case present an ideal situation for release on the defendant's personal recognizance, or at the very minimum, admission to a reasonable bail. The defendant has never previously been charged with a crime. He has absolutely no criminal record whatsoever—*none!*

"There is no evidence that he has ever harmed another human being in his entire life. He was born in Massachusetts and has always lived here. He has established a home here. He lives in Watertown, and has for many years. There's no doubt whatsoever that this defendant will appear for his trial, and that is the fundamental purpose of bail: to guarantee appearance at trial. Mr. Maguire is prepared to post bail in any reasonable amount that the court might order."

The judge nodded and turned to the prosecutor. "I'll hear from the Commonwealth."

Mike sat down. The ADA rose to address the court. Like his district court counterpart, he was a young man, late twenties, dressed in a gray pinstripe suit, white shirt with button-down collar and a red tie. His black shoes needed a shine.

"Robert Sullivan, Assistant District Attorney, appearing for the Commonwealth, Your Honor." He glanced at the papers on the desk before him, continued without further reference to them.

"So far as appears, Your Honor, this defendant has never had any regular gainful employment. He has never filed a tax return in this state. He does not appear to own any property here. The house he lives in is in the name of a trust.

"He was caught leaving a residence where a woman was found dead, drowned in her own bathtub. He was caught coming out of those premises with the owner's jewelry, credit cards and other personal items.

"The grand jury has charged this defendant with responsibility for her death.

"So far as appears, it seems that the defendant's means of earning a livelihood consists solely of breaking and entering domiciles for the purpose of stealing property. There can be little dispute that such an occupation is inherently dangerous to citizens of this Commonwealth. One woman has already died at his hands. That should be enough to persuade the court that he is a danger to society and ought not be released.

"For these reasons the Commonwealth requests that this matter be continued until the court can hold a dangerousness hearing. At that time the Commonwealth will present evidence which in its view will require the defendant to remain incarcerated through the time of trial."

The judge promptly ruled from the bench. "Motion for bail denied at this time. We'll hold the dangerousness hearing as soon as the clerk can make provision for it on the docket. Since we have a full schedule, I will suggest some afternoon next week, if that's all right with you gentlemen?"

Both attorneys agreed, and they arranged for the clerk to provide enough notice for them to procure the attendance of witnesses at the forthcoming hearing.

Mike thought that the young prosecutor was exceptionally well spoken for someone of his limited experience. After the hearing was over, he went up to the attorney and said, "Just wanted to let you know I thought you did a very good job today. I used to do what you're doing when I first got out of law school. It's a great way to learn. Good luck."

The lawyer seemed genuinely surprised, such accolades being entirely unexpected. When Mike extended his hand, his adversary shook it, smiled, said, "Thanks."

Mike conferred briefly with Maguire. "You're not going to be able to testify at the dangerousness hearing," Mike reminded his client. "For the same reasons you couldn't testify today. You'd be decimated on cross-examination. The prosecution would just use it as an opportunity for discovery."

"What's that, 'discovery'?"

"Learning facts injurious to your case—evidence the Commonwealth wants."

"Oh." Maguire leaned toward him. "Something I need to ask you. Judge said bail is denied 'at this time.' Does that mean he's gonna grant it later?"

"No, not at all. That's an unfortunate way judges have of bullshitting people to make them feel better."

"Figures."

Maguire now seemed to be growing resigned to the idea that he would remain incarcerated indefinitely.

Good.

CHAPTER 24

Mike obtained the autopsy report from the Assistant District Attorney, whose office was located in the courthouse building, and began to study it immediately on return to his own office.

The autopsy had been conducted by Dr. Jerome Fishbein, Middlesex Chief Medical Examiner. His report recorded the Manner of Death of Sheila Graham, a forty-three year old Caucasian female, as "Unnatural: Homicide." The Immediate Cause of Death was determined to be asphyxia from drowning.

Dr. Fishbein's autopsy findings correlated with the observations of the assistant ME at the death scene. These findings further disclosed that mucus was found in the decedent's throat and windpipe, consistent with drowning. There was no evidence of lacerations.

Presence of slight contusions (ecchymosis) about the neck at the base of the skull was noted. Although postmortem bruising was possible, this finding essentially indicated that the victim was most likely alive after she sustained a blow to her neck area.

Stomach contents consisted of a small quantity of largely undigested foodstuffs, suggesting that death had probably followed the last meal by less than two to three hours. The report set out no evidence of the exact time when that last meal had been ingested.

A brief review of the autopsy report confirmed Mike's decision to hire a forensic pathologist to testify for the defense. He said to Kaitlin, "Get Dr. Gruber on the line for me. He's in the contacts list." Let *her* bumble her way through the labyrinthine telephone complex at the exclusive practice which Alan Gruber had helped to found.

Kaitlin said, "He's not by any chance related to the Dr. Gruber —"

Mike waited, counting on her to catch it.

"—Never mind." Kaitlin shook her head vigorously. "It's stupid. I just realized . . . ."

Mike smiled at her oblique reference to the physician in *The Verdict* who fled to avoid testifying about the defendants' malpractice. Mike knew that Kaitlin had watched the film a dozen times. "Paul Newman's best," she had told Mike.

He had replied, "Don't let it bother you. Sometimes it seems real to me, too." He remembered that noir movies of the Forties were her favorites.

The doctor came on the line. Mike said, "Alan, good to speak with you."

"It's been quite some time." Dr. Guber said. "How're you doing?"

At the doctor's urging several years previously, Mike had successfully defended a young intern who had been charged with prescribing narcotic drugs to a fictitious patient for his own use. Mike and Dr. Gruber had established a bond as a result.

After chatting a while, Mike said, "I've got a new case for you. Murder. You have time?"

"For you, always, Mike. What've you got?"

"Woman drowned in her bathtub. Looks as though she suffered some sort of head trauma beforehand. May have been in the water an hour or so before discovery. Not too clear."

"You representing the husband, boyfriend?"

"No, nothing like that. Actually, kind of an odd situation." He related a sketch of events.

"Weird. You have the reports?"

"All of them."

"I assume there was an autopsy."

"Yep."

"Who did it?"

"Fishbein."

"Good man. He do the scene too?"

"No, that was a younger guy. Atwater, I think his name was."

"Haven't run into him yet. Okay, email me the reports and I'll have a look at them, then we'll talk."

"I assume your fee—"

"—is still exorbitant."

"Right."

"We'll work it out. Like always."

* * *

Mike made several calls to the Bromfield stamp store during late morning and early afternoon. No live answer, no machine, no voicemail.

Finally, just before 4:00 o'clock, a man answered, "Yeah?"

Younger. Not Weissman's scratchy voice.

"Hi," Mike responded. Might as well be pleasant; more flies . . . . "I'm looking for the owner, Mr. Weissman. He in?"

"Heart attack. He's in the hospital." Click, silence. Line dead.

Mike called right back. The same voice answered and Mike said, "Hey—don't hang up on me like that! I'm sorry to hear about Mr. Weissman, but he's holding some stamps for me I need to get right away. Who'm I talking to?"

"Look, I don't even wanna be here. Nothin' I can do for you." Click, silence.

Next try. "I don't want to cause trouble for you, but you hang up on me again and I'll have the cops over there before you can be out the door."

Silence, but no click.

Mike pressed. "You hear me?"

"I'm only his nephew. Don't know nothin' about this place. Just come in to see—"

"What's your name?"

"Jerry."

"Jerry what?"

Hesitation.

"I'm Mike Ratigan. Lawyer. Like I said, not looking to cause trouble, but I do need to get those stamps back."

No response.

"Jerry what?"

"Silver. Jerry Silver."

"Listen, Jerry, how long're you going to be there? I've got to get those stamps back pronto."

"Can't give out nothin'. They told me not to give out nothin'."

"Well, maybe I can see Mr. Weissman then. He'll give them to me. What hospital is he in? When's he getting out?"

"He ain't gettin' out. He's in a coma and they say he ain't gonna live."

Shit! "Oh. Sorry to hear that." Mike thought for a moment. "I don't suppose if I came in there's any chance . . . ?"

"I ain't givin' out nothin'."

"Well, I appreciate your letting me know what's going on. I'll see what I can do. Are you the one who's going to be in the store most of the time from now on?"

"Not me. Don't know who's gonna be here. Nobody, pro'bly."

"Thanks." Mike hung up. I've got to get those stamps back. What if I can't?

He ran through numerous ideas, ploys he might use. None caught his fancy. Finally, tiring of this effort, he turned his attention to the stamps which he *did* possess.

CHAPTER 25

Through newspaper articles which turned up in a Web search, Mike learned that Willenbrandt's insurer was First Advantage Casualty Insurance Company. The insurer had designated its top attorney, one Charles Thaddeus Oglethorpe, III, to handle the claim.

To make Mike's scheme believable, it had to appear that he was representing third parties, the actual thieves. Which in a way he was.

Plenty to worry about. The insurer might call in the police. Might have Mike followed. Watch his office too. The FBI—anybody—could conceal a device in the "reward" money, follow the signal. Or plant a GPS transmitter on his car. This decided one issue; he couldn't use his own car. Too much risk.

Also, it had to seem that the thieves delivered the stamps to him—again, pretty close to the truth. He could not involve Elaine; she represented a lead to Frankie. Same thing when it came to the money. Make it look as though he was handing off the "reward" to his mystery clients. He could not simply put the currency in his office storage cabinet and leave it there. That would not be credible.

No self-respecting criminal would let an attorney hold the money any longer than absolutely necessary. So the first job was to simulate receipt of a part of the stamp collection. Second was to keep the money in hand while appearing to pass it on.

Mike's initial thought was to use public lockers for both purposes. Although he had not traveled by train since high school, he recalled having seen banks of lockers at the railroad station's grand concourse in Boston's South Station. Those would do just right.

No time better than the present. On the way to South Station he would stop in downtown Boston and purchase attaché cases to carry the stamps.

When leaving the office, he said to Kaitlin, "During trial I'm going to need you to help me in court. There'll be a lot of exhibits and other papers. Motions, memos. I'll depend on you to be my organizer, keep track of everything, take notes, remind me if I forget something. The judge'll let you sit at counsel table with me. Is that all right with you?"

Her smile provided the answer. "Sounds exciting! I can help you and actually see what goes on in the courtroom first hand."

"It's a deal then. You can ride with me each day."

"I'm psyched."

Mike walked to the Davis Square T station, waited for the Red Line train. He got off at Downtown Crossing and walked to Bromfield Street on the chance that Weissman's shop would be open. It was not. He then went to Macy's department store, purchased two aluminum briefcases with faux-leather exteriors. The clerk looked at him with curiosity.

"Gifts," Mike explained with a smile. Immediately he chastised himself for providing an explanation when none was needed.

Originally he had thought that he would walk from the department store to South Station, but carrying his own briefcase along with the attaché cases proved too burdensome. He took the Red Line to the next stop and climbed the stairs to the railroad station.

A large newspaper kiosk dominated the center of the concourse. In the food court dozens of people sat at tables, eating foodstuffs purchased at the numerous vendors on the periphery. He scanned the entire area, saw no lockers.

He approached the Information desk, said to the uniformed attendant, "I'm looking for a locker to store some things for a while. Where are they?"

The man shook his head. "Not here, but I think they have some at the bus station. On the fifth floor." He waved toward the rear of the station. "Over there. Next building. Fifth floor."

Mike thanked him, took the escalator to the second floor and the elevator to the fifth. He looked around. No lockers. Another uniformed employee stood behind a desk. A sign above him said "SHIPPING."

Mike said, "Do you have lockers up here?"

The attendant shook his head.

"The guy downstairs said you do."

The man shook his head again. "No lockers here. No lockers anywheres in the whole country since 9/11. Just ain't no more. Too dangerous, you know?"

"Jesus! 9/11, eh?"

"That's right. Can't find one anywheres in the whole country."

Bombs! Everybody's afraid of bombs. Jesus! What's the country come to?

Mike would have to change his plan.

When he returned to his office, he searched the Web but found nothing satisfactory. He could rent a storage bin, but to do so he would have to use a credit card or give some type of identification, and there was a chance that such facilities would be monitored by closed circuit video surveillance.

Mike discarded the storage bin idea and telephoned a car rental company, arranged for a car to be delivered to his office later that afternoon. After the car arrived and he signed the paperwork, Mike packed the stamps into the new attaché cases and locked the cases in the rental car's trunk, then drove to the parking garage at Alewife Station in Arlington, the end of the Red Line.

He parked on the fourth floor, searched for surveillance lenses, saw no obvious ones. Their presence would make no difference anyway, he believed. He took the stairs down to the train level. After a short wait he boarded an Ashmont train and got off at the next stop, Davis Square, a brief walk from his office.

He disliked the risk involved in leaving the stamps in the car—what if the car were stolen?—but thought theft unlikely. Anyway, a guy has to take some chances.

The plan now set in motion, Mike called First Advantage Casualty Insurance Company. After getting past the receptionist, a chirpy voice said, "General Counsel's office."

"I'd like to speak with Mr. Oglethorpe." Directly to the top.

"Is he expecting your call?" Protective.

"No, but if you tell him it's about the Willenbrandt Collection burglary, he'll want to talk with me."

"Just one moment, please."

"Charles Oglethorpe here." A new voice. Rich, but reedy at the same time, faintly reminiscent of a contrabassoon. No discernable accent.

After exchanging introductions, Mike said, "Some people have approached me about the stamp theft in Brookline, say they may know where the collection is located, would like to help your company save upwards of six million dollars."

"I take it your people aren't charitably inclined. Sounds like you're talking about seven million dollars less seven hundred thousand."

"True."

"Your people say they *may* know where it's located."

"Well, I think they *do* know, but that is what they *said*, all right. Maybe they're just playing it kind of close, at least for the time being, if you know what I mean."

"I think I do. Are these people your clients?"

"They are now." The attorney-client privilege would protect his imagined client communications against disclosure. "I confess I had some hesitation in accepting the matter, because they're people who . . . ." A long hesitation. "They have some associations that . . . . They're men who—who might be vindictive if anything goes wrong and they suspect it was my fault. You understand?"

"I follow you. I might read your name in the newspapers."

"In the wrong section—and yours too." There. Now the idea had been planted.

"Hmmm. Yes." Oglethorpe's turn for a lengthy pause. "Are they reliable? Can you count on them? If they tell you they have the stamps, would you trust them?"

"There's only one person in the whole world I trust, and you're talking to him right now."

"A wise man."

"I don't think trust should enter into it. I wouldn't make a deal with you unless I was *sure*. That way you'd be certain . . . ."

Oglethorpe said, "That expands my comfort zone considerably." He stopped for a few moments before continuing. Mike could hear light breathing over the telephone. "Do you have any timetable in mind, when this could be done? Again, assuming your people have the stamps."

"Not *have*. Have *access to*."

"Yes, yes, of course. Access. But back to the timetable. When do you contemplate . . . ?"

"Not long. A week at most. Probably quicker. Maybe only a day."

"Excellent. Excellent. That would help a great deal." A pause. "I don't suppose you're an expert in stamps?"

"Hardly. It boggles the mind that they can be worth so much. Thirty million dollars, was it?"

"Only insured for seven, thankfully. Actually worth substantially more than thirty million, I'm told. You know how it is; people don't increase coverage even though value goes up." Oglethorpe hesitated, went on. "I assumed you aren't—an expert, I mean. Which raises the question of how you will know that the collection being turned over to you by your peo— clients—is the real thing. You understand we need certainty here before we can release any funds."

Already liable to pay a large claim, First Advantage would be wary, not wanting to be conned in addition to paying for coverage of the theft loss.

"Let me ask if this would do," Mike said. "Say I get part of the collection first, turn that over to you for a percentage of the reward, and so on. Would that work for you?"

"Well, we'd have to figure a way to allocate the reward for the part you're transferring back to us. But it does sound doable, and no problem occurs to me right off the bat."

"How is the collection broken down?" Mike asked. "Do you have some kind of inventory which—"

"We do. Three large binders, I understand. Somewhat like those three ring binders students use."

"So maybe it could be separated in thirds, delivered that way? In exchange for an equivalent amount of money?"

"Sounds straightforward on its face," Oglethorpe said. "Let me run it by our claims department and I'll get back to you. It may well be, for example, that value isn't distributed equally among the three sections, so . . . ."

"Sure, no problem. By the way, my clients insist that we have an explicit understanding that law enforcement be kept entirely out of the picture here. If they're going to facilitate the return of these items, then—"

"Of course, of course. That's clearly a part of any arrangement we make."

"One more thing. The currency has to be *used*. No new bills. Nothing larger than a hundred; nothing smaller than a fifty. And no consecutive serial numbers."

"No problem—sounds as though your clients must be experienced in these matters."

"Perhaps."

Oglethorpe took Mike's telephone number and promised to call the next day.

Now the waiting began.

Only after he hung up the telephone did Mike remember that nine stamps were missing from the collection. Fortunately he had scanned them before he had sold the stamps to Weissman.

Besides, the reward might not be reduced merely because of a few absent stamps. After all, Oglethorpe had himself admitted that the collection was worth more than $30,000,000.

Probably nothing to worry about. Mike would identify those stamps and settle the issue when he talked with the insurer's counsel tomorrow morning.

CHAPTER 26

Mike hadn't spoken with Anne since their dinner at Locke-Ober. Too early for anybody to be tapping his phone, but he would be circumspect anyway. "How are things with The Man?" he asked.

"A bump in the road now and then but quite well, everything considered. He's down in Atlanta now, working on some new project. A science building at Emory University."

"Very pleased to hear it. Same here. What's new with those kids? I haven't seen anything in the papers."

"The school board decided they should all be expelled. The superintendent took it out of the principal's hands and the board took it away from him. Several parents have hired lawyers already and say they're going to sue the city—and everybody else in sight, including me."

"Jesus! Maybe I wasn't such a big help after all. I was actually calling to ask a favor, but now I think maybe that would be a little out of place. Anything I can do?"

"No thanks. The city'll take care of it. They've got a whole bunch of lawyers working in City Hall anyway, but I heard they'll probably hire an outside firm if the parents go through with taking it to court."

"Makes sense. That's what they usually do."

"What's the favor?"

"It's kind of a delicate matter. I really can't get into it over the telephone. I wonder if you've got any time to meet me. Say even later today, if that's possible."

"Sure. Where?"

"How about that chocolate place on—I can't remember the name of the street—right off Walnut in Newtonville."

"You mean Bread & Chocolate. On Madison Ave. Sure, I can meet you. Four o'clock okay?"

"Thanks. See you at four."

* * *

At the deli Mike described the situation to Anne and warned that she might possibly get mixed up in a criminal investigation.

"Mixed up how?"

"There's stolen property involved."

"God, Mike."

"All right, all right! You don't have to do it. I don't even care. In fact, I don't *want* you to do it." He stood to leave.

Anne raised her palm, stopped him. "Don't be that way, Mike. Anyway, you helped me with the cheaters. What do you want me to do? "

He shook his head. "No, I shouldn't ask you."

"So I'm a sucker. What do you want me to do?"

He sat. "It's very simple." He explained the details of his plan to her. "If anybody stops you," he concluded, "you just don't say a word. Not one word. Call me right away. Instantly."

She nodded.

He said, "You have me on speed dial?"

Anne nodded again.

"Test it. Try it right now."

She tapped the keys, and Mike's phone rang.

Anne pressed the end call button. "So I wait 'til I hear from you."

"Right."

* * *

Oglethorpe telephoned the next morning at 9:00. "Looks okay from here," he said. "We can divide the reward into thirds. Assuming these to be genuine, the only problem we see is that after we pay the third installment, your people have no real incentive to turn over the third binder of stamps. My company could possibly get stuck there.

"So we have to deal with that—no reflection on you, of course. We just realize that you don't have perfect control over other people."

Mike thought quickly, said, "Actually that's not a problem, for a couple of reasons. First, when we were talking yesterday, I got a little ahead of myself. After we hung up, I mentioned the plan to my clients, and they said they didn't want any part of three deliveries. Just adds more ways for things to get screwed up. As you might suspect, they're not exactly *trusting* people. So it's got to be one delivery.

"My clients will turn over *all* the stamps at one time. Second, I'll get a sample to you to establish authenticity. Then you can get the reward to me and I'll get the rest of the collection to you. I won't turn over the money until I get confirmation from you that the stamps are as represented. How does that sound?"

"Makes sense to me. I can buy that."

"There are two other things I didn't know until after we talked yesterday. First is my fee. They expect your company to pay my fee."

Oglethorpe cleared his throat. "Your fee."

"Yes, my fee."

"And how much would that be?"

"Five percent."

"I take it you mean five percent of seven hundred—$35,000?"

"Exactly."

A pause, followed by a grunt. Mike could hear Oglethorpe's swivel chair squeak in the background. Finally the other man said, "I guess maybe we could do that. I'll have to get approval from the president, but I don't think it'll be a problem." He sighed. "What's the other thing?"

"Well, when I spoke with my people, they said that a few—nine—stamps are missing from the first folio. I assume that won't make any difference, because the collection is worth so much more than it's insured for anyway, but I did want to mention it."

"What are they?—the missing ones?"

"I don't know. They say they're from the first page. They gave me a copy, so I could fax that to you—or email it. Do you have any means of telling if they match?"

"Our underwriting department has a copy of everything in the collection. But I'll ask them, just to make sure."

"Do you want this to hold up the exchange?"

"No, we're running up against the time when we're obligated to pay the loss under the policy. There are strict limits, as you know, and the claim was filed some time ago. So we'd really like to get the stamps back pronto, else we'll have to pay the claim."

"All right then. Let's do it."

They eventually agreed that Mike would email copies of the missing stamps, plus page eleven from the first volume, page four from the second, and page seven from the third, arbitrary selections to establish authenticity.

Oglethorpe would have these compared with the insurer's copies. Once verified, the insurer would deliver payment to Mike's office. Finally, Mike would personally transport the stamps to First Advantage.

No need to inform the insurer that Mike's "clients" were one individual by name of Francis X. Maguire, currently in jail and not likely to reside elsewhere for a con-siderable period. If ever.

Kaitlin emailed copies of the pages to Oglethorpe; within fifteen minutes the insurer's counsel emailed back that they were identical to his file copy.

From the supply closet Mike withdrew an oversized envelope. "Ratigan Law Chambers" and the return ad-dress were printed in the upper left-hand corner.

First Advantage's corporate offices were situated on Providence Highway in Dedham. The Alewife Garage was on the way, so he would not need to make any detour.

"Good luck," Kaitlin said as he left.

Mike winked. "Thanks."

The temperature was low eighties, the sky cloudless. Fine weather for the last day of May. A good omen, Mike felt. His Boxster started without delay. Before backing out of the driveway Mike lowered the top; the sun streamed onto his uncovered head.

He figured that it did not make any difference if he were followed. No one would have any means of knowing that stamps had been placed in the trunk of the rental car, or when that had been done—as a practical matter, at any time since the car was parked at Alewife.

Besides, it was doubtful that First Advantage could have arranged its own surveillance at this early stage. Nevertheless, Mike kept careful watch on traffic behind him to make sure that he was not being followed; he sensed no one tailing him. One blue, recent-model car did seem to linger behind him for a while, but it turned off the Mystic Valley Parkway before the always-clogged Route 2 exit, and none seemed to replace it in the rela-tively light traffic. Nor did any vehicle follow him into the Alewife Garage.

Mike drove to the fourth level and stopped at his En-terprise rental. He opened that car's trunk and withdrew the correct page from each of the three binders in the briefcase, inserted them into the oversized envelope. He locked the rental car and left the garage.

On Providence Highway a sign on the front lawn identified the two-story, red-brick, colonial-style building with white shutters as First Advantage's corporate headquarters. Inside the entry, a male receptionist dressed in a guard's uniform sat at the front desk. Mike identified himself, told the guard that he had an appointment with Mr. Oglethorpe. The guard made a call, confirmed the appointment, issued a badge for Mike to wear during his visit.

"Second floor," the guard said. "Take the elevator." He nodded to an elevator bay at the end of the corridor.

The general counsel's office was at the front of the building. Mike entered the outer office and introduced himself to the secretary, an attractive brunette.

"Mr. Oglethorpe is expecting you," she said, rising to direct him to the office immediately behind her. A faint floral scent trailed her. The door was open; she stood aside and waved him in. "Mr. Ratigan to see you, sir."

An elegantly appointed, handsome black man rose from a leather-tooled chair behind his desk.

Six-and-a-half feet tall with broad shoulders, the chest of a weight lifter. Except for age, the man could easily have been mistaken as a linebacker for the New England Patriots. Sparkling black shoes, a blue, pin-striped suit, custom-tailored, wide-collar, white, cotton dress shirt, red-and-blue striped tie.

He approached Mike, held out his hand in greeting. Gentle grip for such a large man.

"Very pleased to meet you in person, Mike. I'm so glad we're working things out. Have a seat." He directed Mike to an upholstered chair next to a round, knee-high, glass-topped table. Mike sat, placed the envelope on the table. Oglethorpe took the seat next to him, said, "I see you've brought something with you."

Mike slid the envelope toward him. "Here's the proof. The ones we talked about." His palms felt sweaty; he crossed his legs and surreptitiously wiped his hands on his trouser legs.

First Advantage's general counsel opened the envelope and removed the pages. He glanced at them, said, "I've got a man who can authenticate them for us right here. It'll only take a minute."

He stood and leaned over his desk, pressed a button on his telephone console. "Julie, would you come in?"

When the brunette entered the room, Oglethorpe held out the envelope to her and said, "Would you take these down the hall to Ted? He's waiting for them."

She disappeared and the two lawyers made small talk about the Red Sox quest for another World Series title. Soon Oglethorpe's telephone rang. He answered, listened, smiled. Immediately on hanging up he leaned over and shook Mike's hand. "Deal. They're the real thing."

"Let me hit the road, then," Mike said. "When can you have the money?"

"I ordered it last night; it's being assembled right now. What time do you expect to be back at your office?"

Mike looked at his watch. "Likely take me at least an hour to get back. More if traffic's bad, but it probably won't be now."

"I bet the money'll be there by the time you arrive."

"That would be great."

"Anyway, the guards will wait. You have to sign for it."

"Understood."

"You can get the rest of the stamps to me tonight?"

Mike nodded and they shook hands again.

When Mike returned to Somerville, an armored truck stood in front of his office. He entered to find two armed guards seated in the reception area. A canvas satchel rested on the floor between them.

Kaitlin said, "They've only been here for a few minutes." She held out a paper. "You have to sign this. They wouldn't let me, and wouldn't leave the bag here without it."

In addition to the printed language, the receipt held only the date and the notation, "One package consigned by First Advantage Casualty Insurance Company."

Nothing on the form signified that the bag held money, or the amount. Mike signed the form and handed it to one of the guards, who tore off a yellow under-sheet and gave it to Mike. "This is your copy."

As soon as the guards left, Mike carried the satchel into his library. Kaitlin followed. He unzipped the bag and turned it upside down. Stacks of bills neatly banded in $10,000 segments tumbled onto the table.

"Wow!" Kaitlin mouthed. Mike had much the same reaction, but felt that as employer, and senior, he should not show such emotion.

The piles of currency looked remarkably similar to Pierre Beaulieu's counterfeit money. Mike worried for a moment that he might have been duped, but quickly cast such concerns aside. The bills did not appear new. He picked up one stack and broke the band. The cash did not have the stiffness of new currency. All were fifties and hundreds, as he had stipulated. Adjacent notes bore non-consecutive numbers.

"I want you to count it," he instructed Kaitlin. "You'll have to cut the bands to do it, but don't let that bother you."

She hesitated.

"Not every stack—I don't mean you have to count every single one. Take a couple of stacks and count them. Then riffle through the rest to make sure they haven't interleaved bills of lower denominations."

"Okay."

"By the way, there'll be two or three odd stacks, but there should be $735,000 total. If there isn't, let me know. And look for anything unusual inserted between bills."

"Unusual?"

"Anything at all that isn't a bill, no matter how small. I'm heading out now, but I want you to call me on my cell as soon as you finish—or immediately if you find anything not right."

"Will do."

"You understand that this has to be kept absolutely confidential, right?"

"Of course."

"It is nobody's business but the client's."

Kaitlin looked piqued. "I understand completely."

"I know you do. It's just . . . ."

Mike stuffed the satchel with a week's supply of discarded newspapers and carried it to the T's Davis Square stop. He boarded an inbound car and passed through Harvard Square and Central Square stops, got off at Kendall, carefully watched those riders who exited with him.

He remained in the station; none of his fellow passengers who debarked stayed on the platform. Mike boarded the next train headed in the same direction and rode it to Park Street.

At most of the T's rapid transit stations, passengers exit from the right-hand side of the car. Park Street Station was different. This Red Line stop had a center island in addition to platforms on the outer side of the trains, so passengers there could get off the left-hand side of the car as well as the right.

At the Park Street stop Mike exited on the right, waited until all of the new passengers had boarded, then stepped back onto the car, strode straight across it and passed through the opposite door, to the center island.

No one followed him. He took the next train to Alewife. There he rode the escalator to the top floor of the parking garage. As planned, Anne waited for him in her car.

Mike opened the rear door. "Here," he said, and tossed the satchel onto the seat. "Remember what I told you. If anybody pulls you over, don't say a word, and speed dial me right away."

She shivered, nodded.

He leaned in and kissed her on the cheek. "Thanks. Don't worry. Nothing's going to happen."

She accelerated, entered the down ramp.

Mike descended the stairs to his rental car. He retrieved the attaché cases from the trunk, tossed them onto the rear seat. The drive to Dedham proved uneventful. Again he saw no evidence of being followed. Of course, they could have planted a GPS in his car and be tracking him that way, but that would not matter. No one could know when the stamps had been placed in the trunk. Could they? His grip on the steering wheel tightened.

He parked on High Street not far from the Norfolk Superior Court, walked to the coffee shop on the corner, ordered a mocha latte. "No whipped cream," he told the server, feeling proud of this bow to diet. He felt jittery, hoped the coffee would not make it worse.

After only a few sips, Kaitlin called. "I'm finished," she said. "It's all here. Seven hundred thirty-five thousand."

"Great. I want you to pack it in the two attaché cases and put them in the supplies cabinet."

"You sure you want to leave all this money here?"

"I'm sure."

Mike finished his latte and drove to First Advantage's headquarters. This time Oglethorpe met him in the lobby. Mike passed the cases to him. "Here they are."

The insurance company's lawyer set the cases on the reception desk, opened them, took out one of the binders, thumbed through several of the sheets inside. "If you don't mind waiting," he said, "I'll just have Ted take a look at these . . . ."

"Not at all. Please do."

The general counsel picked up the telephone handset from the reception desk, tapped a number, said, "We're ready." He hung up, turned to Mike. "He'll be right here."

In less than a minute a stooped, early-sixties gray-haired man approached them from the rear of the building. Oglethorpe did not introduce him to Mike. Instead, the attorney handed the attaché cases to this man and said, "Let us know as soon as you can."

The man did not speak. He nodded, accepted the containers and took them with him.

"It'll only be a few minutes," Oglethorpe said. "You don't mind waiting, do you?"

"Not at all." As if he had a choice. At this point Mike half expected police to barge into the room. He pushed onward. "How do you think the Sox are going to do against the White Sox this afternoon?"

"I don't know. I took a peek at NESN a bit ago. Wakefield had been pitching, but they took him out after six. We were behind five to four."

Thus renewed their dialogue concerning the triumphs and perils facing Red Sox Nation with the team in second place, one game behind the despised Yankees. Before long the telephone rang at the reception desk. Oglethorpe answered, listened for a moment, nodded, replaced the receiver.

"We're all set."

* * *

Late that afternoon, after Kaitlin left for the day, Mike showed the money to Elaine. She gasped and pressed against him. "It makes me so *hot*, Mike." He guided her to the examination table. She quickly found the stirrups.

Afterwards Mike stuffed the cash back into the two attaché cases and put them in the supplies cabinet.

"You sure you want to leave all that cash here?" Elaine said. "Aren't you afraid somebody might break in and steal it?"

"Nobody's stupid enough to break into a lawyer's office—unless it's to steal confidential information about a case. Law isn't a cash business, and lawyers have no inventory. So what's to steal?"

"Yeah. I suppose you're right." She moved close, stroked his arm. "Listen, I can stay with you tonight if you want me to." Her eyes seemed to smolder.

"If I want you to . . . . That's a screamer. When wouldn't I want you to?"

"And maybe we can find something to do in the meantime."

"You have anything in mind?"

She moved her hand from his arm, stroked more. "I think something might come up."

*   *   *

They celebrated, walked to Johnny D's, a small club on Holland Street just outside Somerville's Davis Square, near Mike's office. Mike enjoyed a thick burger with sweet potato fries, while Elaine ordered the grilled swordfish tips served with rice. They danced on the small floor. The band was composed of Berklee College of Music students. The lead singer, who also played the guitar, sang R&B and folk music with the purity of a voice reminiscent of a young Joan Baez.

Later, back from the club, lying beside her in his bed, Mike said, "You know, there's something that's been bugging me. I can't figure out why someone let the wrong cat in."

Elaine shivered. "I'm allergic to cats. I hate them."

"No need to worry. None here."

"Why is the cat a problem?"

"When Frankie got into the house, he saw another cat there. Didn't belong in that house. It was somebody else's cat."

"So what?"

"Somebody had to let it in the house. I think the killer did it." A slip. He hadn't meant to tell her.

"Ohhh. So if you can prove that, then Frankie'll get off?" Elaine's face took on a drawn look.

Shit! "That's right. The murder charge anyway. The cat may be the key to the whole puzzle. Trouble is, there's no way to prove it without putting Frankie on the stand, and I can't do that."

Elaine relaxed. "So you can't prove it."

"No, I can't."

"So Frankie won't get off."

"That's the way it's looking."

Elaine nuzzled his neck; her hand traced its way to his crotch. "So he won't need the money after all."

"Except for legal fees." A moment elapsed before he explained. "For the appeal."

CHAPTER 27

Some nights later Mike slept fitfully and awakened in the middle of the night thinking about Sheila Graham's cat. The cat issue nagged at him, but he could not assign a reason. What happened to the animal? Did someone take it in? Or is it still wandering around the area? And what does it matter?

It mattered because of the *other* cat, he felt certain. Maguire said he had seen one in the house. But not the one Burgoyne described, the one in pictures. Did the Graham woman own *two*? All the photographs showed only the tortoiseshell cat.

Obviously Sheila Graham had been a cat lover. If she had owned two, wouldn't she have displayed photos of both? Burgoyne had not mentioned a second feline, but then he was mainly concerned with the noisy "mountain lion." Mike made a mental note to find out how many cats Sheila Graham had owned.

In the morning he reviewed his notes of meeting with Maguire. His memory had been correct: Maguire had told him that he saw a cat in the house. In fact, he had kept another cat from getting into the house because he was afraid they would fight and attract unwanted attention. Mike telephoned the Burgoyne residence and arranged to meet with them that afternoon.

After returning his interview notes to the file, he re-read the transcription of the answering machine messages. In the earlier message, Burgoyne had threatened to call the police if Graham did not immediately rein in her cat. Only on reading this message did it occur to Mike that the killer had likely heard this call, seen a cat at the door, and let it in. That was the reason Maguire encountered the "wrong" cat—if it *was* the wrong one.

*   *   *

At the Colchester jail Mike again met with Frankie Maguire in the interrogation room. They spoke in low voices, heads close together. Although Mike was personally confident that this particular jail was not bugged, his client was infected with the fear of overheard conversations, even those between lawyer and client. *Especially* those between lawyer and client. Can't trust law enforcement.

After being told in cryptic terms about the insurer's payment, Maguire whispered, "Look, I want you to take care of Elaine."

"Take care of Elaine?" You sure asked the right guy.

"Yeah. Don't let her at . . . the whole amount—or anything big. Just give her . . . four thousand a month. She needs that to pay insurance and everything. There isn't no mortgage on it, but there's expenses, you know?"

"Doesn't she have money? What about her business? She said she has a business."

"Nah, she don't make nothin' outta that. Complete waste of time far as I'm concerned." He grinned. "Keeps her out of trouble though."

Sure. Erotic photographs. "Okay. Whatever you say. Four thousand, right?"

"Right."

"Back to your case. Do you remember seeing a cat *inside* the house?"

"Sure," his client nodded. "He was in the den—the computer room—on the chair over near the window-slider."

"Do you remember what it looked like?"

"Fair sized. Black and white. Maybe some gray. Looked like he was asleep when I went in. He kinda raised his head up for a second and laid it right back down again."

"What colors do you recall seeing?"

"Like I said. Regular. Black, white, gray."

"Do you know if that kind of cat has a name?"

"Pro'bly does, but I don't know it. How would I know?"

Mike said, "Next time, I'll bring some pictures with me, see if that helps."

Maguire added. "The other one too."

"Good thought. What about that other one—the one you saw at the door?"

"He was tryin' to get in while I was tryin' to get out. Scrappy devil, but I was able to keep him out. All I needed was for them two to get in a fight." Then he remembered. " 'Course I didn't know a cop was standin' on the patio right outside the door."

"Recall anything else about him—the outside cat, I mean? Color? Size? Markings . . . anything?"

Maguire thought for a minute. "Orangey. Yellowish, maybe. And white. Some dark hair too. Lotsa different colors, you know? Like you see on those horn-rimmed glasses."

Sheila Graham's cat. "You sure?"

"Mostly just noticed him, kept him out, that's all." He grinned. "Had some other things on my mind."

Mike laughed. "You sure did." He returned to his subject. "Anything else?"

"No, that's the best I remember."

On his way back to the office, Mike stopped at a local bookstore and picked up an encyclopedia of cat breeds. That evening he studied photographs and descriptions. He was surprised to learn how many ostensibly different animals meet specific cat-breed standards.

Twenty different sub-classifications constitute the "tabby" breed. The "Classic" tabby has a white "M" on its forehead. The encyclopedia showed tabby photographs with base colors of orange, red, and brown, among others.

The book also identified twenty-six types of tortoiseshell, all with a white undercoat, and generally a white stomach. It seemed quite probable that the "outdoors" cat was a tortoiseshell, while the one in the house was some variety of tabby.

At the jail the next morning Maguire confirmed Mike's guesses without hesitation. "That's it right there," he said, pointing to a picture of the "Classic" tabby. "The one inside, sittin' in the chair."

In another minute he found a photograph of a tortoiseshell cat playing in a pile of fall leaves scattered beneath a maple tree. The colors of the animal matched those of the leaves so closely as to suggest that the cat had deliberately camouflaged itself.

Frankie nodded, pointed again. "The one outdoors. Just like this here. Like those glasses people wear."

Sheila's cat.

"Great," Mike said. "Now all we have to do is find out who let the other one in. The murderer, most likely."

"You think so?"

"I do."

Maguire looked at him steadily. "So you think it wasn't me."

"I think it wasn't you."

The stress lines around his client's jaw relaxed.

When Mike was ready to leave, Maguire leaned forward, lowered his voice. "I hope Elaine's doin' all right. She says she is, but . . . ."

Mike said, "She was asking me what I thought about the case, is all."

"Hope you didn't tell her."

* * *

Mrs. Burgoyne ushered Mike into the living room. He shook hands with the master of the house. "Afternoon, Mr. Burgoyne. Hope you're well today."

"Ralph," the retired officer corrected. "Feelin' fine, thank you. What can we do for you?"

Mike said, "When we were talking before, you told me about the cat that was bothering you so much."

"That bastid is lucky to be alive. If I was still able to get around, I'd have knocked the bejesus out of him, you can believe me that."

"Right. Now I've got a question for you. There's some indication of a different cat on the scene, and I was wondering if you know anything about that."

Burgoyne shook his head. "Heard nothin' 'bout 'nother cat. Whose cat? What's it look like?"

"That's what I'm trying to find out. Did Ms. Graham have more than one cat?"

Again Burgoyne shook his head. "Nah. Just the one—the bad one—the big bastid."

"Do you know if she let any other cat into her house?"

"Don't know of any such. Pro'bly wouldn't though. She wasn't that type."

What type is that? Mike dared not ask. Instead, he raised his eyebrows. "And your wife?"

"Mame!" Burgoyne hollered. When she appeared at the kitchen doorway, he said, "That Graham woman, you know if she let other cats into her place?"

Headshake. "Never seen it. Just the one."

Mike said, "Have you noticed whether there are many other cats in the neighborhood?"

"Not too many." She pointed toward the front of her house. "One over on Warren Avenue—next street over. Comes around sometimes."

Mike felt relieved at this somewhat indirect corroboration of Maguire's version of events.

CHAPTER 28

Kaitlin stood before Mike's desk. "I'd like to ask a favor."

He looked up at her. "Sure."

"I have a friend who does some freelance journalism—actually we were classmates at Tufts—and she'd like to interview you for an article."

Mike smiled. "An article on methods for picking stocks wisely, no doubt?"

"Not quite. It's more like one on criminal lawyers."

"Sure." No publicity is bad publicity. "When does she want to do it?"

"I'll ask her. Do you want me to set it up?"

"Go ahead."

*   *   *

On Friday Kaitlin introduced Nancy Higgins, a petite brunette with a genuine smile and a soft, delicate handshake.

"May I sit?" Nancy asked.

"Please do." Unaccountably, Mike warmed to the young woman instantly. He waved her to one of the chairs on the other side of his desk, took his customary seat. "Kaitlin tells me she knew you at Tufts."

"Yes, we were, like, best friends—still are. We were both on the school newspaper."

"That's one of the many things Kaitlin has managed to keep secret about herself. As time goes on, I'm finding out more and more about her; the more I learn, the more I appreciate what a truly remarkable young woman she is." No harm in laying it on a bit. Besides, it's true. Mostly.

"Yes, you're very fortunate to have her."

"Promise not to tell her, else she'll be insisting on a raise."

"No doubt deserved."

"I think it's time to pass on to a new subject before I get into trouble."

Without making it obvious that he was doing so, he inspected the young woman closely. The reporter wore a pale-green pant suit with a cream-colored blouse, matching shoes and over-the-shoulder bag. A dash of lipstick appeared to be her only cosmetic. Clear complexion, bright eyes, smooth, rounded cheeks; breasts unremarkable; small waist; tight mouth—all the better for . . . .

He wondered what it would be like to have her sit on his lap, facing him. Riding. He broke the thought, leaned back, put his hands behind his head. "You have some questions for me?"

Nancy nodded, opened her handbag and withdrew a mini-recorder. "You mind if I record this? I'm not a good note taker, and, like, I hate to misquote anyone."

"Not at all."

She also removed two small microphones from her handbag and plugged them into a Y connector, then inserted the jack into the recorder, switched it on, spoke.

"This recording is being made at 71 College Avenue, Somerville, Massachusetts, on June 10 at approximately 2:30 in the afternoon by Nancy Higgins, interviewing Attorney Michael T. Ratigan at his law offices here." She looked at Mike and said, "Mr. Ratigan, do you understand that this interview is being recorded, and do you consent to the use of this material in an article to be written by me?"

Mike nodded. "I do."

"Let's start, then. How did you first become interested in law?"

"Back when I was just a kid. My uncle had, I think, every book ever written by Erle Stanley Gardner. You know, the Perry Mason series, and he also wrote under the name A. A. Fair, and a half-dozen or so other pseudonyms. I read them all, ate them up. And of course the TV shows."

"The Perry Mason ones, you mean?"

"Oh, that and the others too. They all excited my interest."

"Did you want to be, like, a criminal lawyer?"

"That's what really interested me, to tell the truth, even though I knew that's not where the money is."

"And where *is* the money?"

"Corporate law, finance, IT, getting in on the ground floor of startups. Personal injury law can be very rewarding too if you get the right cases. Some guys around here have made piles of money in PI work. That sort of thing."

"Have you practiced in any of those areas?"

"No, not really. I've pretty much stuck to criminal law and domestic relations, but I've given up the latter, so now it's just criminal cases." No need for the young lady to know why I no longer handle divorce cases.

"When I knew I was going to have the opportunity to interview you, I looked you up on the Web. I didn't find, like, a site for you, but in the places where you were mentioned, I saw the firm name Ratigan & Johnson. Were you in, like, a partnership at some time?"

Jesus!—I didn't think this would come up. The question brought back memories of that final night—the night

of the breakup with his law partner. The final night with
Simone.

*   *   *

Around 8:00 o'clock one evening almost three years
earlier, Mike had been sitting at his desk, drafting a motion on his computer. He had heard no sound of entry, no
suggestion of another presence.

The first hint came gradually, the familiar pungent
odor drifting toward him. Immediately he suspected the
intruder's identity. He stood and went to the reception
area. Interior lights were off, but light from the street
showed dimly through the front windows, casting everything in shadow.

Mike saw the red glow of a cigarette in the area of the
leather-upholstered wing chair. He flicked one of the
bank of wall switches. The reading lamp on the table between the wing chair and sofa came on.

From the chair Simone stared up at him through nar-
rowed eyelids. She wore an ecru silk blouse and a short,
tan, leather skirt. His partner's wife had slid forward on
the cushion, her shoulders hunched against the seat back.
She had cast her shoes aside; her legs were fully extended
in front of her. Simone took a deep drag and held it in.
Her gaze did not shift.

He made no effort to conceal his irritation. "What are
you doing here?"

Simone said nothing, exhaled slowly, letting the
smoke drift lazily in front of the lamp light. She took another deep drag and held the joint out to him. He waved it
off.

"Come on, take a hit," Simone said. Her voice held
that throaty timbre Mike always found so tantalizing.
Full of secret promise.

"No thanks."

She raised her torso off the seat a little, drew her knees up at the same time and moved one leg outward, separating her knees.

He could not help but wonder whether she was wearing any panties—or even the crotchless ones he had bought for her. God, this is the last thing I need to be thinking about. "Thinking" wasn't the right word for the impulses scorching his brain. He shook his head to clear it.

"You've got to get out of here," he said, urgency threading his voice. If Dick were to walk in and see this— thank God he's out of town.

Simone tilted her head back and started another drag. With a casual yawn, she lifted her legs and hooked her thighs over the thick, padded arms of the wing chair. Her meager skirt inched back, revealing her core amidst a dark forest. Mike could not resist gazing upon that treasure so willingly displayed. He moved toward her.

Simone placed the remainder of the roach on the lamp base, creating a makeshift ash tray. "Give me your hand," she said. She knew her victim.

He foresaw what was coming. It was as though the entire encounter had been preordained, fully orchestrated in advance, even rehearsed. He reached toward her. She took his hand; her own felt warm and dry to his touch. Without hesitation she drew his hand to her crotch, rubbing the back of his hand against her prickliness. His face was close to hers. She offered her lips, and he took them. Quickly their tongues explored, probed. They kissed wetly.

"Right now I think you ought to do something we both like," Simone said. "*Love*," she amended.

No longer woozy, Mike sank to his knees. She slid her buttocks forward even further, offering the feast. He sensed the moisture trapped there. A complete assault would come in the fullness of time. Simone's thighs gripped his cheeks tightly. She closed her eyes and moaned. "Oh, God, Mike! I had to see you." Her grasp tightened. "I couldn't help it," she crooned.

In the next instant something smashed into the back of Mike's skull and drove him deeper into the crevice he had sought.

"You dirty rotten fucking son of a bitch!" his partner roared. "I'll kill you! I'll kill you both!"

Fortunately, Dick Johnson did neither. He had brought with him no weapons other than fists and shod feet. Yet the damage done to Mike was sufficient to hospitalize him for four days. Simone escaped relatively unscathed. Her husband's unexpected early return from a trip to Wichita had surprised both her and Mike.

During Mike's hospitalization, Johnson withdrew all but $100.00 from the firm bank account, rented space and opened a new office, took the firm's secretary and paralegal with him. He arranged to have the Ratigan & Johnson telephone numbers assigned to his new location, so as to receive all calls directed to the firm.

After Mike's release from the hospital, he and his ex-partner worked out a dissolution agreement. Mike kept the house, which was his anyway, and the meager library, plus some of the office furnishings. Johnson, perceived to be the injured party, got most of the collectible accounts receivable, plus all of the firm's clients except for two whom Mike was representing *pro bono.*

In Wichita, Johnson had settled a case generating a fee of more than $200,000. Mike received no part of the Wichita settlement. Simone was not included among the divided assets. Scuttlebutt had it that she and her husband reconciled.

* * *

"A partnership?" Nancy Higgins repeated.

Mike returned to the present. A moment passed before he remembered the question.

"Yes, I had a partnership for a while. Actually, Dick Johnson and I met while we were both working in the DA's office. We left separately and set up our own offices, but we were talking over a couple of beers one night and decided to give practicing together a shot. It didn't work out, but that's the way things go sometimes."

"So you've practiced mostly in the criminal area. Have you specialized in any particular type—white-collar crime versus, like, violent crime, for instance?"

"My cases tend to run the gamut. I've never really analyzed it, but I suspect that they probably split about evenly. Recently I had a rash of DUI—driving-under-the-influence—cases, which can be difficult but financially rewarding, and I've had remarkable success with them. I don't suppose that they fall under either of your classifications though."

"Do you ever feel responsible for people who were driving while drunk, but you get them off?"

"Feel responsible?"

"I mean, like, if they get drunk again and have an accident and kill somebody. Like, wouldn't you feel . . . guilty, maybe?"

Mike had actually thought about this. Several clients—men, and a couple of women too—roaring drunks for whom he had received Not Guilty verdicts. It had occurred to Mike that some dark night on a lonely road he might himself become their victim. He had shuddered at the thought. But whenever one of them called with a new arrest, Mike had needed the money and put aside such notions.

"Possible. You never know."

Nancy continued. "Kaitlin mentioned that you have a murder case now."

"Yes, but it wouldn't be proper for me to discuss a pending matter."

"I understand, but can you comment generally?"

"Sure. Go ahead."

"You must feel an enormous sense of responsibility in representing someone who might spend the rest of his life in jail—or even, like, be executed."

"Well, Massachusetts doesn't have the death penalty any more. It's still on the statute books, but the Supreme Judicial Court has held it to be unconstitutional. But the essence of your question is right. It is a great responsibility. It weighs heavily, I'm sure, on any trial lawyer who handles such cases."

"Have you ever found yourself in a situation involving a potential conflict of interest?"

Surely Kaitlin hasn't mentioned my involvement with Elaine. "Do you mean where I'm representing more than one defendant in the same case, and one wants to cop a plea and put the finger on his co-defendant?"

"Anything like that."

"Whenever that type of situation has come up, I always insist that each co-defendant be represented by separate counsel. That way they'll feel they received adequate representation, and nothing is likely to come back on the individual lawyer.

"After a defendant is convicted, you know, he doesn't have a lot to do except sit around in prison and try to figure ways to get out. One way is to attack his lawyer.

"A common ground of motions for new trial—and appeals too—is ineffective assistance of trial counsel. So the losing defendant is seeking to blame you, his trial lawyer.

They all do it. That's just the nature of the beast though, and we all live with it."

When the interview ended and Nancy left, Mike said to Kaitlin, "Your friend is cute. Adorable, in fact."

"She's not sophisticated enough for you."

Another way of saying, "You're too old for her?" Probably.

A few days passed and he forgot about the interview, but it soon impacted his life in a way he would not have predicted.

CHAPTER 29

Well past midnight Mike's cell phone rang. Groggily he snatched the device from the night stand. The screen showed the calling number and "Eastern Massachusetts," but not the name of the caller. Mike took a chance and answered. "Hello?"

"Mr. Ratigan. Mr. Ratigan." Slurred voice. "This is Dan Ferguson. You remember me?"

It would have been hard to forget Dan Ferguson. Mike had defended him against four DUI charges, the most recent three months ago, and had secured Not Guilty findings in all of them.

"Listen. I've got a little problem here." Mouth full of marbles. "I'm at the police station in Woburn. They arrested me for being stopped at a red light."

Mike shook his head, thinking that he had not heard right. "They arrested you for being stopped at a red light?"

"Yeah."

Well that's a new one. "Was the light red?"

"Yeah."

"I think I'm missing something here."

"Yeah."

A new thought occurred to Mike. "How long were you at the red light?"

"They say fifteen minutes."

Ah. "Was it red all the time?"

"No."

"Did they give you a field sobriety test?"

Hesitation. "I couldn't walk."

Oh. "Did you take a Breathalyzer?"

"No. You told me nev—"

"Right." For no readily accountable reason, an image surfaced in Mike's mind, one of Dan Ferguson on a dark highway driving at blinding speed toward Mike himself, a crash imminent. In that instant Mike's decision was cast. "I'm sorry, Dan, but I'm not taking any more DUI cases."

"What! I need you to help me here, Mr. Ratigan." Mouth stuffed with cotton batting. "I need you. You've got to do it. Just this one last time."

"Sorry, but I made up my mind and that's the way it is. Good luck." Mike hit the end button.

* * *

The next day, Mike met with Maguire to discuss trial strategy.

"I *want* to testify. I *have* to testify," Maguire pleaded.

Mike's lectures hadn't stuck. "I thought you understood. You *can't* testify. You do realize that, right?"

"How else am I going to get off? I'm the only one who really knows I didn't do it. Why can't I testify?"

Mike put his hand on his client's shoulder. "Look, we went over that. You know you can't testify. Every defendant wants to get up on the stand and say he's innocent. Jurors expect to hear that, and tend to discount it automatically. Same as they tend to disbelieve the defendant's mother, or wife, or girlfriend when they provide an alibi."

"What's our defense then?"

"It's not easy." Maybe impossible. "You were in the house for the purpose of burgling. And you did walk out of there with credit cards, money and jewelry. So we have a lot of explaining to do right from the get-go."

"Yeah, I see that. But—"

"You want to get on the stand and start explaining what you've been doing to earn a living your entire adult life?"

Maguire's forehead creased.

"You want to tell the jury that you found a woman's wallet in her home with her credit cards and money—and driver's license—in it, and you thought she wasn't home?"

Maguire's expression remained stolid.

"How likely do you think the jury'll buy that?—it'll swing them right over to your side?"

"What's our defense then?"

Same question. Again. A good one.

"I'm working on a couple. Our best defense may be accident. The woman's death could have been caused by some kind of mishap. I've engaged a forensic pathologist who is prepared to testify that the physical condition of the body is consistent with a fall in the tub.

"So if we can't find someone else to point the finger at, our best defense is probably to attack the Commonwealth's medical evidence. Their premise is, I think, that you knocked the woman out in her office and carried her upstairs, where you drowned her. Her sandals on the floor in the office are consistent with that theory. But their case is built on surmise, conjecture.

They have no *direct* evidence that you struck her, carried her upstairs, or did anything else with her at all. Their circumstantial evidence is not powerful, but it's strengthened by the fact that you were an unlawful intruder, and you stole items from her when you had to know she was in the hou—"

"But I *didn't* know!" Maguire interrupted. "I never even *saw* her!"

"What actually happened is irrelevant. No one on the jury is ever going to know what *really* happened. The *facts* are *irrelevant*. No one ever knows the facts. What people *think* are the facts is what's important. So it's my job to make it appear that either someone else killed her, or that she suffered an accident.

"One of the problems with the 'accident' defense is that you could be found guilty of murder even if she did die of an accident. Say, for example, that she was taking a bath and you went into the bathroom and startled her. She stood up, slipped, fell backward and struck her head, drowned.

If the jury found that this occurred during the commission of a felony by you—burglary, breaking and entering, larceny—then they would be justified in finding you guilty of her murder."

"Jesus!—But if anything like that ever happened, I wouldn't let the woman drown."

"How is the jury to know that? People might think that a man who broke into a house and stole things while the woman was home might not have been too sensitive when it came to protecting her against physical harm."

"Shit."

"Yeah."

"So there's no out?"

"I didn't say that. I'm still working on—"

"You didn't need to."

"—finding out who actually killed her. That's a common defense. It's called the 'third-party-culprit' defense. Or you might have heard if it as a 'red herring' defense."

Maguire seemed to brighten. "So you really don't believe it was me?"

"In my own mind I'm firmly convinced that someone else killed Sheila Graham."

His client seemed relieved. Relieved enough to attempt a joke. "Is there any way you can sit on my jury?"

"No problem." Mike smiled, went on. "We also have a number of technical legal defenses. The problem with them is they're *technical*, and juries don't like them.

"But basically, the prosecution doesn't have any direct evidence that you killed the Graham woman, so they have to prove their case based upon circumstantial evidence and the inferences which can be drawn from it.

"We have to do the best we can to knock holes in those inferences. I'm not going to get into the niceties of this with you now, because you're not directly involved."

"Not directly involved! Who's more directly involved than me?"

"Right. Right—of course. Sorry, my imperfect expression. Anyway, bottom line, our best chance of acquittal rests upon persuading the jury that somebody else did it. Too bad we can't use your testimony to establish that someone else was in the house immediately before you got there. But that would be too risky. Furthermore, it has the appearance of being cooked up."

"Cooked up? How's that?"

"It's a little too neat to be credible. Something a smart lawyer might think up."

Maguire leaned forward, obviously agitated. "But I *saw* that stuff on the computer! I did!"

"I know. I know. I believe you. That's not the point. The problem is *proving* it. We would need evidence that some text was on the screen when you went in the house. The fact that the Recycle Bin had been emptied might offer some support, but again, that's subject to the same frailties: you could have done that, or even I could've. And you can't testify anyway. So we've got to get it some other way."

"How?"

"I've been digging around, trying to find out if Graham had any enemies, anyone who'd likely want her dead. So far I haven't come up with anything in that direction. She didn't have a boyfriend—or girlfriend either, for that matter—and everyone at the college where she worked seems to have liked her."

"Maybe you'll find something. I sure hope so."

"We both do. I'll keep on it."

CHAPTER 30

Mike's birthday fell on a Monday this year. Over the last several days he had developed a new but persistent erotic image of Elaine. Because the vision involved pearls—she had worn pearls on her second visit to his office—Mike decided to buy a strand of pearls for Elaine for *his* birthday. Knowing nothing of pearls, he searched the Web.

Research disclosed that there are no generally accepted standards for pearls. The buyer depends on the reputation and integrity of the seller, usually a jeweler. In other words, the buyer is on his own. Pearls are frequently rated on an "A" scale (from A-AAAA, with the last being the best).

Criteria include source, smoothness, shape, size, luster (the fancified spelling "lustre" raising the price), color, overtone, rarity, match, and flaws. "Source" means natural or cultured; most pearls sold are cultured, but natural pearls—exceedingly rare now—are the most costly. In a strand of pearls, closeness of match affects value.

"A" pearls are poor quality, not worthy of jewelry; they are used in ornaments. "AA" pearls are fair in quality but have notable imperfections. The next higher grade, "AAA," exhibits superb quality but has imperfections, probably not noticeable to the inexperienced observer.

The highest rated, "AAAA" pearls (called "collection quality" by some dealers), show no notable imperfections. These are the most expensive. Just right for Elaine.

It is "nacre" which gives pearls their luster and color. Nacre is the substance which the oyster secretes to surround an impurity, either one implanted (as in the case of cultured pearls), or one which migrated naturally.

Color is confusing to the uninitiated because there are two kinds. First is body color, which can be white, rose, cream, yellow, gold, black, or gray. Second is overtone, which is rose, silver, blue or green. The "color" of the pearl is a combination of these, Mike learned. A white/rose pearl would have a white body color and a rose overtone.

Shape, which refers principally to roundness, affects price too. The more perfect the sphere, the more valuable the pearl. Size also influences price: the larger, the more costly. So too, surface appearance impacts price. Noticeable blemishes, scratches, or other similar defects will reduce cost.

Obviously, the more pearls in a strand, the more expensive the necklace will be. Individual preferences tend to be based on the wearer's flesh tone, white pearls thought to be suitable for all skin colors.

Finally, Mike discovered, pearls come from numerous areas, including China Freshwater, Akoya (Japan), Tahitian (French Polynesia Atolls), and South Seas, the last two sometimes grouped together, and being the most expensive.

* * *

The evening before his birthday, he told Elaine how they would celebrate. "I'm buying you a present. Something I think you'll like."

"Buying *me* a present! No way! *I'm* getting *you* a present, goofy."

"You can do that too if you want, but I insist. We'll pick it out together, and then we're going to have a conclave of two. How's that sound?"

"I like the 'conclave of two' part best." After a moment she said, "Can you give me a hint?"

He shook his head.

"Just a little one?"

"Nope."

Elaine rolled her tongue around her lips slowly, tantalizingly. "Not even a teeny one? I can make it worth your while."

Mike laughed, untempted, knowing that he would receive the hinted reward no matter what he did now. "The first time I saw you—when you came to the office that day—I thought that was the sexiest thing ever, the way you do that."

"Do that?—do what?"

"Lick your lips that special way you have. Jesus, it's so, so . . . titillating. I figured you were doing it to turn me on."

She threw her head back, laughing. "Not at all. I do it because I have dry lips."

"You're serious?"

She nodded, still laughing.

"You weren't trying to . . . ?"

"No, but now I'll have to remember it, whenever I feel you need a little extra prompting."

"Only with me," he cautioned. "Only with me."

"Of course. Of course. Besides, I know you never need extra prompting."

Later, lying beside him, she said, "I can tell that Kaitlin likes you a lot." She looked at him, waited a moment, said, "You ever 'do' her?"

"No. No, of course not. Besides, I think maybe she likes females."

"So what's wrong with that? I'm a female. You think she might like to join us sometime?"

"That's not going to happen. I guarantee it."

Mike felt disturbed by Elaine's remark. Was she introducing the idea of an additional partner designed to enhance *his* pleasure—or her own? Or both? The pearls might help to dispel any such ideas.

* * *

The next morning, when Mike came down from breakfast, Kaitlin sang Happy Birthday to him. Mike did a jig, twirled and said, "I don't feel a day older. How do I look?"

"Youthful! Charismatic!"

"That's what I like: a truly perceptive woman. So rare these days."

"Not to discombobulate you, but did you happen to renew your license yet? This is the last day."

"No sweat. It's already in the schedule for today. But thanks for reminding me anyway."

"If they had an 'Ultimate Procrastinator' TV reality show, I think you'd be guaranteed to win."

Mike smiled. "I suspect you're right." Immediately he went into his office and checked the Registry of Motor Vehicles website, learned that he could *not* renew online because RMV required an updated photograph.

In the afternoon he removed $20,000.00 from the supplies cabinet and stuffed it into an oversized, thick envelope. Elaine arrived on time, parked in his driveway. They took his convertible, put the top down, enjoying the mid-eighties temperature and relatively low humidity for this mid-June day.

"You look ravishing," he told her.

"I'd prefer *ravished.*"

"Well, that too, soon to come. But first we have to go to Watertown. That's the only place open late today."

"Is that where we're getting the present?"

"No," he said. "I have to get to the registry first to renew my driver's license. We'll go to the store right after that."

The breeze was brushing her hair back. Her skin tones looked fabulously appealing, her mouth ripe. His heart beat faster. How lucky I am!

After he renewed his license, Elaine said, "Where's the store?"

"Don't be so impatient. It's our next stop." Mike fastened his seatbelt. "You remember what you were wearing that first time you came to my office?"

"Yes."

Good. This confirmed his suspicion that she had planned what to wear that day, calculating how she might influence him. "Well, I'm going to buy you a necklace, a pearl necklace, and I want you to wear it with that outfit you had on that first day. Those short black boots with the stiletto heels. That black leather skirt and the black blouse—except you're not to have any bra on. And the pearls are to dangle between your breasts. I'm going to sit in my chair and you're to kneel on the rug in front of me and suck me off. How does that sound?"

"I love all of it, but I love the sucking you off part best." Her hand strayed across the center console, touched him, bringing an instantaneous response. "Do we have to wait? We could do it right here. We have before."

Mike arched his legs, looked around the parking lot. It would be exciting to do it now, here in the open, with the heightened pleasure that risk of discovery brings. But he had enjoyed his "first day" fantasy so extensively that he did not want to deviate from it. He said, "It's *my* birthday, don't forget, so it goes down *my* way."

"Okay." Elaine slowly withdrew her hand. "If you're sure."

He reached the Natick Mall, a much-ballyhooed upscale shopping center. He parked near an entrance. It took less than thirty minutes to choose and pay for the necklace, an 18-inch "Princess" length of 8-8.5 mm South Sea white pearls graded AAA, one grade down from what he had intended.

They chose the Princess length partly because it was suitable for plunging necklines—although this was not Elaine's planned clothing for tonight's adventure. The low neckline would come later. Often, Mike was certain. Price: $17,000.00, paid in cash from the $35,000.00 which he had extracted from First Advantage as his "fee" in the stamp collection ransom. Found money, he felt. What better way to spend it?

*   *   *

The initial round of his "first day" fantasy went as planned. Afterwards they adjourned to the conference room, and Elaine was ensconced on the now-familiar leather surface of the gynecological examination table. Mike quickly found his target at the V between her thighs and began a gentle massage. Thick curls prickled his palm.

"Ohhh," Elaine said, "*doc*-tor!" She spread the word out.

"Yes." He kneaded gently. "Would you like to know my specialty?"

Elaine leaned her head back. She had left her shoes on. The stiletto heels locked in the stirrups.

She raised her hips; her heated center pressed against his palm.

"Ohhh," she answered, throatily now, riding his hand. "I would, I would, I would *love* to know your specialty." A pleasure pause. "What is it?"

His finger easily slid into that place of eternal mystery. Welcomingly warm, moist, taut. "Cuntologist," he explained. "A specialty worthy of sustained and penetrating study." He punctuated his thesis by driving deep within her.

No further remarks were warranted. Both had lost all interest in speech.

CHAPTER 31

One morning in mid-October, Kaitlin came to work looking a little ragged.

"Tough night at the books?" Mike asked.

"Quite the opposite," Kaitlin answered. "Watched *The Big Steal.*"

"Robert Mitchum. How did you like it?"

"The movie itself was okay, but we got a colorized version by mistake. I can't stand those."

"Some of them *are* pretty awful."

"Too bad I couldn't be colorblind for the length of the movie. Or there isn't a button to make the screen go black and white."

At the mention of 'colorblind,' an idea burst into Mike's consciousness. "My God!— you've got it! He's colorblind! Has to be. That's why he let the wrong cat in!"

"Who? What're you talking about? What do you mean?"

"The Graham woman's cat was a tortoiseshell—all sorts of different colors. The one the murderer let in was basically black and white. This would explain it. He was in the house, listened to Burgoyne's message, let a cat in to forestall the police coming to the house—but it was the *wrong cat.*

"Because the killer is colorblind. He couldn't tell from all the pictures in the house that the woman's cat was colored. He sees everything as gray and white. That's the answer. You got it!"

"So you're saying we have to find a colorblind murderer?"

"That's right."

"Not exactly a routine task."

"No, but—" Immediately came a vision of Dr. Fessenden struggling to decipher the T's red, blue, orange and green lines on his computer monitor when that grad student called from Logan Airport.

"It's Fessenden!" Mike exclaimed. "Has to be!" Kaitlin looked at him in surprise.

"The professor?"

Mike nodded. "He's on the prosecution's list of witnesses. The only purpose I can think of for him to testify is to establish time of death."

Mike described the occasion where the professor had been unable to tell the difference among the various MBTA trolley and commuter rail lines.

"So he's the killer, and that fits right in with your 'Somebody else did it' theory."

"Our third-party-culprit defense," Mike elaborated. "The *Bowden* case."

He thought for a few moments, went on. "And there's something else that bothers me about Fessenden. When I met with him, he told me that he destroyed Ms. Graham's hard drive, but that wouldn't make any difference because nothing on it would help me. First, how would he know what might be helpful to me and what not? And second, how could he conceivably know what was on there, because he said that he hadn't looked at the files?"

Kaitlin said, "Okay, but how are you going to get it in evidence? You can't testify."

"He'd likely admit if he's colorblind."

Kaitlin looked doubtful.

"Or we could put something on the screen—a test for colorblindness."

"But even if he says he's colorblind, I can't see him ever testifying that he let a cat in, or even admit *being there* when the neighbor called to complain about the cat."

Mike was persuaded. "You're right. We need more, something else."

"A lot more. But what?"

"That's a tough question. Let's get a start on finding the answer. I'll go over the discovery materials. You review the notes."

"I'm on it, but I should mention something else too. I did read the police report, but didn't see anything in there about the police finding any water on the bathroom floor. You'd think there would have been water all over the place if she fell."

"Good point. We'll keep it in mind as we dig through these materials."

* * *

They conferred a couple of hours later.

Mike said. "Fessenden's call on the answering machine came a little after nine. He must have called the Graham house from his cell phone. He couldn't have called from his office because he was *not at* the University. He was at Sheila Graham's house. He *had* to call on his cell phone. And that's conclusive because his cell phone number is the one that appears on the answering machine as having made the call."

He went on. "His phone probably has a GPS feature. That would pretty much tell exactly where he was located when he made the call. Even if it doesn't have GPS, its location could be identified by cell tower triangulation."

Kaitlin said, "How can you be so sure he made the call from the Graham house?"

"He had to. He killed her before Frankie got there."

"How do we know that?"

"The timestamp on the answering machine."

"But what if he changed the time?"

"Hmm. I hadn't thought of that. Give me a couple of minutes." After some time went by, Mike said, "I think the time stamp has to be right, because we know from Burgoyne's message what time he called. Only about a minute before 9:00 o'clock. And that's been independently verified by Burgoyne. So we can take that as being true.

"And right afterwards, somebody—presumably Fessenden—let a cat in. The *wrong* cat. Then Fessenden went about his business for a few minutes.

"But Burgoyne called the police at 9:10. Fessenden had no way of knowing that. Three minutes later, at 9:13, he called Sheila's house number and got the answering machine, left the phony message about their meeting. It must have been about this time—maybe a couple of minutes later—that Frankie rang the front bell. This scared Fessenden off, and he left through the side door."

"That sounds right," Kaitlin said. "It wouldn't have made any sense for him to reset the answering machine clock for a time *after* he actually made the call, and it would have been equally senseless for a him to set an earlier time. His whole reason for making the call had to be to put distance between himself and the murder scene around the time when he killed her."

* * *

Later that afternoon Mike received a telephone call from the courtroom clerk. "Sorry to give such late notice," he said, "but trial will start Monday morning, 9:00 o'clock sharp."

Mike's pulse jumped. "What happened? Another case fold?"

"You're right. Defendant pleaded out."

"Okay. We first case on the list?"

"Yeah. In fact, you're *it*— the *only* one."

So there would be no continuances.

CHAPTER 32

Mike and Kaitlin entered the courtroom at 8:30 AM. No spectators were present. Maguire had agreed that it would be wise not to have Elaine attend. However, his sister might come if she chose.

When trial reached the evidence stage, media observers and others would be there, Mike felt sure. The case had reached a minor degree of notoriety. News headlines drew attention. "Nude body of Slain Professor Found in Bathtub." "Woman drowned in Tub." "University Professor's Naked Body Discovered During Burglary Investigation." And so on. One energized soul had established a blog for "Floor Plan Robber," which fostered the initial impression that some thief was stealing floor plans.

The courtroom clerk, Reginald Fortras, short-cut gray hair, was speaking on the telephone, one hand shielding the mouthpiece. The Assistant District Attorney assigned to try the case was already at the prosecution table. Thomas Armstrong Barton, age fifty-four, had tried more than two hundred major felony cases, including many dozens of murder cases. A canny trial attorney, his conviction rate stood just short of one hundred percent. In brief, a formidable adversary.

Mike had done battle with Barton on two previous occasions, ending with convictions each time (Barton had refused to plea bargain). Mike knew Barton to be independently wealthy from trust funds passed down through generations of a family prominent in the forest-products industry. Affable in manner, around six-five in height, weighing two hundred and sixty pounds, with a full head of brown hair, the attorney struck an imposing presence, both inside and outside the courtroom.

He drove a $200,000-plus Bentley Continental GTC red convertible, favored designer three-piece suits except on summer's hottest days, always wore a bow tie with a matching pocket square, saving ones with polka dots for trial dates, and was never seen in a button-down collar, using only collar stays.

Mike said hello to Barton and introduced Kaitlin to him. Mike and Kaitlin took seats at the defense table, situated on the right-hand side of the courtroom, to the judge's left. While they were emptying their briefcases and arranging papers, court officers escorted Maguire to the table and released his handcuffs. The client sat at the far right of the table, closest to the jury. Mike sat in the center. Kaitlin, on the left, set up Mike's laptop, plugged it in to the courtroom network.

Mike leaned over and said to his client, in a low voice, "We got a piece of good luck. Judge Brenda Spencer has been assigned to the case."

"Is a woman better?"

"In this case, yes. Judge Spencer is considered to be very fair. A lot of judges are perceived to side with the Commonwealth in their decisions—rulings on motions, objections, that sort of thing. She isn't. So that's a piece of good luck."

"Let's hope we get some more," Maguire grumbled.

In a while a few visitors drifted into the courtroom. Mike recognized only one of them, a reporter for a local newspaper, the Colchester Reporter, a weekly.

At precisely 9:00 AM the court officer opened the door behind the bench and announced, "All rise."

Judge Spencer entered the courtroom. Sixty-eight years old, two years before mandatory retirement, she measured five-feet eight inches tall, had a kindly face, dark hair, wore wire-frame eyeglasses, was thick-bodied, meant business. She took command of the courtroom from the moment she entered it, her manner communicating the idea that no shenanigans would be tolerated.

She introduced herself to all present. When the members of the jury pool were called, for their benefit she identified the attorneys, the defendant, described the nature of the case, and gave the names of probable witnesses. No juror answered affirmatively to the questions whether they knew anyone involved in the case.

Over the course of several hours, jury selection went relatively smoothly. One juror was dismissed because she was related by marriage to a police officer who would testify. The judge excused nine jurors for potential prejudice, including one who worked at the victim's college, had known of her and thought her fate "terrible." Another juror excused was a man whose brother was a sheriff's deputy in western Massachusetts, and felt that he held a bias against "these criminals." Seven reported that they held views about the defendant's guilt or innocence. Ten were excused due to personal hardship.

A number of jurors had read about the case in the newspapers, but had formed no judgment about guilt or innocence, they said. The judge did not discharge them for prejudice.

Mike made no challenges for cause, and only four peremptory ones. Barton made one challenge for cause, three peremptory ones. The judge seated sixteen jurors, allowing for four alternates, available in case replacements were needed. Eight of the regular jurors were women, four men.

The jury presented a reasonable cross-section of the community. The four males were comprised of an Hispanic building inspector for the City of Cambridge, a black biochemical engineer, a software engineer from India, and a network cable installer. The women were a black dentist, an Hispanic high school teacher, a Native American grocery clerk, two retirees, a nurse, an MBTA bus driver, and a real estate saleswoman.

The judge designated the biochemical engineer as foreman, and instructed him to change places with juror number seven so that he would occupy the most prominent seat. The four alternate jurors were divided evenly between male and female.

After the jury were seated, the judge described the case in outline, and gave brief instructions about how the jurors were to proceed during the course of the trial.

"Members of the jury are not to have any discussions or deliberations of any kind prior to receiving my instructions at the conclusion of the evidence and after final arguments of counsel. That includes discussions or conversations even among yourselves.

"You are not to watch any televised accounts of the trial, nor are you to read any newspaper or other reports of it. Nothing on the Internet, no emails, no blogs. You are not to do any research on the Internet, or in person. For example, you are not to go to any place mentioned in the evidence, in particular the home of the decedent.

"In other words, simply stated, you will not permit any outside interference. You must leave your consideration of the evidence and of the case until such time as you retire to the jury room for your deliberations.

"You may take notes during the trial if you wish. If you have any question about these procedures—or any other subject—at any time, do not hesitate to ask me. You should submit any such question to me in writing, and I will respond after I have conferred with counsel."

The judge consulted her watch and announced that the court would stand in recess and the trial would recommence the following day at 9:00 AM. "At that time," she said, "the prosecution will make its opening statement, and defense counsel will make his opening statement if he chooses. Then the presentation of evidence will begin."

She concluded with her standard "end of day" remarks instructing the jurors not to discuss the case with anyone or permit themselves to be exposed to any information about it, including newspapers and television.

CHAPTER 33

On Tuesday morning the trial resumed promptly at 9:00 o'clock.

"The Commonwealth may proceed with its opening statement," Judge Spencer stated.

Assistant District Attorney Barton rose and stood beside the prosecution table while he addressed the jury.

"Ladies and gentlemen of the jury, you will find that the evidence in this case demonstrates beyond any reasonable doubt that this defendant," he turned, walked directly to the defense table and pointed straight at Maguire—"this defendant," he repeated, "Francis X. Maguire, did on the morning of May 18 of this year break into the home of Sheila Graham in Colchester, Massachusetts."

Barton paused in his speech, turned away from the defendant and back toward the jury; with deliberation he walked to a spot in front of the jury box at its very center. Slowly he met the eye of each member. "When Sheila Graham discovered this defendant, Francis Maguire, in the den of her home, he knocked her unconscious, carried her upstairs and placed her in her own bathtub. Then he filled that tub with water and brutally held Sheila Graham's head under that water *for several minutes until she drowned*. In sum, he *murdered* her with full intent, deliberation, and malice aforethought.

"But that was not enough for Francis Maguire. He then callously pursued the very purpose for which he broke into her home in the first place: to steal items of personal property from her to the value of more than $250. Those items included cash, credit cards and jewelry."

Again Barton's discourse ceased. He stepped away from the jury box and moved back toward the prosecution table, finally turned toward the jurors once more.

"That, ladies and gentlemen, is what the overwhelming, uncontradicted evidence in this case will show. That, ladies and gentlemen, is the evidence which will require you to find this defendant, Francis Maguire, not only guilty of breaking and entering a dwelling house for the purpose of committing a felony, and guilty of grand larceny, but also guilty of *murder* in the first degree."

Barton sat, and the judge addressed Mike. "Does counsel for the defendant wish to make an opening statement at this time?"

Mike stood. "A brief one, Your Honor."

Mike walked slowly toward the jury box and stood at the end farthest from the judge's bench. The four alternate jurors were seated in chairs to the right of the jury box. In his address Mike included not only the twelve regular jurors but the alternates as well.

"The prosecutor has stated his view of what the evidence in this case will be. Now it is the defense's opportunity.

"As you doubtless know, and the judge will later instruct you, the defendant has no burden of proof whatsoever in a case of this nature. In other words, the defendant does not have to prove *anything*. Nothing at all. Not one single thing.

"Nevertheless, I say to you that when this trial is over, when you have heard all the evidence, you will be *fully satisfied* that, first, the Commonwealth possesses *no* evidence that Mr. Maguire entered the home illegally, second, that he did not unlawfully deprive Sheila Graham of any personal property, and—most importantly—that *Mr. Maguire did not kill Sheila Graham.* Thank you."

In this presentation Mike had violated the cardinal rule which his first—and only—mentor had taught. Janine Madore, then Middlesex First Assistant DA, now Superior Court *Justice* Madore. She had insisted that he *never* over-promise and under-deliver; *always* under-promise and *over*-deliver.

Mike would not have been able to explain why he transgressed here. Perhaps because of his certainty that Maguire was innocent of the murder charge. Perhaps not. At root he hoped that somehow he would be able to fulfill his promise to the jury, rather than have another client go down to defeat at Barton's hands.

While Mike was returning to the defense table, the judge said to Barton, "Call your first witness."

The Assistant DA stood and said, "The Commonwealth calls Ralph Burgoyne." He gestured to the witness, seated in a row near the rear of the courtroom. "Come forward, please."

Burgoyne stood and limped to the front of the courtroom, where the clerk swore him in. He then took the stand.

"You may sit if you wish," the judge told the witness.

"Thanks, Your Honor. I will."

When Burgoyne seemed to be settled, Barton began his questioning. The witness stated his name, followed by the next question.

"Where do you live?"

"Colchester." He gave the address.

"Are you employed?"

"Retired from the Colchester police." He then ampli-
fied without being asked, "Out on disability."

Although Mike often objected to a witness—especially
an adverse witness—offering information not sought by
the question, he ordinarily refrained from doing so when
the answer brought no harm, as here. The prosecutor
could easily have secured the information by asking a
series of questions, including, "Are you retired?"

"You state that your address is 74 Brandywine Road,
in Colchester, Massachusetts?"

"Yes."

"Where is that property in relation to Ms. Graham's
home?"

"Right next door. She's at 76 Brandywine. Sorry—
was."

"Did you know Ms. Graham?"

"To say hello to, that's all."

"Did you have occasion to speak with her on the telephone from time to time?"

"Yes I did."

"What did those occasions concern?"

"Well, she had this cat, see? And that cat was the
loudest thing you ever heard in your whole life. Screeched
like you wouldn't believe. I'm out on disability, like I said,
see? And I have trouble sleepin'. A lot of trouble. Have to
sleep in the daytime a lot. But that cat had the nasty
habit of jumpin' up on the air conditioning unit right outside my bedroom window and screechin' something awful,
terrible." He stopped, as though his answer was complete.

Barton said, "And did that have something to do with
your speaking with Ms. Graham on the telephone?"

"Oh, yes. Sorry. I called her to tell her what was goin'
on, and that I couldn't sleep. So she would take the cat
in."

"What, if anything, did Ms. Graham say in response?"

"That she'd take care of it."

"And did she?"

"Almost always."

"How many times did this happen?"

"I don't know. Maybe quite a few, goin' back over the years."

"What happened this last time?"

"Nothin'. She didn't answer the phone."

"Had this ever happened before?"

"So I left a message on her answerin' machine."

"Thank you for explaining. Did you ever have to leave a message previously?"

"No. She always answered the phone. I knew when I called that she was home because she never let the cat out unless she was home. If the cat was out, she was in. So I knew she was there that day too. Because the cat was out. Sometimes she even answered the phone when she was in the tub."

Some jurors tittered.

"Objection!" Mike roared, leaping to his feet. Without knowing why, he sensed this to be dangerous territory. "I move that the last sentence be stricken and the jury instructed to disregard it. It's not responsive, and not within the witness's knowledge."

"Sustained. The part about Ms. Graham answering the phone when she was in the tub is stricken, and the jury are to disregard it."

One problem with objecting is that doing so tends to emphasize the "stricken" testimony.

The prosecutor immediately found a way around the objection. "Did you ever have a telephone conversation with Ms. Graham concerning her physical location?"

"You mean in the tub?"

More jurors laughed this time, and the judge could be seen hiding a smile behind her hand.

"Well, wherever."

"Yes. She said she was in the tub."

"How did that arise?

"There was noise in the background, and I have trouble hearin' too—out on disability, you know. So I said to her, 'What's that noise I hear?' And she said, 'It's the motor—the tub motor—the whirlpool motor. I'm in the tub, but I'll get right out and bring her in.' "

"So that's how you knew she was in the tub when she was talking to you on the telephone on those particular days?"

"Right."

"How many times did that happen?"

"I don't know. Two, four, maybe five over the years. Somethin' like that."

"And on each occasion previous to your May 18 call, had Ms. Graham told you that she would bring the cat right in?"

"Yes."

"On those occasions did she?—bring it right in?"

"Yes. Except a coupla times the cat didn't come when she called it, and I phoned the station and they came over."

"You say that happened twice?"

" 'Bout that."

"Now on this particular day, May 18, describe what happened that led to your call."

"Well, the cat was drivin' me crazy. I hadn't slept hardly at all for several nights, and I was tryin' to get some shut-eye early in the mornin'. But the cat was right there on the air conditioning unit, screechin' away, drivin' me crazy. So finally I called her. She didn't answer—so I left a message."

"Have you listened to the audiotape?"

"Yes."

"And did you read a transcript of that recording?"

"Yes."

"Can you identify it?"

"It's the one I left—the message."

"On that day, May 18?"

"Yes."

"I will play the tape and post the transcript on the screen."

The audio came on: "You're cat's at it again! If you don't get that little bastid out of here within ten minutes, I'm gonna call the cops. I've had it! I toldja! This is the last time—I toldja!" This message was followed by a mellifluous female voice announcing, "Thursday, May 18, 8:49 AM."

Mike observed that the jurors could easily follow the text on the screen. When the tape was finished, Barton said, "Does that tape accurately reflect the words which you spoke?"

"Yes."

"And does the transcript accurately reflect those words?"

"Yes."

"The time stamp on the answering machine stated that you left the message at 8:49 AM. Is this consistent with your own recollection?"

"I wasn't lookin' at the clock, but that sounds 'bout right."

"Did you take any other steps regarding this matter?"

"I called the station house. The cat kept on, and I just got completely fed up. You can believe me that."

"What did you say?"

"I told them about the situation, and they said they'd send somebody over."

"Thank you. No further questions." Barton turned to Mike. "Your witness."

Mike rose and moved to the lectern. The prosecution had at a minimum established a time by which the jury could infer that Sheila Graham was no longer alive. Mike saw no way to minimize this fact, or even a need to.

"Mr. Burgoyne, you had been bothered by this cat from time to time over the years?

"Yes."

"Always the same cat?"

"Yes. Same one."

"How many cats did Ms. Graham own?"

"The one. Just the one."

"Thank you, Mr. Burgoyne. No further questions."

Mike resumed his seat and Barton indicated to the court that he had no redirect.

"All right then," the judge said. "Call your next witness."

Barton gestured to a man dressed in a police uniform who was sitting on a bench at the rear of the courtroom. "Come forward."

The man passed through the swinging gate at the bar and ambled to the witness stand. The clerk swore him in. The witness assumed the stand, remained standing. Barton took a position at the lectern.

"Please state your full name."

"Theodore Dane Driscoll."

"Are you a police officer with the town of Colchester?"

"Yes, I am."

"And were you such on May 18 of this year?"

"Yes."

"What was your position?"

"Corporal."

"How long had you been in that department?"

"About eight years."

"On May 18 did you have occasion to go to the premises at 76 Brandywine Road in Colchester, Massachusetts?"

"Yes I did."

"Tell the court and jury what led you to go there and what you observed when you arrived."

"I was out on routine patrol when I received a radio call to go to that property because of a disturbance. I was on the other side of town when I got the call, and it took me eight or nine minutes or so to get over there.

"When I got there I parked the squad car on the street and went to the front door and rang the bell. When nobody came, I tried the door, but it was locked. I had only been there—oh, I'd say even less than a minute or two—when Officer Tosca arrived on the scene."

"Pardon me for interrupting, officer, but what time was this?"

The patrolman glanced at his notes. " 'Round 9:30, 9:40 AM—in there."

"Thank you. Please go on."

"Officer Tosca got the same call I did. When he came up to the front door, I told him to check the side. He did and a minute later he called out he had somebody in custody. So I—"

Barton interrupted. "Before you proceed further, Officer Driscoll, tell us if the radio message said anything about the nature of the disturbance that you were being called to at 76 Brandywine Road."

Driscoll answered, "Well, I kind of knew what it was about, because I had been there before."

Although this and some earlier responses had gone beyond the DA's questions, and in addition included hearsay evidence, Mike again chose not to object. These errors were essentially harmless; the evidence would come in soon anyway. The prosecutor would simply reword the question or offer the testimony for a non-hearsay purpose.

"Had there been a disturbance at that address previously, to your knowledge?"

"Well, sort of. One of the neighbors was being bothered by the victim's cat—couldn't sleep—"

Several spectators chuckled, and a few jurors smiled at the notion that police were called because a cat could not sleep.

Mike rose. "Objection! We have a *victim* already, without any evidence that a crime has been committed."

"Yes," the judge agreed. "The reference to a victim can be stricken." She turned to the officer and said, "Did you mean to refer to the decedent, Sheila Graham?"

He nodded. "I did."

"The record shall so reflect," the judge said. "In the future please refrain from using the term 'victim' or any other similar word." She turned to the jury. "Please ignore the reference to a 'victim'." To the DA she said, "Let's proceed."

Barton took up the reins. "So you were familiar with a complaint having to do with Sheila Graham's cat? Bothering one of the neighbors?"

"That's what had happened, I understand."

"And that is the reason you were familiar with the property?"

"It is."

"I believe you were at a point where Officer Tosca told you that he had someone in custody, is that correct?"

"Yes, that's right."

"Please go on from there. Tell us what you did and what you observed."

"I went around to the side of the house where Officer Tosca was standing with this man. Officer Tosca was in the process of putting handcuffs on him."

"Let me stop you there. Do you see that man in this courtroom today, and if so, can you identify him?"

Officer Driscoll looked at Maguire and said, "That's him right there. The defendant, Francis Maguire."

The jurors all looked at Maguire, who sat rigid and stared back.

"What happened after Officer Tosca put the handcuffs on defendant Maguire?"

"Officer Tosca showed me some of the things the defendant stole from the house."

Mike jumped to his feet. "I guess we're not going to need a trial if this witness is the determiner of guilt and he's free to share his conclusions with the jury."

"Is that an objection?" the judge said.

"Indeed it is, Your Honor. This testimony goes to an ultimate issue in the case, is a conclusion which invades the province of the jury, and is not within the capacity of the witness, and the officer knows better."

"Sustained. The reference to things which the defendant quote stole from the house unquote may be stricken and the jury will disregard it."

Still standing, Mike said, "Would Your Honor be good enough to instruct the witness to refrain from stating his conclusions and just simply describe the facts as he saw or heard them?"

"Yes, the witness is so instructed."

From Mike's viewpoint his objection and request for jury instruction were possibly counterproductive. The request for instruction tended to emphasize something which Mike did not care to do, that is, the characterization of Sheila Graham's personal property as "stolen." Further, in the grand scheme of things this parrying over an issue which might actually become a non-issue would not have made sense to a casual observer. This would be especially so if the trial reached a point where Maguire might plead guilty to breaking and entering, and larceny.

Why quibble over legal niceties in such circumstances? Answer: because the *next* conclusion that the witness expressed might be a devastating one. Trial lawyers widely recognize that a judge's instruction to the jury to disregard a witness's particular testimony tends to be ignored by the jury. Quite simply, it is ineffective.

No one can truly erase testimony from his memory, but the judicial supposition to the contrary persists. In Mike's judgment it was best to cut off any attempted transgressions at this point rather than wait until too late.

Barton said, "Will the stenographer please read back the last question?"

The court reporter read from the tape. "What happened after Officer Tosca put the handcuffs on defendant Maguire?"

"He showed me some items."

"What items?"

"Some pearls, earrings, cash—bills—a necklace type thing. Credit cards. A clipboard. Stuff like that—and the gloves—latex gloves."

"Did you have any conversation with the defendant at that time?"

"No."

"Did you have a conversation with the defendant later?"

"No."

"What did you do after Officer Tosca showed you those articles?"

"I started to go in the house. There was a slider there—one of those glass doors—the door was shut, and there was a cat trying to get in. I opened the door and let the cat in—another one jumped out at the same time— and I went in myself. I didn't think anybody would be home, but I went through the house to check."

This time Mike chose not to object to the witness's "thoughts."

"What, if anything, did you discover?"

"I found the body. In the bathtub."

"Officer, exactly what did you observe?"

"A woman in the bathtub. It was a big tub. Deep. She was under water—her head—and it was obvious she was dead."

"What did you do then?"

"I called the station, spoke to Detective Leonard."

"All right. And did Det. Leonard come to the scene while you were there?"

"Yes he did."

To the judge, Barton said, "May I approach the witness, Your Honor?"

"You may."

At the stand, Barton said, "I show you a photograph and ask if you can identify it."

He handed a color photograph to the witness. Officer Driscoll glanced at the picture and said, "Yes, this is the way she looked—the bathtub looked with her in it—when I first went in."

Barton passed the print to Mike, who had already seen it, a gruesome depiction of Sheila Graham, nude, drowned in her own bathtub, head below the water, hair strands suspended in wispy tendrils.

Mike handed the photograph back to Barton, who gave it to the clerk and said, "I ask that this photograph be marked in evidence as the Commonwealth's next exhibit."

The clerk passed the photograph up to the judge, who peered at it, said to Mike, "Any objection?"

"No, Your Honor," Mike answered. "It's on the agreed list."

The attorneys had previously agreed on exhibits, including which of the many morbid photographs could be admitted in evidence. Had they not done so, no valid objection could have been made anyway. An objection based on undue prejudice would promptly be overruled, with no chance of reversal on appeal.

The judge nodded, smiled with approval. "It may be so marked." She passed the document to Barton, who handed it to the stenotypist. After she marked it, Barton retrieved it and walked to the jury box, handed the picture to the foreman of the jury. The foreman looked at it a moment, blanched, passed it to the juror seated next to him, looked sternly at Maguire.

"If it please the court," Barton said, "We will display this exhibit on the courtroom screens while the print makes its rounds among the jury."

The judge said, "There being no objection, you may do so."

In a moment the photograph flashed on the giant projection screen as well as on the multiple smaller screens throughout the room. Jurors who had not already seen the color photograph gasped. The photographic print had a similar impact on each successive juror. While the photograph made its trip among the jurors, the prosecutor returned to the podium at a leisurely pace.

Barton proceeded to secure the admission in evidence of two more photographs, showing different views of Sheila Graham lying in the tub. While these pictures were being displayed, he said, "After discovering the body, did you make a search of the premises?"

"Yes, I did."

"What, if anything, did you find?"

"The drawers of a jewelry box were open, and there were no credit cards or cash in her wallet, which was lying on the bed in the master bedroom."

The prosecutor needed to pin it down. " *'Her* wallet' being . . . ?"

"The vic—Sheila Graham's."

"Anything else?"

"Downstairs in her office. Her sandals. Her sandals were—"

The officer stopped as he saw Mike rising to object. Before Mike stood fully erect, the witness amended, "—a *woman's*-type sandals—I don't know whose—were on the floor in the office—a home office, right inside the slider— the door I went through to get into the house."

Barton concluded by having Officer Driscoll identify a photograph of the sandals, one turned on its side. The photograph was marked in evidence and displayed.

"At some point did you make an inventory of telephone handsets in the house?"

"I did. That was a couple of weeks later when Det. Leonard asked me—"

"Objection!" Mike said.

"Sustained. Next question."

"What did you find?"

"There were five portable handsets in the house. One in the home office—at the answering machine, one in the kitchen, and one in each bedroom."

"On May 18 did you observe any telephone handset in the bathroom when you discovered the body?"

"No."

"Or cellular telephone?"

"No."

"Does Exhibit 1, the photograph of the tub and the area surrounding it, show any telephone handset?"

"It does not."

"Cellphone?"

"No."

"Do any of these other photographic exhibits show either of those items?"

"No."

"Or slippers?"

"No."

"And does your testimony accurately reflect your memory of your observations of the bathroom that day?"

"It does."

"And your memory is . . . ?"

"There was no telephone handset or cellular telephone in the bathroom when I went in there and found the woman."

"Or slippers?"

"Or slippers either."

"Aside from slippers, was there any other kind of footwear in the bathroom at that time?"

A headshake. "No. Nothing like that."

"When you entered the bathroom, was the bathtub water running?"

The witness shook his head. "No."

"The tap was in what position?"

"Off."

"Was the tub full?"

"Yes. Right up to the overflow drain, as far as it could go."

"Was there any water on the floor alongside the tub?"

"None."

"Or in the vicinity of the tub?"

"No."

"Was the whirlpool motor running?"

"No."

"Did you do anything else with respect to the premises that day?"

"Detective Leonard asked me to secure the crime scene, and I—"

"Objection!" Mike interrupted. "There's no determination of any cri—"

"Sustained. Reference to a 'crime scene' will be stricken and the jury instructed to disregard it. It is for the jury—not the attorneys, or even the court—to determine whether a crime has been committed."

"What did you do?"

"I secured the scene."

Barton said, "Thank you, officer," and turned to Mike. "Your witness."

Mike quickly assessed the damage. The patrolman had tied Maguire to the death scene, a fact not disputed. The importance of the absence of slippers was unclear, but to Mike the telephone handset issue presented a lurking danger.

Burgoyne had testified that at times he had spoken to the decedent while she was in the tub. If it were her practice to take a phone to the bath, this would undermine the defense claim that she had fallen in the tub and drowned as a consequence. Had she gotten to the tub by herself, she would have had a telephone—tele*phones*—with her.

The ADA would likely offer further corroborating evidence on this point. If Ms. Graham did not get to the bathtub by her own locomotion, someone carried her there. From the evidence, Maguire was the logical carrier —thus the killer.

One of the greatest dangers in cross-examination is that the questioner will not only do no good, but will actually elicit new evidence harmful to his client. Thus the basic rule to follow is similar to that of the physician: First, do no harm.

Tread lightly, Mike cautioned himself. He rose and stepped to the lectern. Barton had often addressed the witness as "Officer," seeking to lend greater weight to his

testimony by cloaking it in "officialdom." Mike would refrain from doing so.

"You did not find any burglary tools on the defendant,
did you?"

"No."

"And you did not find any burglary tools in the house,
did you?"

"I didn't look for any."

Ah, a wiseguy. "So clearly you did not *find* any, is that
correct?"

The officer shifted his weight from one foot to the
other. "That's right."

"You did not have any conversation whatsoever with
the defendant, is that so?"

"I did not."

"You have absolutely no information whatsoever as to
how the defendant gained admission to the house, do
you?" If the witness did not now admit seeing the house
key, Mike would ask him directly.

"Well, he had a key in his pocket—a key to the
house."

Good. "And you do not possess any information of how
he acquired that key, do you?"

"No, I don't."

"Did you try the key to see if it fit the lock?"

"I did."

"And did it fit?"

"Yes. It opened the front door of the house."

"Thank you for clearing that up. So far as you are
aware, Mr. Maguire was given that key by Ms. Graham,
is that so?"

The officer again altered his stance, this time looked
at the DA.

Mike bored in. "Mr. Barton can't answer the question
for you, sir. You have to answer it yourself. Do you have

any knowledge of how Mr. Maguire came into possession of the house key?"

"No."

"It was because Mr. Maguire held a key to the house, that you did not look for burglar tools, is that right?"

"Yes."

"So far as you know, Mr. Maguire was invited there, is that true?"

"I have no knowledge—he did have graph paper with him."

Although a seeming *non-sequitur*, Mike welcomed the answer. "He had what?"

"Graph paper—like for floor plans."

"You saw it?"

"On a clipboard. Along with some floor plans—but not for this house."

"So, in summary, today you have absolutely no knowledge whatsoever of the means by which the defendant came to be in the house, is that correct?"

"That's right—unless you count the key."

"Which of course you do, correct?"

"Yes."

"And you do not have any knowledge as to his permission to use the key, do you?"

"Correct."

"And you saw *two* cats at the house."

"Right."

"One came out when you went in, and the other went in with you."

"True."

"Do you remember what either one looked like?"

"Sorry, I really don't. My attention was somewhere else."

"Thank you. No further questions."

The judge inquired of the prosecutor, "Any rebuttal?"

"Yes, Your Honor." Barton rose and turned to the witness. "Did you search for a house key in a container adhered to the bottom of the mailbox, located at the front door?"

Mike unconsciously held his breath.

"Yes."

"What did you find?"

"I found a magnetic key case, but it was empty."

"That's all, Your Honor."

"Any further cross?" the judge asked Mike.

Mike figured that any further question about the key would likely only make matters worse.

"No, Your Honor."

The judge said to Officer Driscoll, "You may step down."

Barton said, "I call the next witness."

The judge raised her hand, said, "Sorry, but I have an unplanned-for meeting I need to attend. We will recess until tomorrow morning, 9:00 o'clock." She rose and left the bench.

CHAPTER 34

When Mike arrived in court the next morning, Thomas Barton was already present. The clerk, Fortras, saw Mike enter the courtroom and waved for him and his adversary to come to the front.

"There's been a change," the clerk said with gravity. "Last night, Judge Spencer was involved in an accident. A car ran a red light and broadsided her. She's in the hospital and they don't expect her to get out for several days at least, and they say she may be laid up for quite a while—maybe a month or more. I got a call from the chief administrative judge's office saying another judge is going to come in this morning and decide what should happen. I just wanted to give you both a heads up."

Mike said, "Jeez, that's too bad. She's a nice woman. I hope it's not too serious."

Barton nodded agreement.

Fortras shrugged his shoulders, said, "I don't know how bad." He turned to the court stenographer, a slender woman in her early forties. "Did you hear anything?"

"Just that she's in the hospital—not life-threatening."

"Thank God," Mike said.

Barton said, "Who's replacing her?"

The clerk answered. "I don't know if anybody is. They didn't say. We'll just have to see. They did say somebody would come in and tell us."

At ten-forty the bailiff held open the door to the judge's lobby. Judge Janine Madore appeared at the doorway, entered the courtroom and stepped up to the dais.

Upon seeing her, Mike muttered, "Holy shit!"

Both his client and Kaitlin turned toward him with questioning looks. "What's the matter?" Kaitlin said.

"Nothing—nothing. Don't worry."

As the judge entered, the bailiff proclaimed, "Hear ye, hear ye, hear ye. Please rise. All persons having anything to do before the Honorable, the Justices of The Superior Court in and for Middlesex County, draw near, give your attention, and you shall be heard. God save the Commonwealth of Massachusetts and this Honorable Court. Court is open. You may be seated."

Mike's mind raced. Janine Madore had been both his boss and mentor at the Suffolk County District Attorney's office, his first job after graduating from law school. She had also become his lover. As an assistant district attorney supervising the prosecution of major felonies in Boston, Janine had developed a distinct interest in Mike wholly apart from the rather modest legal talents which he then presented.

Even though he had not yet progressed to the point where he appreciated that pleasing his partner should be foremost in his objectives—because this led to his own greatest pleasure—his general appeal to her and more specifically his adroitness and sensual awareness brought her focus to him.

In short, his lovemaking abilities had grown far more important to her than his skills as a trial lawyer, and Janine brought to their unions her own considerable experience in matters carnal.

While Mike appreciated the extra tutelage, over time his libido had naturally turned interest elsewhere. As had all his affairs except for that with Anne, this one too had ended badly.

On the last August Sunday evening before Labor Day that summer, when no one was expected to be in the office, his mentor had discovered Mike tending to the needs of a busty intern who was then sitting firmly ensconced on the corner of a desk, thighs spread, audibly enjoying her impalement.

Janine had proved adept at playing the injured party. The intern was gone from the office the next day. Mike left a month later, trailed, he felt—albeit without evidence—by Janine's rancor. Although he had not encountered her as a judge in the three years since she had been appointed to the bench, he feared those feelings might injure his client's cause in this case. Nothing good could come of this, he was sure.

As soon as she was seated, Mike rose and spoke. "Your Honor, it is a pleasure to appear before you. This is the first occasion on which I have had the opportunity to address you since you were appointed to the bench. However privileged I would feel to try this matter before you, it is incumbent upon me as an officer of the court to inform my brother that you and I for some two years served together on the staff of the Suffolk County District Attorney, and indeed worked closely on several cases during that period.

"While I am certain that Mr. Barton would have no doubt that Your Honor would always rule wisely and consistent with the law, without any bias or prejudice, even unknowing, it would doubtless be best for Your Honor to recuse herself. That way there could be no possible basis for any suggestion of impropriety. Therefore, in order to relieve the Commonwealth of the potential embarrassment associated with doing so, I move on behalf of the defendant that Your Honor recuse herself from hearing this matter. Please note that this is done with all due respect for the court."

Judge Madore smiled and said, "The court appreciates your candor, as I am sure Mr. Barton does as well. In that spirit, the court acknowledges that defense counsel and I did serve as assistant district attorneys in Suffolk County at the same time, and had the pleasure of working together." Any irony intended?

The judge continued. "However, I feel that it should also be disclosed that this work relationship occurred more than nine years ago, and there has been no communication between us during that time—or at least any communication which I recall." She stared at Mike. "Unless Mr. Ratigan might correct me?"

"No, no, Your Honor. You are absolutely correct."

The judge turned to Barton, who had also stood during this exchange. She continued. "I will tell you that I do not have the slightest natural sympathy for Mr. Ratigan or the cause which he represents. Indeed, I know nothing about it whatsoever. Now if you feel that there might be any shade of impropriety in my presiding over this case, I urge you to speak with absolutely no hesitation at all. Should you wish, I would be happy to withdraw from this case and pass it on to another member of this court."

Mike hoped that he held the upper hand, but a sidelong glance at Barton suggested that his adversary sensed otherwise.

"Your Honor," the ADA said, "the Commonwealth appreciates your position, but I have the utmost confidence in your impartiality and the fairness of your rulings. Hence there is no need for you to recuse yourself from this case. I respectfully suggest that we proceed as we would were Judge Spencer still sitting."

"Fine. That settles it." She turned once again to Mike. "I assume that you are satisfied?"

"Of course, Your Honor."

Actually, Mike had thought of moving for a mistrial based upon the inability of a new judge to come into the case after testimony had already been admitted, along with numerous exhibits. However, he felt certain that the motion would be denied, and that it would not present a sound basis for appeal. What it *would* do is alienate the judge. Probably she already harbored feelings potentially antithetical to Maguire's best interests. No sense in irritating her further.

Judge Madore looked at the papers on her desk and said, to no one in particular, "Did you arrange for daily transcript here?"

The stenographer nodded and Barton and Mike both spoke at once. "Yes, we did, Your Honor."

"Is there a copy being provided to the court? I don't see one here."

The stenographer stood and handed several volumes to the clerk, who passed them up to the judge. She thanked the court reporter, looked at the covers, placed them on the desktop.

"Call the jury," she said to the court officer.

When the jurors were assembled and seated, Judge Madore explained to them the situation concerning Judge Spencer. "Thankfully she does not appear to be hurt critically, although she may be out for some time. I've been called in as a substitute and will try to carry on and do as good a job as Judge Spencer would herself have done.

"In order for me to do that, it will be necessary for me to review the transcripts of the testimony and to become familiar with the exhibits. I apologize for this inconvenience to you, but it is necessary, as I'm sure you can see—unless we start all over again, which no one wants.

"Also, I have just finished sending another case to the jury, and I expect that I will at some point be called away to take a verdict in that case, and maybe for other things too, such as hearing arguments on motions.

"So what I'm going to do is give you a few hours to yourselves. You can read a newspaper—as long as it's not about this case, of course—do a crossword, play cards, go for a walk around the block, or do whatever you like—except discuss this case.

"We will reassemble at 2:00 o'clock and go on from there. Thank you for your patience."

*   *   *

After the recess Barton called another uniformed officer as a witness. The man came to the front of the courtroom, held his hand up to be sworn, then assumed the stand but did not sit. He identified himself as Patrolman Ronald Sheffield Tosca, a five-year veteran with the Colchester Police Department.

The Assistant DA moved quickly to the Graham house, through leading questions to which Mike did not object. Then he came to the essence of the officer's testimony.

"When you arrived at 76 Brandywine Road, Officer Driscoll was already there?"

"Yes, he was."

"What did you do when you arrived there?"

"I had a conversation with Officer Driscoll and then I went around to the side of the house."

"What happened then?"

"I saw a man coming out through a slider door. He closed it and when he turned around, he ran right into me. Before I could say anything to him, he said, 'Alarm?'"

"What did you say or do?"

"I asked him who he was. He didn't answer. I asked him his name. He didn't say anything. I asked him if he was the owner of the house. He would not answer. I asked him if anyone was home. He would not speak. He was wearing a suit, and his side pockets looked as though they were sort of stuffed with something—and he was wearing gloves—those latex ones."

"Gloves? He was wearing gloves?"

"Like I said, those latex ones."

"What did you do next?"

"Fearing a possible weapon, I patted him down. I asked him to empty out his pockets, and he did. There was some jewelry, cash, credit cards, keys. I looked at the credit cards and saw a woman's name on them.

"I placed him under arrest, hollered to Officer Driscoll to come around to the side of the house, that I had caught somebody. Then I put handcuffs on him, gave him his *Miranda* warnings."

"By 'him,' to whom do you refer?"

"The defendant." Officer Tosca pointed at Maguire.

"Are you pointing at the man sitting at the defense table, next to Attorney Ratigan?"

The witness nodded. "Yes sir. That's him right there. The defendant."

Maguire slouched and looked down at the tabletop. Mike leaned over and whispered sharply, "Don't forget what I told you. Look at the witness, or look at the judge, or look at the jury, but *don't ever* look down—don't lower your eyes. And sit up straight."

Immediately Maguire assumed an erect posture and focused his gaze on the officer testifying.

Barton said, "At some point did you make an inventory of the personal property that the defendant had in his possession?"

"When we got to the station house."

"Do you have that inventory with you?"

"Yes I do."

"May I see it?"

The witness held up a paper.

The prosecutor asked the judge, "May I approach?" When he received permission, he took the paper from the witness and said, "Did you prepare this list yourself?"

"Yes."

"When did you do it?"

"Right when we got to the station house."

"Officer, can you tell the court and jury whether it contains all of the items which the defendant had at that time?"

"Well, not his clothing, but it does have his personal stuff."

"You mean driver's license, his own credit cards—items like that?"

The witness nodded. "Yes, he did have those, and we inventoried them too."

Barton showed the paper to Mike, then had it marked as the next exhibit. "Referring to Exhibit 5, the list includes an item labeled 'clipboard with floor plans,' does it?"

"Yes."

"You didn't mention those in your testimony yet, did you?"

"No, I didn't."

"Did you retrieve a clipboard and floor plans from the defendant?"

"Yes I did."

"Please describe them for us."

"Well, he had this clipboard with some papers attached to it. When I looked at the papers, I saw that the ones that weren't just blank pages—there were a lot of blank ones, only they weren't really blank, they were like graph paper with lines on it, you know—anyway, the ones that weren't blank were floor plans."

"Were you able to determine whether those floor plans or any of them were plans of 76 Brandywine Road?"

"They were not."

Technically, Mike could have objected here because the witness did not answer the question, which was "Were you able to determine" something. As is common, the witness here jumped to the answer to the next question which would have been asked: "What did you determine?" Mike refrained from objecting because no good purpose would have been served.

"Thank you, Officer Tosca." Barton then asked the judge for permission to approach the witness again.

"For the time being, at least," Judge Madore said, "it will not be necessary for counsel to ask for permission to approach *your own* witness. If the need arises, I will let you know. Please proceed."

"Thank you, Your Honor." The Assistant DA went to the stand and handed a clipboard to the witness. "Can you identify this?"

"This is the one—the clipboard the defendant had with him."

The clipboard and papers were marked as the Commonwealth's next exhibit and passed among the jurors. "Did the defendant say anything about the clipboard or papers?"

"No, the only thing he said about anything at all was the alarm, which I already told you about."

Next, Barton had the witness identify the jewelry items found on Maguire's person: a strand of pearls, a diamond clasp, two sets of diamond earrings, an emerald pendant on a gold chain. All were introduced in evidence and marked as exhibits, photographs of the pieces also marked and displayed on the screens. The policeman also identified the house key, which too was marked in evidence.

Next he established that Maguire had $390.00 in cash, now tagged and marked as an exhibit. Maguire also carried a business card, which listed a false address and a out-of-service telephone number. Barton's final step was to have the policeman identify the credit cards.

"Officer, how many cards did you find on the defendant's person?"

"Well, if you mean all of them, eleven."

"Some were in his own name?"

"Yes."

"How many?"

"Three."

"Did you find any in someone else's name?"

"Yes, eight."

"Are these those cards?" Barton placed a group of eight credit cards on the surface at the front of the witness stand.

"These are the ones I found, yes."

"And are they on your list?"

"Yes."

Barton picked up one of the cards. "This is a VISA card, issued by Chase?"

The witness looked at it and said, "Yes it is. That's one of them."

The credit cards were placed in evidence as separate exhibits without objection and marked accordingly. With that completed, the Assistant District Attorney passed one of the VISA cards to the witness and said, "What is the name on the card?"

"Sheila B. Graham."

"And the names on the other cards?"

"They are all Sheila Graham, but one of them doesn't have any middle initial."

"Officer, do any of these cards bear the name Francis Maguire?"

"No. They do not."

"Or any name other than that of Sheila Graham, with or without a middle initial?"

"No."

"With your permission, Your Honor, I'll pass these among the jurors and project them on the screens."

"There being no objection, you may do so." Had Mike objected, the judge would simply have overruled it.

Barton handed the eight credit cards to the foreman and said, "Thank you, Officer Tosca."

To Mike, Barton said, "Your witness."

At the podium Mike began his questioning.

"What burglary tools did you find in the defendant's possession?"

"We didn't find any."

"None at all?"

The witness shook his head. "No. We didn't find any."

"Well, in the house then, how many did you find that he left inside?"

Headshake. "None."

"Did you search for burglary tools?"

"I did not personally, no."

"Did you see anyone else do so?"

"No."

"Did you instruct anyone else to do so?"

Officer Tosca shook his head. "No."

"Did you instruct anyone *not* to do so?"

"No."

Mike's next question held the capacity to be dangerous, but after consideration he decided to take a chance. "So you have no information about how Mr. Maguire gained admission to the house, is that correct?"

"Aside from the key, that's correct."

"Yes, the key. So far as you are personally aware, Mr. Maguire may have been given permission to use that key, is that right?"

"I have no knowledge."

"And if so, he had every right to be on those premises, is that correct?"

"I have no knowledge."

"Thank you, Officer Tosca. No further questions." Mike returned to the defense table.

"Any redirect?" the judge asked.

Barton stood. "No, Your Honor."

Judge Madore stood and said, "I apologize to all, but as I indicated at the outset what might happen, I have to take up another matter in a different session. We'll adjourn until tomorrow morning at 9:00."

CHAPTER 35

"Are you ready for your next witness?" Judge Madore said at the start of the next day's session.

"Yes, Your Honor," Barton answered. "The Commonwealth calls Pamela Stevens."

The woman had not been present in the courtroom before being called to the stand. Mike remembered her from their meeting at the Graham house. As she passed him in walking to the swearing-in area, she scowled. Doubtless she recalled his subterfuge.

After the witness was sworn, she sat. Barton said, "Where do you live?"

"Madison, Wisconsin."

"Were you related to Sheila Graham?"

"She was my sister. Just a year apart. She was older."

"Did you visit one another from time to time?"

"Yes. Every year we would have at least one visit. Usually two. She would visit me, or I would go to her house."

"How long would those visits last?"

"A week. Usually a week."

"During those visits did you become familiar with her household living practices?"

"I did—and of course when we were kids growing up, too. They didn't change much."

"Were you familiar with her practices concerning bathing? Specifically with regard to telephone devices?"

"Yes. She always took her telephones with her. Both the house one and her cellphone, after she got one of those."

"I show you a photograph, and ask if the scene is characteristic of your sister's lifestyle in this regard."

The witness glanced at the picture, gasped, covered her mouth, looked away.

"I apologize for subjecting you to this, but it is necessary."

Mrs. Stevens dabbed at tears, composed herself. "There's no phone—and no slippers. My sister always wore slippers in the bathroom. She couldn't stand the cold marble floor."

"Thank you. I realize this is difficult for you."

Mike rose. "Can we do without the heartwarming speeches?"

"Let's move along," the judge said.

"So does the absence of a phone and slippers lead you to any conclusion consistent with your sister's habits and practices?"

"Certainly does: She didn't get to that bathroom by herself." The witness quickly added, "There's something else, too."

"Which is?"

"She never filled the tub until she was actually sitting in it. She would only run a little bit of water to get the temperature right, then step in and sit down."

"So in your experience she would not have fallen into a full tub?"

"That's right. Not the way she did things."

"When you visited your sister, did she give you any means to gain access to the house?"

"She always gave me my own key to use, and she also kept a spare one hidden under the mailbox, near the front door. It was held up there by one of those magnetic key holders."

"Was that key accessible to anyone who looked for it there?"

"It was."

At this point the bailiff's telephone sounded a partially muted tone; he answered it, then walked to the bench. The judge wheeled her chair to the sidebar and they spoke.

The judge then addressed the courtroom as a whole. "I'm sorry, but I have to take this call."

She spoke on her receiver, hung up, again addressed the assemblage. "I have to hear attorneys in that other case I have responsibility for. I think it will not take very long, but we'll have to take a recess. I apologize once again." She rose and departed with the court officer's, "All rise . . . ."

Mike turned to Kaitlin and said, "Let's step out into the corridor." He did not want Maguire to overhear their conversation. In the hall Mike said, "That Barton is too smart. Do you see what he's doing?"

She nodded. "Undercutting our 'accident' defense. She wouldn't have fallen and struck her head. Besides, if she had fallen when the tub was full, water would have splashed all over the place. Someone had to carry her to the tub, put her in it, then fill it with water. And the *hidden* key—that knocks out our 'assent' defense."

"Seems to. But maybe not. I think I see a way around it. She could have told him about the key, where it was kept."

"But he wouldn't have needed a key if she was going to be home—which she was that day."

"But he didn't have to know that," Mike said. "She was planning to be at a meeting with Fessenden that morning, and she didn't need to be home for him to make floor plans."

Kaitlin disagreed, pressed on. "And it gets worse: the absence of telephones and her slippers, showing she did not navigate to the bathroom by herself."

"Smart of Barton."

"And the floor plans. What're you going to do?"

"I don't know. I don't have any idea what I *can* do. Anything occur to you?"

Kaitlin shook her head. "Sorry. Bottom line is, it looks like they're right. Somebody did carry her to the tub and drown her."

Mike nodded. "That actually fits with our own theory of what happened. Only thing is, it leaves us with what seems to be a virtually insurmountable problem."

Kaitlin agreed. "As a practical matter we're stuck with proving who *really* did it." She hesitated, added, "A burden that constitutionally is not ours, but the state's."

"Lot of good that does." He thought for a moment. "Maybe the best thing to do is let it lie, not pursue it with this witness."

"You think so?"

Mike shook his head slowly. "I'm not sure. I'm just not sure. But one thing's certain: I don't want to delve into uncharted territory and make her testimony even more damaging."

At the end of recess, the ADA resumed questioning the decedent's sister.

"To your knowledge, was your sister in the process of placing her house for sale on the real estate market?"

"She was not. She had thought about it a year ago, when she was considering taking a position at another university, but definitely decided against moving when she decided not to change jobs."

"Was she planning any renovations which would have entailed the use of floor plans?"

"No. And she had floor plans anyway. She got them when she bought the house from the developer."

Barton said, "Thank you, ma'am. No further questions." He returned to his seat.

Mike announced, "No questions, Your Honor." He glanced at the jury; some seemed surprised.

Barton said, "The Commonwealth calls Detective Sergeant Sargent."

A burly man with the body of a weight lifter entered the courtroom and strode to the area in front of the witness box. The clerk swore him in and he took the stand, remaining on his feet.

"You may sit, if you wish," the judge said.

"No thank you, this is fine."

In Mike's experience, witnesses who insist on standing tend to be excessively self-assured, often arrogant. Police officers in particular usually stood while testifying, thus lending an increased aura of importance to their evidence, adding to the air of "officialdom" created by their uniformed presence. Thankfully, Det. Sgt. Sargent wore a suit.

Barton went to the podium and, without notes, began his questioning.

"Please state your name and employment."

"Sargent Sargent, Detective Sergeant with the Colchester Police Department."

Mike could not avoid wondering if the officer had the middle initial "S," and if so whether his middle name is Sargent. Mike was tempted to ask on cross-examination if the detective's parents were fans of Joseph Heller. More particularly, had they read *Catch 22*—and had the witness himself read it—and thought of the naming scheme.

Mike knew that he would refrain, however. Not the place. Or the time.

"How long have you been employed there?"

"Fourteen years."

Thereupon Detective Sargent testified in succinct terms that he secured the scene, cordoned it off, surveyed it. He was present when photographs were taken by the state police photographer. He took possession of the sandals in the den after they were photographed, marked them as exhibits and cataloged them.

The detective measured and made note of the bath water temperature, ambient room temperature, and the ambient exterior temperature. He checked the heating system, verified that the air conditioning system was on, set to 76 degrees.

He waited for arrival of the medical examiner and the state police criminalist, stood by while they completed their duties. He made recordings of the two messages which callers had left on the digital answering machine. Before leaving, he ensured that all doors were closed and locked.

However, he did not indicate that he had viewed the answering machine redial numbers or the caller ID feature to identify calls made to or from the house. He did not mention the computer.

Mike's cross-examination was brief. There was little which he could gain from Det. Sgt. Sargent, and much potentially to be lost.

"You measured the bathroom ambient temperature, right?"

"Yes."

"And that was 76°?"

"Yes."

"The same as the thermostat setting?"

"Yes."

"And the bathwater was what temperature?"

"81°"

"You had no way of knowing what the bathwater temperature was at the time Ms. Graham died, is that correct?"

"Yes."

"Yes, meaning that you had no way of knowing, right?"

"Yes."

"Or knowing how long Ms. Graham had been in the tub at the time of her death, is that correct?"

"Yes. No way of knowing."

"Do you know how the bath water temperature came to be higher than the 76° room temperature??"

"No. It could happen in two ways that occur to me."

"Which are?"

"That the water temperature was initially much higher and cooled down over time. Or that her body temperature raised the bath water temperature." He stopped, added, "Or a combination of both."

"And you don't know which of those circumstances—if either—created that condition?"

"Yes, I don't know."

"Or how long it took to go to 81°?"

"Correct."

These answers provided no particular use to the defense, Mike knew. The truly devastating testimony would come from the medical examiner and the criminalist. He hoped merely that any confusion about such details might make the circumstances of Sheila Graham's death sufficiently murky to create doubt in the mind of at least one juror.

One juror. All he needed.

Mike finished his cross-examination and the judge took the luncheon recess at 1:00 o'clock.

CHAPTER 36

When court reconvened at 2:00 PM, Barton turned to the judge and said, "I call Dr. Carl Fessenden."

A court officer opened the door at the rear of the courtroom and admitted Dr. Fessenden, who ambled to the front of the courtroom. Today the professor was dressed in a dark-brown suit with a tan pocket square, wide-collar white shirt, conservative brown tie, and freshly shined brown shoes. His trim mustache and Vandyke beard added an elegant air to his presence. After being sworn, he stepped into the witness box.

"You may sit if you prefer," the judge said.

"No, that's all right. I'd rather stand."

From the lectern Barton addressed the first question. "Please state your full name."

"Carl Gregory Fessenden."

Barton elicited the witness's age and home address and continued. "What is your employment?"

"I'm on the faculty of Harvard University."

"What is your position there?"

"I am the Rittenhouse Professor of Cellular Biology."

"Is that an endowed chair?"

"Yes it is."

"How long have you been at the university?"

"As an employee, thirty-seven years—ever since I graduated." Apparently feeling a need to explain, he added, "I went right into the PhD program and just never left."

"What is your area of concentration?"

"As the title suggests, cellular biology."

"Thank you, doctor, for that background information. Did you know Sheila Graham, the decedent in this case?"

"Yes I did."

"What was your relationship with her?"

"First she was my student and thereafter we collaborated on a joint project."

"Were you working on such a project with her at the time of her death?"

"I was."

"Did you have an appointment with Sheila Graham on the day of her death?"

"I did."

The jurors seemed to become more attentive, sat forward.

"Please describe to the court and jury the specifics of your appointment."

"Well, Sheila—Ms. Graham—had arranged to meet me at my office at 9:00. When she didn't arrive, I became concerned—she was always punctual—and before long I called her at her home. No one answered, so I left a message. As more time went by, I became increasingly concerned—upset, even—that something might have happened to her, and I decided to drive to her house and see. I was afraid she might have had an accident, a heart attack, or something—I don't know what."

The prosecutor said, "Counsel for the defendant and I have agreed that the compact disc which I have furnished to the clerk is an accurate representation of a message which was found on Ms. Graham's answering machine. I will play this message and ask you to listen to the recording and tell us whether you left this message that day."

Barton pressed a button on the controller at his desk, and the audio system played these words: "Sheila, this is Dr. Fessenden. I'm waiting for you. Where are you? Did you forget? Call me. Let me know you're all right." This was immediately followed by an announcement in a young woman's voice, "Friday, May 18, 9:13 AM."

"Did you leave that message?"

The doctor rubbed his eyes with the back of his hand. "I did—of course not the date part."

Barton said, "Of course not. And did you leave that message on Wednesday, May 18, at around 9:13 AM."

"Yes. That was the time."

"Ms. Graham did not answer the telephone?" A leading question, but harmless and Mike let it pass.

"True. That's why I left the message."

"Did Ms. Graham call you back?"

The professor shook his head. "No."

"Did you ever hear from her again?"

"No."

"What did you do after you left the message on Ms. Graham's answering machine?"

"I thought she might be on her way, so I waited a while. But then I got concerned again and drove to her house to see if she was all right."

"And did you go there?"

"Yes, I did. I drove right over."

"When did you arrive there—at the house?— approximately, if you don't know exactly."

"It must have been about quarter to ten, somewhere in there."

"9:45 AM?"

"Yes, AM."

"What did you do then?"

"I went into the house, met the police officer, who told me Sheila—Ms. Graham—was dead."

"Thank you, Dr. Fessenden."

To the court, Barton said, "No further questions." He turned to Mike. "Your witness."

Judge Madore glanced at her watch. "I have to hear attorneys argue motions in that other case I have mentioned to you. We'll adjourn until tomorrow morning at 9:00 o'clock." To Mike she said, "You can begin your cross then." She tapped the gavel on her bench and stood.

"All rise!" the court officer boomed.

CHAPTER 37

Returned to his office, Mike's thoughts moved to Jeri Thompson and the video she had made. In thinking back to their meeting, in his mind's eye he saw the master bedroom, quickly followed by an image of the master bath where Sheila Graham had met her death. Then his memory tracked Jeri through the house as she videoed each room. He recalled trailing behind her, and their amiable chat.

After a while he broke this chain of concentration, decided to review the actual recording rather than rely upon his memory. He went to the evidence drawer and pulled out Monument Video's DVD. At his desk he slid the DVD into the slot on his computer. Immediately the title page of the case, date, and time came onscreen. "Commonwealth v. Francis X. Maguire," the screen announced in large letters. Oddly, the arrest report itself hadn't given a middle initial. Mike speculated that most people would know automatically that his client's middle name had to be Xavier.

The video ran for a while, progressing from the master bedroom to the bath, on to the other rooms on the second floor, then downstairs. From the first floor Jeri had taken a view of the staircase leading up. Next came the kitchen, followed by the home office and living room, finally the first-floor bathroom.

Nothing seemed remarkable in the first pass, but some lurking thought impelled Mike to look through the video again. *Something* bothered him.

He clicked on the play arrow and leaned back in his chair to watch the recording again. Everything seemed just as it should until the video got to the point where Sheila's office filled the screen again.

All seemed to be in place. The high-back leather computer chair was swivelled toward the entrance. The computer desk stood against the outside wall, the monitor screen dark. The keyboard sat ready for use. Large-format inkjet printer at the rear of the desk, to the right of the monitor, the answering machine beside it, LED's dark.

Bookcases full of issues of the Journal of Cellular Biology were shelved immediately opposite the desk. Two wooden chairs finished in black and bearing the Tufts University seal were grouped around a small table; several magazines lay on its top. From his earlier visit Mike knew that these were issues of American Psychologist, and some of Psychology Today. In the corner near a window, an antique-brass floor lamp with a frosted-glass globe stood next to a wing chair.

He let the video run to the end, ran it twice more, stared at the immobile screen. Why was he watching this? Something had jogged his memory, bothered him, but try as he might, he could not grasp what it might be. Whatever the thought was, at that moment it resided too far beneath the surface of awareness for him to disgorge it.

Displeased at his inability to pierce the darkness, he decided to take a break from the video. He reviewed the autopsy and criminalist's report, hoping to find something—*anything*—of use.

Later Mike took a hot bath and lay back in his whirl-pool tub, letting the powerful jets roil the steaming bath-water, thrusting it against his flesh. He wished that Elaine were with him. She would soothe his psyche.

The thrum of the one-horsepower motor driving the tub's water pump battled the whoosh of the water spray for supremacy. His limbs relaxed and his thoughts drifted in a seemingly aimless path.

An image of Sheila Graham's computer desk kept re-turning. He could visualize the desktop. Monitor, key-board and mouse, inkjet printer, answering machine, a pencil holder, easel, some papers. Why did his mind keep coming back to this scene? He had no ready answer, but felt that there must be one. He would find it.

After drying himself, he donned bathrobe and slip-pers, went downstairs to watch the video again. The im-ages came on screen. He immediately fast forwarded to the part where Jeri had returned to Sheila Graham's home office.

At the sight of her desktop, he paused the motion and then placed it in slow play. At first the camera focused on the answering machine, which showed a red LED blink-ing the numeral 2.

Mike watched as the images progressed. At this speed sound was not reproduced, so he could not hear the audio playback of the two messages—his original purpose in making this part of the video. Jeri had used a wide-angle lens, which in addition to the answering machine showed the front of the Epson printer located next to it.

He caught sight of the printout which sat in the ejec-tion tray. He stopped the motion, ran back a few frames. Jeri had set the tripod high enough that the camera lens aimed downward toward the surface of the answering machine—and the printer as well. The still frame showed a photograph sitting in the printer's output tray. Mike stared at the picture.

The photo showed a cat sitting on the computer desk. The cat, with a coat of a distinctive pattern, matched the animal depicted in the oversized photographic enlargement displayed prominently on the wall above the computer desk, and in the many others scattered throughout the house. But this picture differed from the others: a rectangular object roughly the size of a postage stamp dangled from the feline's collar.

Mike peered closer. He pressed the Control and + keys simultaneously to enlarge the display, did so again and again, appreciating that Jeri had recorded in high definition. On close examination the plastic container appeared to be the type of case made to hold a secure digital card: flash memory in a miniature case.

Sheila Graham had been a computer aficionado. Maybe she used the cat's "ID" as a way to preserve important information! Even while appreciating that this is the kind of hunch which can easily be mistaken, Mike felt confident in the accuracy of his suspicion. He had to find the cat. What is its name? He did not know. Where is it? He did not know.

Realizing that he would need a photo of the cat, he sent the frame to the printer, which whirred through two color copies. Burgoyne had told him that the cat was only around as recently as two nights after the murder. What happened to it? Maybe the local Animal Control Officer picked it up. Mike located the number through an Internet service and called.

"I'm trying to find out if a particular cat was picked up by your office around the beginning of last month," he said.

"We don't give out that information over the telephone," a female clerk answered.

"What if I come in?"

"You can give it a try, but I wouldn't promise anything. We get an awful lot of animals in here. It might be pretty hard to tell—it *is* pretty hard to tell. When did your cat disappear?"

"It isn't mine."

"Oh." Obvious disinterest. Nevertheless, the clerk gave the hours of operation. Mike thanked her and hung up. The animal control office would not reopen until tomorrow morning.

Time was short. Frustrated, Mike decided to use another approach: canvass the neighborhood. Immediately he dressed and drove to Brandywine Road in Colchester. He began with the house on the far side of the Burgoyne's property, away from the Graham residence.

From the exterior the home seemed identical to Burgoyne's. There was no car in the yard and Mike could not see into the garage because the door had no window. At the front door Mike rang the bell and waited. No answer. He went to the next house.

A woman wearing a white terrycloth bathrobe came to the door. She kept the door on a chain, eyed Mike with suspicion. He held up the cat's photo, explained his mission. Looking frightened all the while, the woman glanced at the picture, shook her head, snapped the door shut.

Too bad he had to do this at night, but he felt a sense of urgency. He had no time to wait. The trial would not cease to move forward simply to benefit his quest.

Mike left and rang the doorbell of the house opposite Sheila Graham's house. No one answered, and no one came to the door of the next two homes either. On the fourth visit he found a cooperative husband.

"Yeah," the man said, "I know that cat, but haven't seen it since—you know." Mike thanked him and continued. Forty minutes later Mike walked up the bricked pathway to the front door of another house and pressed the button. After a two-minute wait he rang it again. No one responded. This time he leaned on the bell. Still no one came to the door, and despite an interior light, he could not hear any sound from within.

He was about to turn away when the door shot open. An unshaven man, late forties, glared at him. Barefoot, he was wearing jeans and a white tee shirt spotted with coffee dribbles.

"We don't want any." Gruff. Started to close the door.

"Wait a minute," Mike said. "I'm looking for this cat." He shoved the photographic printout in front of the man's face.

The man looked at the picture, hesitated, smiled. "That's Ms. Graham's cat—Agnes. She used to come here a lot. I'd feed her once in a while. She was a good cat. Noisy sometimes, though. She went into a lot of houses 'round here—she knew evbuddy in the neighborhood. Why'n't ya say so in the first place?" He held the door ajar, offered his handshake. "C'mon in. I'm Fred Jarvis."

Mike handed his card to Jarvis, who glanced at it. The man's use of the past tense worried Mike. "Have you seen her—Agnes—recently?"

Jarvis rubbed his jaw a moment, said, "Not for a while. She was 'round some after . . . after the—you know. She was 'round then but I haven't seen her for a while. A few weeks now—months, maybe."

Mike asked if he knew whether Agnes favored one neighbor more than the others—visited one more often.

"Naw," he said. "Might've, but not to my knowledge. Maybe Lili knows." He turned toward the rear of the house and bellowed, "Lil! Lil!"

After a few moments a squat woman with dark hair, wearing a yellow jumpsuit, poked her head into the hallway, approached. Her midsection protruded mightily.

Mike thought yellow to be a poor color choice for her, drawing unwanted attention.

"Whaddya want?" She saw Mike, added, "Who's he?"

"Just a lawyer," Jarvis said. "He's lookin' for that cat—ya know, Agnes, Mrs. Graham's cat. You seen her lately?"

The woman shook her head.

Mike asked, "Know if she liked anybody around here special—went there more often?"

Another headshake.

"Well, thanks," Mike said. "I appreciate your help." Jarvis started to return the business card, but Mike stopped him. "Keep it. If you think of anything else, I'd appreciate a call."

"No problem. Will do." He looked at the card and then at Mike. "You're Ratigan." He said it as a statement, not a question.

"Right."

"I heard'a you. Seen ya in the Herald. And on Channel 7."

"Yeah." Mike thanked him and left.

Luck turned positive after a few more houses. An over-large, pleasant woman clad in a pink bathrobe, her hair in curlers, opened the door wide without hesitation or any sign of fear. The odor of frying beef clung to the air. The Graham woman's cat, she volunteered after hearing Mike's quest, had been taken in by the Jamison family, living in the yellow house on the corner in the next block. When Mike turned to leave she said, "But I'm not sure anyone's home now, because . . . ."

With thanks trailing behind him, Mike hurried to the street and raced to the Jamison house. As he neared the house, one of the garage doors began to rise, and a car started to back out into the driveway. Mike ran behind the car and waved his arms in the air, shouting, "Stop! Stop!" The brakes squealed and the car halted.

Mike moved alongside the vehicle until he was at the driver's window. A woman, mid-seventies, stared out at him, her mouth agape. Mike was glad that he had worn a suit; at least he did not give the impression of being an "undesirable element."

Without thought he pulled his card case from his jacket pocket and thrust it against the side window so the woman could see "Michael J. Ratigan, Attorney" prominently emblazoned in cobalt-blue raised lettering.

The woman glanced at the card, pressed a button to lower the window. Quizzical look, but no words. For assurance Mike continued to hold the card for her to see,.

"I'm terribly sorry to bother you like this," he explained in a rush, "but I'm a lawyer working on a case and it's very important that I be able to find Sheila Graham's cat. I know it may sound a little odd—" *a little odd!* "—but the cat has a collar—"

"That cat!" The woman interjected. "I just can't take it any more. I'll tell you quite candidly—" she glanced at his card again "—Mr. Ratigan—that this cat has simply got the best of me. I didn't let it out because I didn't want it to run away and get lost." She stopped, continued. "I can't deal with it any more, screeching all the time. In fact, I had just about made up my mind to take it to the pound and let them deal with it. So if you want to take it off my hands, you have my blessings."

Mike sighed. Miracles like this just don't happen.

Mrs. Jamison went into the house, located Agnes, put her in a cat carrier, and handed her off to Mike. Before he accepted the animal, which remained completely silent during this interchange, displaying none of her alleged misbehavior, Mike peered through the screened entrance to make sure that the cat still wore the collar. It did, the miniature plastic container dangling from its neck.

"Thanks," he said.

"Thank *you*," the woman answered.

He started to walk toward the sidewalk when a thought occurred to him. He asked Mrs. Jamison, who was just about to get back into her car, "Does it bite or anything like that—is it kind of wild?"

She shook her head energetically. "Not the least bit. Noisy, that's all. Noisy. That's what I couldn't stand."

Mike transported the carrier to his car and placed it on the rear seat.

Filled with excitement, he shouted, "We're on our way, Agnes! We're on our way!"

CHAPTER 38

On the way back to his office, Mike made a detour to a pet supply store and picked up a bag of cat litter, a litter box, cat food, and bowls for food and water. Upon return to his office he set the carrier on the reception desk, opened its door with caution. Immediately Agnes emerged, sat down on the desktop, looked at him with disdainful curiosity. He approached the animal warily, stroked it for a few moments.

After gaining assurance that she would not attack him, he removed the collar. The cat seemed relieved by this action, scratched its neck, jumped to the chair, then to the floor, began to prowl.

Mike peered at the miniature plastic container attached to the cat's I.D. medal hanging from the collar. The case was semi-transparent; he could see that it contained a 16 GB mini-SDHC card. He released the snap lock, opened the case, withdrew the memory card, and plugged it into his computer's card reader.

Immediately Windows Explorer opened with the card's directory. Of the five files on the chip, the one titled "ReadMeFirst.doc" signaled an obvious starting point. He opened it, shuddered when he read the first few sentences.

Written this 17th day of May, 2011. My name is Sheila Graham. If anybody else is reading this, then I've had an accident, or something worse has happened than I thought might. So please turn it over to the Colchester police.

By way of background: Jonathan Wright and I knew each other in college and we both received graduate degrees in the same field, cellular biology, studying under Dr. Carl Fessenden, who is now quite famous. We lost contact over the years, but recently I got a call from Jonathan's sister, who told me that he had died some years ago (which I did not know), and wondered if she could send me some technical papers he had left with her. Naturally I said okay.

I read Jonathan's manuscript the day I received it in the mail. Right away I knew that Carl Fessenden had plagiarized it and used it as his own article, which led to his international recognition, and getting the Balzan Prize and others.

I know this isn't the place for it, but I was astonished by Jonathan's brilliance, by the magnificent way in which he expressed his dissertation. Never had I read anything written so cogently. I was sure conflict with Dr. Fessenden would bloom and there was nothing I could possibly do to prevent it if I were to deal with the situation honestly and with forthrightness.

I placed Jonathan's original ms. in my bookcase at home on the bottom shelf next to several years of the Journal of Cellular Biology issues. Out of an excess of caution (I do appreciate it's unlikely that I'll be in any personal danger), I've made this digital copy and attached it to Agnes' collar. Just in case, on my computer I have deleted any reference to these portable files. I know this sounds kind of desperate, but . . . .

As soon as I realized the implications of what his sister had sent to me, I ran Jonathan's whole ms. through a scanner and converted the text to a file. The file, on this portable memory, is named "JDissertation.doc." I also scanned the Fessenden article in question and named the file "Questioned.doc."

I used a free on-line program to compare the two and generated a third file named "Comparison.doc," which shows all identical passages in the two sources along with the pagination of both documents. The last file, named "Similarities.doc," contains passages which are similar, although not 100% verbatim. There are very few of these (because most are identical).

Almost all of the textual changes are slight (such as merely changing the preposition "in" to "on" in some cases). In all situations the quotations are set forth (in landscape layout) with Jonathan's dissertation on the left and the Fessenden article on the right. Any differences in the two texts are highlighted, making comparison and contrasting extremely easy.

Anxious to look at the other files, Mike returned to the file list and double-clicked on "JDissertation.doc." The title page of a new document filled the screen: "Draft Dissertation Concerning Aging," with the subtitle "Inhibiting the Aging Process Through Manipulation of the Telomerase Rate." Information at the bottom of the display showed the paper's length: Mike was viewing page 1 of 96.

He studied the files for long enough to see that the Fessenden article published in the *Journal of Cellular Biology* was almost identical to the Wright work.

Satisfied that the two works were in essence the same, Mike telephoned Elaine. He said, "We just got a real break in the case. I think I may be able to get Frankie off on the murder charge."

The line remained silent for several moments. Finally he said, "You still there? Did you hear me?"

Elaine said, "That's wonderful, Mike . . . . Have you told Frankie yet?"

"I don't want to get his hopes up and then have something go wrong, but I can't reach him at this time of night anyway."

"Yes. I hadn't thought of that." Again he waited until she spoke. "What's this going to mean for us? He'll want the money."

"I don't know. Don't worry. We'll figure it out."

"We have to. We have to. The money is for *us*."

"I'll call you tomorrow, let you know how it plays out in court."

Mike decided to search the Internet to see if by chance Jonathan had registered his manuscript with the United States Copyright Office. He quickly found the copyright office's home page, clicked on the "Search the Catalog" option and was redirected to a search page. He chose "Name" and typed "Jonathan Wright." The search engine returned seventy-eight results. Number twenty-seven was "Jonathan A. Wright," author of "Draft Dissertation Concerning Aging." He slapped his hand on the desktop. "Jesus!" he exclaimed to himself. What if . . . ?

He telephoned Kaitlin, briefly described Sheila Graham's last testament and what he had discovered on the Web. "I figure it must be the original manuscript. I certainly hope it is."

A whoosh escaped from her. "My God! That's—that's *everything!*"

"A motive for murder."

"But are you going to be able to use it—get it in evidence?"

"I haven't thought it through yet, but there has to be a way. I realize it's hearsay, and there's a clear problem with authentication, and it's not on our exhibit list."

"The last one might be the biggie. The judge seems to be pretty much a stickler with that list. Until you mentioned it, I didn't see the authentication problem. You'd have to be the witness, wouldn't you? And you can't be."

"I'm not certain, but it may be self-authenticating."

"How?"

"Good question." Mike had no witness to show that Sheila Graham's records were what they purported to be—that they were "real." One record—the published *Journal of Cellular Biology* article—was authentic beyond dispute, and bore Fessenden's name as author. It was Jonathan's manuscript that required authentication. Anyone could have drafted it—including a dishonest defense lawyer.

Kaitlin said, "You have to do it through cross-examination, don't you?"

"You may be correct . . . . Can you come in the office right now? I want you to go to Washington and pick up a certified copy of the Jonathan Wright article at the Copyright office, and get back here as soon as you can. So come in, pick up some cash, and be off."

"Do you think I'll be able to get a certified copy right away?"

"I don't know. Usually there's a delay in getting them from any government agency, but from the website it looks as though there's a work-around—an extra charge for expedition. That's why I want you to leave as soon as you can."

She seemed to think for a moment. He could hear her breathing. Finally she said, "Even if I'm able to get a copy tomorrow, it's not likely I can get back in time for court."

Being practical. That's good. "Don't worry. I'll handle it. You get the copy. Obtaining an expedited certified copy may take a little extra . . . manipulation—at which you're an expert."

"Well, I don't know about that."

"Don't argue. Get a move on."

"I'm on my way."

Next he called Jeri Thompson, the videographer, whom he had not seen since meeting her at the Graham house.

"Hi. This is Mike Ratigan. I know it's a little late to call, but—"

"I remember you. How're you doing?" Sounded friendly, even at this late hour.

"Great. The reason for my call—I'm in the middle of the trial on that case, and I think I may need you to put something together for me, maybe testify too. Are you available this weekend—and Monday?"

"No problem this weekend. What time would you want me on Monday?"

"Well, all day basically. You'd probably be on standby, in case we need you to authenticate the video you took."

"I can make that work, move some things around. When do you want me this weekend?"

"Saturday morning, plus. I need you to edit the video, set up a section which shows her home office, especially where I had you video the incoming and outgoing telephone numbers on her answering machine—you remember doing that?"

"Sure."

"And also the recorded messages. There were two."

"I remember."

"Now another question. Could you do the work on our computer, or would you need to take it to your office?"

"I'll need the right software, and I'd be surprised if you have it on your machines. But I do have it here at home. Best bet is to meet with you so you can show me what you need, then I can make a copy at your office and do the actual edit here."

"Great. Say 10:00 o'clock Saturday morning—here at my office."

"See you then." She hesitated, added, "A question: since I'll be doing this work on my own time, not the company's, would you mind if I bill you directly?"

"Not at all. Works great. See you Saturday morning."

After hanging up, Mike located the business card which Dr. Fessenden had given to him when they met. It listed the professor's email address, university telephone number, facsimile number, and last, his mobile number. Comparison of the mobile number and the one in the answering machine memory showed them to be the same. A Web check of the cellphone's number revealed Verizon Wireless to be the carrier.

Kaitlin arrived at the office within the hour. She saw the cat carrier sitting on her desk. "What's this for?"

Mike explained, added, "You'll get to meet her. She's wandering around now, checking out the place, but she'll make an appearance. I've decided that if we win this case,

I'm going to keep her. Her name is Agnes, but we're going to call her 'Barrister' instead."

"I'm anxious to meet her. . . ."

"Also, I need you to do a couple more things before you take off. Dig out my latest Verizon bill and make a copy of it—three copies. Be sure it shows the Verizon logo. In color."

"Okay. What else?"

"Draw up a subpoena to Verizon Wireless for all of Fessenden's cellular telephone records for May 18 of this year specifically. Stick in some language that picks up GPS coordinates, cell tower positioning data, and spell out 'all other data in your possession, custody or control reflecting or indicating the location of the cellular telephone to which that number is assigned, more particularly the location from which calls were initiated and to which calls were received on that date.' "

"I'm on it."

In fifteen minutes Kaitlin handed the Verizon subpoena to Mike. He reviewed and signed it. "On your way to the airport, drop this off at the constable's house. Wake him up if necessary. Tell him we need service forthwith. I've paid him enough over the years."

"Got it."

Mike said, "Take $5,000.00 out of the supplies cabinet to cover your expenses. Get back here ASAP, but call me on my cell before you head to the courthouse."

"But I moved . . . ." She saw that he was not paying attention. "Never mind, I'll explain later." Her look grew worried. "What're you going to do if your cross-examination of Fessenden ends before I get back?"

"That can't happen. Don't worry. I've got a plan; if it works, we won't need the certified copy until Monday."

"And if it doesn't?"

Mike scowled.

Kaitlin said, "Okay. I'll call you once I get it, and be back as soon as I can."

CHAPTER 39

Early Friday morning Mike ate a breakfast of six fried eggs sunny side up with an English muffin and drank five mugs of black coffee. In his office he retrieved a spare trial bag from the file room, stuffed it with ready-to-be-discarded papers from a years-ago trial, and left for the courthouse.

On the way he stopped at a pharmacy and made a purchase of a 30 ml.-size medicine, along with a bottle of Pepto-Bismol. In his car he set the Pepto-Bismol on the passenger seat. He released the clasp locks on the trial case and placed the other bottle in it, closed the case.

Upon entering the courthouse he took the elevator to the sixth floor and went directly to the men's room. He entered a stall, removed the medication bottle, drank its entire contents, returned the bottle to the case, and covered it with papers. Only then did he go to the courtroom.

Mike set his trial case on top of the defense counsel table, opened it and waited for the court officers to escort his client into the courtroom. Immediately he felt his stomach begin to churn. He stepped to the prosecution table and told Barton that he did not feel well. "I'm going to ask for a recess."

"What's the matter?" No look of obvious concern.

"Not sure, but upset stomach."

Mike signalled to the nearest court officer. "Would you tell the judge there's a preliminary matter she needs to address?"

"Sure." The bailiff went to the entrance to the judge's chambers, knocked on the door, and after a short wait opened the door and went into the room beyond it.

Soon the judge came into the courtroom, took her seat during the usual "Hear ye's . . . ."

She looked at Mike. "I understand there's something I have to attend to, Mr. Ratigan?"

"Yes, Your Honor. I regret to inform the court that I feel quite ill this morning, and am not at all sure that I will be able to represent my client adequately. In fact, I think . . . ." Suddenly the urge to throw up overwhelmed him. He leaned forward and vomited into his briefcase. His breakfast spewed over the paperwork inside. The retching sound reverberated throughout the courtroom, accompanied by the powerful stench of vomit.

Startled, Maguire jumped away, then leaned back toward his lawyer. "You all right?"

Mike blanched, gagged. He placed his palms on the table top and leaned his weight on his arms, his head directly over the open case. A putrid odor rose. He heaved again. The discharge saturated the papers. Perspiration began to dot his brow. His mouth held a bilious taste. He puked once more, took several deep breaths and sat down, hung his head.

"Do you feel that you need to see a doctor, Mr. Ratigan?" the judge said.

Mike looked up at the bench. "No, Your Honor. I think I'll be okay—must be something I ingested. I hope that's all. A day or two, I think."

"All right." She looked at the Commonwealth's attorney. "I assume that the Commonwealth has no objection to a recess until Monday?"

"None, Your Honor."

"We'll recess until Monday morning at 9:00 o'clock. Bring the jury down."

Maguire said, "You sure you're gonna be all right?"

Mike nodded, stood, left the courtroom as soon as the jury was excused. He went directly to the men's room, rinsed his mouth and gargled. He returned to his car, drank a full-dose cup of the Pepto-Bismol. His stomach began to settle.

* * *

Just after 3:00 o'clock at his office, Mike's cellphone chimed. The screen showed Kaitlin's name and mobile number.

"Hi," he said. "How'd you make out?"

"I got it!" Her voice was filled with jubilance. "I got it!"

"Fantastic. Where are you?"

"On the way to Reagan National."

"You won't be back for quite a while then. Come to the office when you get in."

"I will. How did it go today?" Her voice was tinged with concern. "Were you able to drag it out so we get to go back with Fessenden on Monday?"

"No problem. We didn't have court today. The judge gave us a day off."

"A day off! How—?"

"I'll explain it when you get to the office."

* * *

When she arrived, Kaitlin handed the package to him. He opened it, briefly checked the certification, glanced at the first few pages of text.

"Great. Just what the doctor ordered—pun intended. How did you manage to get it so fast? And how much did it cost?"

"You don't need to know everything. Like you said, a woman has her methods . . . . All it cost was for the copying and certification, airfare, taxis, and two lunches."

Mike briefly wondered who had joined her for lunch. Male? Female? He did not ask, but instead said, "Okay. Here's what I want you to do. Scan this entire document. Then scan the article in the cellular biology magazine.

"After you do that, set up a PowerPoint file that displays the certified copy on the left-hand side and the Fessenden article on the right. I want it so that each slide shows a page from the dissertation on the left and the corresponding page from the article on the right, so they can be read together, line by line. Because of differences in typescript and formatting, the two pages won't be identical, but get them as close as you can."

"Sure. I can do that, but before I start, I have a question for you."

"Shoot."

"How did you manage to get a day off from court?"

He described what he had done that morning.

"God, that was ballsy. What made you think of it?"

"Actually, I learned it from the judge herself when she was in the D.A.'s office. She used it once when we had a case on trial and she needed to produce a witness who wasn't available, but we didn't have a good excuse—or *any* excuse. So she came up with the idea, and that's what she did. Right in court, just like I did today."

"Wow! You were taking a big risk though; she had to know what you were doing."

"Right. I was taking a chance, but we needed to do it. And somehow I don't think she minded it that much. In a way, it's a compliment to her. And there's no way I could've cross-examined Fessenden for long enough to get through the whole day. Without that, our defense would have been over."

Kaitlin moved to go to her desk, turned back. "You don't expect me to clean out that trial bag, do you?"

"Absolutely not. That's a goner. I already tossed it. We'll just pick up a new one."

CHAPTER 40

On Monday morning the jury was assembled and counsel ready at their tables when Judge Madore assumed the bench. She nodded to Mike and said, "Mr. Ratigan, we are pleased to learn of your swift recovery, and hope that those symptoms will not revisit you."

Mike discerned no suggestion of sarcasm. "I appreciate the court's indulgence during my brief indisposition."

The court officer signaled to Professor Fessenden to take the stand again. He did so, once more declining a seat. The judge leaned toward him and said, "You are still under oath, professor."

Mike strode to the lectern. "Good morning," he said to the witness.

"Good morning," Dr. Fessenden answered. He stood straight-backed, but avoided seeming to be rigid. His face was serious, but held no hint of sternness.

Mike turned toward the jury box. "Good morning, ladies and gentlemen." The jurors nodded, some returning the greeting out loud.

Mike feared the beginning part of his cross-examination because it had the appearance of being irrelevant and of little weight. Moreover, his questions would be somewhat divorced from the witness's direct testimony, which had touched on the professor's credentials only in passing.

Although no Massachusetts evidentiary rule prohibited opening new lines of inquiry on cross, the best approach would be to ease into the subject by way of questions expected to make the witness comfortable.

In Mike's judgment, Fessenden was a consummate egotist. So long as his credentials were the subject of testimony, he could be expected to preen his feathers before the jury.

Mike watched the man closely to gauge his reaction.

"Dr. Fessenden, you are an expert in cellular biology, is that correct?"

"I am," he admitted, with only the slightest nod. He did not expand. Perhaps the prosecutor had taught him well: Answer the question, answer *only* the question. Do *not* go beyond it. Do not volunteer anything. Ever.

"And you have been at the university for many years now?"

Another nod. "Thirty-seven—forty-one if you count my undergrad years."

"During one period you were chairman of the department, is that correct?"

"Yes."

"That is an honor, is it?"

"It is thought to be, although many might disagree." A slight smile.

"After a time, you resigned in order to concentrate more fully on pursuit of your research?"

"Yes."

"You resigned as chairman," Mike said, consulting his notes. "Let's see now, just a little over eleven years ago, is that correct?"

"Yes."

The witness seemed to relax, to grow comfortable with the flow of questioning, but plainly he would give no help by volunteering information. When the slogging became difficult, Mike conjectured, he would have to use verbal pliers to extract the answers he wanted—needed.

"At that time you assumed the position of Rittenhouse Professor of Cellular Biology?"

"True—an endowed chair created especially for me by the Rittenhouse Foundation."

The Great Educator had, for the moment, forgotten his instructions; he had expanded his answer beyond what the question required. He seemed even more relaxed now, moderately puffed up as well. The stiffness had gone out of his back.

Mike himself now began to feel a little better, more comfortable. He was at his best like this, when he got a witness at ease, thinking that Mike presented no danger—perhaps might even be a fool.

"Yes, and the Rittenhouse Foundation is a creation of James B. Rittenhouse, is that correct?"

"True."

The professor seemed still to have no inkling where Mike was headed.

"Mr. Rittenhouse is the Chairman of Rittenhouse Pharmaceutical, is that correct?"

"Yes." At this point Dr. Fessenden must have begun to suspect that something wasn't just right with the information being elicited. It was too favorable to him, to the prosecution.

He glared at the prosecution table, frowned, turned to the judge and said, "Your Honor, do I have to answer all these questions? They don't seem to have anything to do with this case."

Barton stood. "I agree, Your Honor. I object on the grounds of relevance—and materiality as well."

Judge Madore looked down at Mike. "What do you say, Mr. Ratigan? It does seem somewhat far afield. Are you just trying to establish the witness's percipience—or lack of it—through his education, knowledge and experience? I hadn't thought that would be an issue, but of course . . . ."

Mike shook his head. "Not at all, Your Honor. I think it'll be eminently clear in just a few moments, if I may have your ruling."

"All right, proceed," she said.

Mike resumed. "Two years ago you were awarded the Balzan Prize?"

"Yes." The professor could not help but smile once more. He placed his hands on the front edge of the stand. His posture grew more erect.

"That is one of the highest awards achievable?"

"Next to the Nobel, I would warrant."

"But unknown to many people—perhaps most—the Balzan Prize awards are of equal or even greater monetary value than the Nobel itself?"

"This is true." His pride showed, and jurors smiled with him.

"A little bit more than one million dollars?"

"You are right."

"Roughly the same as a Nobel award?"

"Yes."

"You received the award for your work in—if I may put it in layman's terms—the causes of cell death?"

"Yes."

"And the *prevention* of death?"

The professor nodded, did not answer orally.

The jury had been attentive all along, but their interest now picked up even further. They leaned forward in their seats, cocked their ears, looked at the witness intensively.

Mike glanced at his client, who sat at the defense counsel table, hands in his lap. His countenance wore a look of concern, but not comprehension. Mike had told him nothing of his plan, partly out of fear that it might not be successful and also because his client might inadvertently reveal it—or somehow sabotage it.

"You *nodded* in answer to my question, but for the record, Dr. Fessenden, you agree, do you, that the subject of your work concerned the prevention of cell death?"

"It did."

"And you received some considerable publicity—even fame—at the time of the award of the Balzan Prize, did you?"

"Yes. The popular press dubbed me 'Dr. Everlast.' I made the cover of *Time* Magazine, which called my quest 'The Search for the Holy Grail'."

"That is because, based upon your research, you posited that under the right conditions cells can live forever?"

"Yes. They can. I proved it unequivocally."

"The Fountain of Youth."

"That's right: The Fountain of Youth."

"What Ponce de León failed to find . . . you did discover."

"This is true."

Barton stood. "Your Honor, this is all very interesting, but I fail to see—"

Mike cut the prosecutor off. "One more moment, if it please the court."

"You may have it." The judge had become as interested as everyone else in the courtroom.

"As a result of your research."

"Yes."

"And your creative thought."

"Indeed." The doctor's chest visibly expanded and his mustache seemed to vibrate.

The other shoe was about to drop.

"You wrote a journal article about it?"

"Yes."

"What was the subject of your article?"

"Cellular longevity."

"How long ago did you write it?"

"Nine years ago."

"And its title?"

"The title was 'Inhibiting the Aging Process Through Manipulation of the Telomerase Rate'."

"You remember that quite well, do you, doctor—after all these intervening years?"

Fessenden seemed to realize that he might have slipped, but recovered quickly. "I was just reading the article again last week. In fact, in preparation for my meeting with Professor Graham."

Mike shifted gears. "You had a research assistant, a graduate student named Jonathan Wright?"

Now Fessenden faltered, apparently beginning to see his adversary's direction. He turned toward the judge and said, "Your Honor, this is getting so far astray. I don't really have to answer any more of these questions, do I?"

Barton popped up. "Yes. Objection. Plainly irrelevant!"

"Mr. Ratigan?" the judge inquired. "I gave you leeway, but . . . ."

"One more brief exchange, Your Honor, I promise, and it will all become clear."

"It better," she snapped. "Go ahead."

"Do you have the question in mind, or would you like to have it read back?"

Mike could be so polite, so considerate.

"No, I don't need to have it read back." Churlish. "I had a graduate student working with me by that name —some years ago."

"He was a Ph.D. candidate?"

"Yes."

"His area of research coincided with your own?"

A nod. "Of course. He was working with me, helping me."

"Did he get his Ph.D.?"

"No. Regrettably, he never submitted the final draft of his dissertation."

"He submitted interim drafts to you, as his supervisor?"

A lengthy pause before the answer came. "Yes, I believe he did."

"What was the subject of Jonathan Wright's *draft* dissertation?"

The other shoe had dropped.

Fessenden grasped the rail of the witness stand. He sputtered, "I am not going to answer any more of these questions!"

His face had taken on a violet hue; perspiration beaded his brow, and spittle oozed from the corners of his mouth. He looked as though he were about to have an apoplectic seizure.

He continued, "They have nothing whatsoever to do with this case."

The professor glared at the prosecutor. "Can't you control this—this obfuscation? Can't you do *anything*?"

Barton remained seated, said nothing.

"Dr. Fessenden," the judge interjected. "Please answer the question."

Fessenden's chin jutted out like the carved figurehead at the prow of an ancient ship.

"May I have an answer?" Mike asked. "Or perhaps you don't remember the subject of Mr. Wright's dissertation?"

Fessenden spoke through gritted teeth. " 'Inhibiting the Aging Process Through Manipulation of the Telomerase Rate'."

"The very same title as your own paper." Mike left no rising inflection at the end of the sentence. It was not a question.

The witness answered anyway. "Yes."

"Now I will show you the first page of Mr. Wright's paper alongside the first page of your own." Mike activated the digital projector, clicked on the first slide. The two manuscript pages splashed across the courtroom screens side by side.

Barton sprang to his feet. "Objection! Hearsay. Relevance. Not properly authenticated. Lack of foundation. Immaterial. Not on the exhibits list."

The judge, ignoring the computer monitor right before her on the bench, peered at the larger screen. The two pages were similar in title and identical in text. One single difference stood out.

Without waiting for a defense response, the judge said, "I assume that this evidence relates to your *Bowden* defense?"

"Yes, Your Honor. It does."

"Overruled."

Mike glanced at the jurors. Their gazes too were riveted on the display.

Mike said to the witness, "Are these the first pages?"

"Yes," Fessenden begrudged. His face had grown the color of eggplant.

"Of your paper and Mr. Wright's?"

"Yes," again, voice lower this time.

"Is there any difference?"

"The titles," Fessenden croaked.

"But the *subtitle* of Mr. Wright's paper is the same as the *title* of your own, is that correct?"

"Yes."

"And one other difference shows, does it?"

Fessenden frowned, seemed not to understand.

Mike explained. "The names of the authors are different, are they?"

Fessenden's mouth dropped open. After a moment he nodded.

Mike tied it down: "That is a 'yes'?"

"Yes." Weakly.

"Now we can go through the entire manuscript page by page, but that's not necessary, is it, doctor?" Uncharacteristically, Mike did not wait for an answer. "If we do that, we both know what we will find, don't we?"

Fessenden glared at Mike.

"And what is that?" Mike asked.

The doctor squeaked the answer. "They're the same."

The jurors sat in rapt attention.

"Yet Mr. Wright's paper was written in advance of your own, is that true?" Before the witness had answered, Mike added, "If it will help you in your answer, perhaps you will accept my representation that a copy of the original document—Mr. Wright's dissertation—has been filed with the United States Copyright Office. Moreover, we have a certified copy of that document in court at this very moment."

Fessenden began to recover, shook his head slowly back and forth. "No. Absolutely not. I can't believe he did such a terrible thing as this—copying *my work*. I just can't believe it."

Kaitlin's prediction was accurate: Fessenden would claim that Jonathan Wright had copied his mentor's paper rather than vice versa. Consequently Mike's challenge remained.

"May I have a moment, Your Honor?" Mike asked.

"We'll take a fifteen minute recess," she said.

CHAPTER 41

After the recess Fessenden resumed his place on the witness stand.

Mike stood at the lectern. "So you claim that your paper was written before Mr. Wright's, is that so?"

"Without question."

"Mr. Wright submitted his paper to you as his supervisor and mentor, did he?"

"Yes."

"Did you copy Mr. Wright's manuscript?"

"Absolutely not!"

"Mr. Wright was living out West at the time, was he—in Wyoming, was it?"

"That's my recollection."

"And Mr. Wright's submissions were transmitted to you by email, were they?"

"Yes."

"So if we look at the emails back and forth between the two of you, and compare the dates of transmission with the date when you authored your prize-winning article, we could determine which came first?"

The ADA rose and objected. "Your Honor, for the life of me I cannot fathom what this has to do with the issue here: did Francis X. Maguire murder Sheila Graham."

The judge looked at Mike. "Mr. Ratigan?"

"I promise, Your Honor, that shortly the relationship of this evidence to the *Bowden* defense will become absolutely pellucid."

"Hmm," the judge murmured.

Mike went on. "But in deference to my adversary, I will for the time being take up a different subject."

"Go ahead," Judge Madore responded.

Mike again directed his attention to the witness. "You were in Professor Graham's house the day she died, were you?"

"As I testified." Fessenden's posture seemed to stiffen. "I was there briefly. After she . . . after she died."

"After she died."

"Yes: after she died."

"How long does it take to drive from your office to Ms. Graham's house?"

"Well, I—"

"Let me change that a bit. Assuming that you are in your office, how long does it take to leave your office, go get your car, and drive to Ms. Graham's house?"

"Well, a lot depends on traffic, but I'd say at that time of day it would probably be around a half hour or so. Maybe a little more."

"What did you do while at her house?"

"Nothing. The policeman told me she . . . she was dead . . . so I didn't really do anything."

"You told the police that you were to meet Professor Graham at your office at the University the morning she died?"

"Yes."

"At 9:00 o'clock?"

"Correct. Nine o'clock."

"But she didn't show up."

"Right."

"And you became concerned."

"Yes."

"So you called her."

"Yes."

"That call was made at 9:13, according to Ms. Graham's answering machine."

"I don't know, but it sounds about right."

"I have it on video, if you want to see it."

Fessenden shook his head rapidly. "No. No, I accept that."

"You have no reason to contest the accuracy of that clock?"

"None."

"So you called at 9:13."

"Yes."

"And you made that call on your cellular telephone, is that right?"

The witness did not answer immediately. He appeared to be struggling to remember.

"Frankly, I don't remember right now. Could have been from my office, or I might have used my mobile telephone."

"Do you remember that you made the call *from your office*—as distinct from *which telephone* you used to make it?"

Fessenden looked at Mike with growing suspicion. "No, I don't." His hands gripped the side rails of the witness stand.

"Well, let's see if we can get any help for your memory. The video indicates that the call came from an instrument with the 339 area code."

"Oh, then that's my cellphone. The University uses 617."

In exaggerated fashion Mike now focused his attention on the papers he held. They prominently bore the distinctive Verizon logo, white lettering on a bright-red field. He looked up at the professor. "That's a Verizon number, right?"

The answer came out hesitantly. "Yessss."

"So you made that call at 9:13. And according to the police report, you arrived at Ms. Graham's house at 9:32. Is that consistent with your memory?"

"Sounds close."

"You know of nothing to contradict it?"

"True."

"You state that it takes about a half hour to go from your office to Ms. Graham's house. Since you made the call at 9:13, and arrived at Ms. Graham's house at 9:32, does that suggest to you that you made the call from some place other than your office?"

Fessenden seemed to stiffen a little. He said, "Must have, but I don't remember."

"Well if the timing is right, in order to arrive at the Graham house at 9:32, you had to leave your office around 9:00 AM—or perhaps even earlier, is that so?"

"Sounds logical, but I don't remember."

"Your appointment was at 9:00, correct?"

"Yes."

"So you would not have become concerned as early as 9:00 that Ms. Graham was going to be late for her appointment, would you?"

"Doesn't seem so."

"Unless you knew something else?"

"Something else?"

"That Ms. Graham would not keep her appointment with you?"

"Not keep it?"

"Not keep it because she was already dead."

The professor shook his head vigorously. "Ridiculous."

Mike pushed a button on the remote. A giant version of the Verizon logo appeared on the screen. "Dr. Fessenden, you can read the writing on the screen, can you?"

"Yes. 'Verizon.'"

"Thank you. Incidentally, what is the background color?"

Barton objected. "Completely irrelevant, Your Honor!"

Judge Madore said, "It does seem—"

Mike cut her off. "Very soon the court will see exactly how relevant this is, Your Honor."

"All right. You may have it."

The witness answered, "I can't tell."

Mike said, "You can't tell. Do you remember letting a cat in while you were at the house?"

"A cat?"

"Yes, the *wrong* cat. A black and white cat."

"I don't know what you're talking about." Fessenden turned to the judge. "Do I have to continue putting up with this nonsense?"

"There is no objection. Answer the question."

"I already did. I don't know what he's talking about."

"Next question," Judge Madore said.

Mike pushed the remote button again. Photographs of two cats flashed onto the screen: a tortoiseshell and a tabby. "What colors are the cats displayed on the screen, Dr. Fessenden?"

The professor mumbled something inaudible.

"I'm sorry," Mike said. "I didn't quite hear you. Could you speak up a little, please?"

"I can't tell." Barely audible.

"Did you say, 'I can't tell'?"

A nod.

"You nodded 'yes'?"

"Yes."

"And you can't tell, doctor, because you are colorblind, is that right?"

"Yes." A weak croak.

"And you particularly have trouble distinguishing the color red, is that correct?"

"Yes." Another croak.

"So you see the cats on the screen as gray, is that right?"

Extreme reluctance. "Yes."

"Going back a bit, we established that you made the call to Ms. Graham's home by your mobile—not through the telephone exchange at the University, is that so?"

"Yes, that's right." Seeming relief at getting off the colorblind questions.

"Are you aware, doctor, that wireless service providers track the location of their users—even if their mobile telephone is turned off, so long as the battery is not removed—or dead?"

Fessenden seemed to ponder this for a moment. "Sort of."

Mike went to the defense-counsel table and picked up a paper. "And you use Verizon, do you?"

"For my mobile, yes."

"Do you know that as a matter of routine practice Verizon does this: that is, tracks cellphone locations?"

Barton rose to object. "Your Honor, there is no evidence of this; perhaps the jury could be so instructed."

The judge said, "I'm sure that by now the jury understands that questions by themselves are not evidence." She turned to the jury box. "Ladies and gentlemen of the jury, I will simply remind you at this point that questions do not constitute evidence. Just because a question may assume a fact does not mean that the assumption *is* fact. If the witness's answer adopts the assumption, then you may or may not accept as fact that answer and the proposition which it encompasses, as your sound judgment determines." She then instructed the stenographer to read the question back.

The stenographer read, "Do you know that as a matter of routine practice Verizon does this: that is, tracks cellphone locations?"

"Probably," Dr. Fessenden answered. "I don't know for sure."

Barton, who had remained on his feet, smiled, as though to say, "There! Gotcha!" He sat down.

"Well, perhaps you'll accept my representation that we have issued a subpoena to your telephone service provider, and that Verizon has independently confirmed that it does indeed track the location of its customers."

Barton's smile soured, but he did not object this time.

"I accept that," the witness answered.

Mike passed near the prosecution table, holding his own bill so that Barton could see the face page, with the Verizon color logo in prominent display, but not close enough for him to see detail.

Mike said, "As stated, I have subpoenaed records from Verizon covering your telephone usage on the day of Sheila Graham's death." He moved past the prosecution table so that the cover page was even more visible to Barton. Mike stared at the paper in exaggerated fashion before proceeding to his next question.

"Records show that you made a call to Sheila Graham's home on May 18 at 9:13 AM. That's the same time the answering machine indicated." He pressed a button on the remote. A video clip started to play. It showed the answering machine display of Fessenden's incoming telephone call, identifying his mobile number, and played the audio:

"Sheila, this is Dr. Fessenden. I'm waiting for you. Where are you? Did you forget? Call me. Let me know you're all right."

Barton belatedly jumped to his feet. "Objection! We do not have a copy of the record that counsel is holding in his hand. If counsel is going to examine the witness about a document, we have a right to a copy."

"Your Honor," Mike said calmly, "I haven't even finished asking a question yet, or more important, shown any record to the witness or offered any paper in evidence. Right now I am only seeking to test the witness's memory by reference to material already in evidence. If he doesn't remember where he was when he made the call, then we may resort to records. If he does, however, there may be no necessity for further burdening the record in this case with more documents."

"You may have it. Objection overruled."

Mike turned to the professor. "You don't need a record to remember making that telephone call, do you, doctor?"

The witness remained silent, staring at Mike from his standing position.

"In fact, you left that message on Sheila Graham's answering machine, didn't you?"

"Yes. Yes. I did."

"And you used your cellular telephone to make that call, didn't you?"

Warier now, the witness nodded. "Yes."

"Not your office phone."

"Yes. I already said that about fifty times."

"Because you were not at your office when you made the call."

"I don't remember where I was."

Mike held the Verizon telephone bill—his own—in prominent view. "But you don't need a record to remember the place from which you made that call, do you?"

No answer.

"You understand, as you already testified, Dr. Fessenden, that cellphones emit signals even when a call is not being made?

Barton rose. "Objection! No conceivable relevance."

Before Mike could respond, the judge said, "I think otherwise. Overruled." She turned to the professor. "Answer the question."

"Yes, I've heard that. Yes."

"In addition, you already acknowledged that cellphone carriers can track users?"

"Yes."

"Your cellular telephone has a GPS function, does it?"

"I don't know. I don't use it."

"Do you know that your mobile telephone communicates with the GPS satellite system even when the GPS function is not utilized?"

"No, I did—"

"Objection!" Barton interrupted, jumping to his feet. "He's trying to make an expert witness of this man in a field where no competence has been demonstrated."

Judge Madore said, "What do you say to that, Mr. Ratigan?"

"I rather thought this to be common knowledge nowadays, Your Honor, but if counsel for the Commonwealth prefers that I introduce this through expert testimony, then I will do so. On my representation to that effect, I assume that the Court will permit me to pursue this line of questioning *de bene*. In the event that it is not connected later, then it could be stricken, but I promise that it will be connected."

"On that basis, objection overruled. Proceed."

"Can you accept my representation, Dr. Fessenden, that cellular telephones which contain the requisite GPS chip communicate constantly with the GPS system, even when that function is not invoked on an individual telephone—as long as the battery has not been removed—or dead?"

"Through GPS, you mean—not what you asked me about before?"

"Yes, through GPS—the global positioning system, using satellites."

"It doesn't sound like an outrageous proposition. I can accept that." The profesor did not want to appear unreasonable before the jury.

"And similarly with respect to my representation that GPS tracking can pinpoint a telephone to a position accurate within about half an inch?"

"You mean, can I accept that?"

"Yes."

"Yes, I can."

"And even if your phone doesn't have GPS, its location can be identified by cell tower triangulation."

"I do know about that. I think probably everybody does nowadays."

"But in this situation there is no need to look at cell tower records, or GPS records, is there?"

Fessenden did not answer, instead gave Mike a hard look, as though he knew Mike's next questions.

"Did you hear the question? Do you want it repeated?"

Still no answer.

"There is no need to look at Verizon records, because you remember exactly where you were when you made the call, don't you?"

Again no answer.

"We all know what those records show, don't we Doctor Fessenden?"

Silence.

"Everyone in this courtroom knows where you were, don't they?"

No response.

This was one of those occasions where it was wise not to press for an answer. "You were in Ms. Graham's house, weren't you?"

Again no answer.

Barton remained stuck to his chair.

"And you were there when the neighbor's message about the cat came in." At the end of this statement Mike left no inflection signifying a question.

Mike continued. "And that is what led you to let a cat into the house. In order not to have the police come."

Unanswered.

"But you made a mistake. You let the *wrong* cat in. Because you are colorblind. Is that so?"

Silence from the stand.

"May I have an answer, Your Honor?"

"You may." To the witness Judge Madore said, "Answer the question." Her voice had taken on a sternness not shown before.

The professor now seemed to deflate, much as an air mattress with a sudden leak. He stared at Mike, with resignation said, "So you know everything."

Mike sensed that the plagiarizer was ready to crack. He bore in. "Yes, we do. Everything! You stole the Wright manuscript and published it as your own. Ms. Graham discovered your wrongdoing and threatened to disclose it, correct?"

"No! I did not steal *anything*! This was *my* idea. My whole life's research work. Wright stole *my* idea. You have no understanding at all—people like you cannot possibly comprehend the dimensions of my discovery. Someone like you could not conceivably appreciate it."

"In truth it is Mr. Wright's paper which won the Balzan Prize, not your own?"

"No one like you could ever possibly comprehend the immensity and complexity of my work—its enormous value to society."

Mike waited.

From deep purple earlier, the doctor's face had now become pallid. Suddenly he looked thinner, almost gaunt. He shook his head, seemed to collect himself, but his hands gave him away. They gripped the sides of the witness box, his knuckles white, reminding Mike of the Charles Bragg "Cross Examination" print on his office wall.

Without warning, Fessenden erupted. "She was going to expose me! Destroy me! Ruin my entire professional career, make a mockery of me. I could not abide it. I had no choice."

"You killed her, Doctor Fessenden, didn't you?"

"I had no choice," he raged. Spittle flew from the corners of his mouth. "I had no choice." He banged his fist against the stand. "The stupid bitch left me with no choice."

The judge stood, gestured to a court officer. "Bailiff, take this man into custody."

She called the attorneys to the sidebar and addressed Barton. "Do I hear a motion from the Commonwealth to dismiss the murder indictment against Mr. Maguire?"

Barton responded, "Your Honor, I do not have authority to do that."

"Well then, I suggest that you call District Attorney Peters and obtain that authority."

"I will, Your Honor."

"*Right now*, counsel. Right now! We will take a recess and wait for you to report."

Judge Madore looked at Mike. A smile barely traced the corners of her lips. "At this time I will entertain a motion for admission to bail."

Mike said. "So moved, Your Honor. And defendant further asks that he be released on personal recognizance."

Barton objected. "The Commonwealth is opposed to extending bail to this man for the same reasons explicated previously."

The judge shook her head. "The remaining charge—basically of burglary—does not warrant incarceration pending trial. This man has no criminal record. Motion allowed. Defendant is released on personal recognizance.

"We stand in recess until Mr. Barton receives instructions from the District Attorney. If he does not receive guidance soon, we will adjourn until tomorrow morning. I suggest that the Commonwealth would be well advised to confer with defense counsel prior to our reconvening."

She hesitated, said, "I've changed my mind. No sense in keeping the jury waiting until the District Attorney gets around to making up his mind. We will recess forthwith until tomorrow morning at nine."

She ended the sidebar conference and turned to the jury. "The jury is excused until tomorrow morning at 9:00 o'clock. Do not discuss this case with anyone or expose yourself to any materials about it. I hope you all have a pleasant evening."

A court officer said to Maguire, "You want to come back with us to pick up your stuff?"

Maguire said, "No. I'll get it tomorrow."

"You'll need your license if you're planning on driving."

"Hadn't thought of that. I'll hitch a ride over tomorrow." He smiled at the officer. "No offense intended."

The officer chuckled. "Understood."

CHAPTER 42

Once out of his client's hearing, Mike called Elaine to tell her of Frankie's release.

Elaine answered, sneezed mightily.

"What's the matter?" Mike said. "Are you all right?"

She sneezed again. "Yeah, I'm okay—just my allergies acting up, I guess. You don't have a cat here, do you?"

"Oh, you're at my office."

"Yes. I thought—" another sneeze—"I'd wait for you here."

"I did get a cat—never occurred to me it might bother you."

"I think I'll have to wait outside."

"What I called about . . . . We got Frankie off on the murder charge, and he's been released on bail."

"That's great! But . . . what're we going to do about . . . about *us?*"

"Don't worry. We'll deal with it. Frankie's coming with me. We'll be there soon."

"Uh. What're we going to tell him?"

"We'll figure something out."

* * *

On the way to Mike's car, Maguire said, "I know it sounds crazy, but I've been dying for one of those Dunkin'

Donuts butternut doughnuts. Suppose we can stop and get one?"

"Sure. No problem. I'll ask Kaitlin to pick some up for us. How about coffee too?"

"Sounds good."

"Any preference?"

"Nope. Regular's fine. Light."

As they got into Mike's car, his mobile chimed. The display read "Peter Kagan" with a 617 area code. Mike knew him to be a *Boston Herald* reporter.

"Mike, Pete Kagan from the *Herald*. I just heard you pulled off a miracle. I'm lookin' for comment. Interview if you can make time."

Previously Mike had never spoken to this reporter. Now they were on a first-name basis. "How did you find out so fast?"

"I have my sources. How'd you work this bit of magic?"

"Superior representation, that's how. Look, I'm in my car, on my way back to the office."

His phone chirped; the display showed another call coming in, this from a WBZ number. Mike didn't want to lose the opportunity for coverage. It would pump up his caseload for sure, get him back on financial track.

"Can you call me there, say around six?"

Kagan agreed.

Mike answered the next call, started the engine.

"Jack Spurlong, 'BZ TV. Just heard you pulled another one out of the hat. 'Murder One Walks' is how I see it. How'd you do it?"

Mike particularly liked that this reporter referred to "another one," recalling past successes. Perhaps his report will include references to Mike's earlier string of victories. Mike told him that he could not speak right now, but promised to call him later that day. "I can use the number you called from, right?"

"Right. I'll wait to hear from you."

What other choice did he have?

Mike maneuvered out of the parking lot.

Maguire said, "Jesus, am I ever glad to get out of that fucking hole. What do you think's gonna happen now?"

"I suspect that Barton will call and suggest a plea deal, but we'll just have to wait and see."

"What kind of deal?"

"Maybe conviction on a lesser charge—trespassing, something like that, maybe a sentence to time served— that might be your best deal. On the other hand, you did have the key, and that should raise considerable doubt concerning whether you had permission to be in the house. You might have had the owner's authority. So it isn't clear cut by any means. Except for those gloves— they don't help."

"Yeah, there's that. If I plead to something like trespassing, I wouldn't have to go back in?"

"Not if time served is the deal. Which it should be."

"Jesus, I hope so."

Maguire looked out the side window, watched as they drove by commercial and industrial buildings on Route 128. "It's nice to just be able to see this crappy old landscape, not have to look at bars all day."

"Enjoy it while you can. Odds are, the cops'll have an eye on you from now on. You'd be wise to take up a new line of work."

"May do that. That money you have stashed for me will sure help me get a start." After a few seconds he said, "Where is it?"

"In my office. It's secure—don't worry."

"Step on that pedal. I'm psyched to see it, get my hands on it—*feel* it."

"Sure do appreciate that."

They rode in silence for a while. Eventually Frankie said, "After I pick up the money, I'll have Elaine drop me at my house in Watertown. Or if she's tied up, I can call Meridee and have her pick me up."

Stunned, Mike jerked the wheel. The car veered sharply toward the breakdown lane. "Meridee?"

"Yeah, my niece. I'd have my sister do it, but she couldn't get off work today."

Mike corrected his steering. "Your niece's name is Meridee?"

"Yeah. Unusual name, eh?"

"That's the same name as Ela—your girlfriend's sister."

"Elaine?—Elaine doesn't have any sister."

"A twin sister: Meridee, I thought."

"No, she doesn't have a sister. Never did."

Mike tensed, felt that his chest had collapsed under enormous pressure. He took a deep breath before speaking. "Didn't she have a sister die—get killed or something?"

Maguire chuckled. "Somebody's pulling it. Elaine tell you that?"

Mike forced himself to look indifferent. "Must've misunderstood."

"You did. Don't worry about it."

When they entered the office, Maguire called out, "Elaine! Elaine!"

Silence.

Mike put his trial bag on his desk and led Maguire to the file room. Mike opened the supplies cabinet and swung the door back so they had a clear view of the contents. The cabinet contained no attaché cases.

Shaken, Mike said, "They're not here." He looked about the room in a dazed fashion. The attaché cases did not magically appear.

Maguire held his fist in a menacing gesture. He growled, "If this's some kind of fuckin' scam . . . , somebody's gonna wind up very sorry. *Very* sorry."

Mike recalled Elaine's reference to Maguire's "friends." Clearly agitated, Mike said, "Do you think I'm that stupid? If I had any plan like that, do you think I'd be winning the case for you, getting you out on bail?"

This profoundly logical explanation seemed to mollify his client.

Mike heard Kaitlin enter the reception area and hurried to her. "We've got a problem," he said. "His money's gone."

The telephone rang. The display showed a call from CNN. Mike let the call go to voicemail. "There may be a lot of these calls," he said to Kaitlin. "I'll get back to people later. Let's deal with this now."

She said, "Calm down, Mike." She placed two Dunkin' Donuts bags on her desk, stacked a pile of doughnuts on waxed paper, removed coffees from the other bag. The rich aroma of the coffee was refreshing.

Overcome with worry about the money, his hand shaking, Mike passed a cup to Maguire and removed the lid from one of the other containers, sipped carefully without spilling.

Kaitlin said, "You looked in the supplies cabinet, right? I put *Beaulieu's* money in there. Remember? It's not there? Should be. I tried to tell you about Mr. Maguire's money the other day, but—never mind. Come with me."

She opened her desk drawer and took out a key bearing a green tag, grasped Mike's elbow and steered him toward the sunroom. Maguire trailed. Kaitlin went to the middle window seat, picked up the cushion and tossed it aside. This action revealed a wooden lid with a cutout for a brass spring-release button. She pressed the button, and a brass finger-pull popped up.

Kaitlin raised the lid. Beneath it was a safe. She inserted the key into the lock, twisted, raised the cover. Two attaché cases sat in plain view. "Here they are. I tried to tell you, but . . . ."

She removed the cases and set them on another cushion, released the clasps of the first one. They clicked open with a loud snap.

She opened the case. Stacks of banded $50 and $100 bills packed the container. She did the same with the other case, and waved her hand at them. "It's all here."

Maguire said, "Thank God!"

Mike looked at Kaitlin with wonder. "You sure this isn't . . . ?"

Kaitlin shook her head. "No, it isn't Beaulieu's. This is Mr. Maguire's money. All of it."

Maguire began to lift banded stacks of currency from the case, holding them with obvious pleasure.

Mike said, "But how . . . ?"

"I tried to let you know that day the clerk called to tell you the trial would start on Monday, but everything got so busy, and I . . . . I put Mr. Maguire's money here and left the Beaulieu money in the supply cabinet, where this used to be."

"Well it's not there now."

Maguire interrupted. "I thought Elaine would be here. I'm going to try her again. Can I use your phone?"

Mike pointed to Kaitlin's desk telephone. "Use that one."

Maguire tapped out the number and let the telephone ring for a long time. Finally he said, "It went to voicemail.

I hope she's all right. I can't understand why she wouldn't answer."

"We'll just have to wait," Mike said. "Now how about those donuts—or would you rather have a drink? It's been quite a while for you."

Kaitlin indicated the stack of doughnuts on her desk.

"Can I choose both? I'll take a coupla butternuts with the coffee, then a drink. Love one. What've you got?"

Mike said, "Just about anything you want. You name it."

When Maguire attacked the doughnuts, Kaitlin said to Mike, "I've got to speak with you," and drew him into the adjoining room. "I was going to tell you about switching the money, but just forgot in all the excitement. And then . . . ."

"No problem. But now it looks as though Pierre's money is gone. You know anything about that?"

She shook her head, avoided his eyes. "It was in the supply cabinet the other day."

"Well, somebody took it."

The telephone rang again. Another newspaper reporter. The next call came from a well-known blogger. Mike let them all go to voicemail.

CHAPTER 43

Mike had never owned a cat, but Aunt Julia had bought a dog for him soon after he started living with her. "Bone" was a giant St. Bernard with a heart equal to his size. It was not even a close call whether Mike loved any human nearly as much as he did Bone.

Occasionally nowadays he thought of Bone, remembering him with great fondness. He did not expect Barrister to achieve that exalted status, but felt that he would always appreciate her. After all, she provided the means by which this signal victory was attained.

Thoughts of Elaine now stood in sharp contrast to those of Bone. She was not to be remembered with fondness. Memories of her caused his chest to ache. At times he felt as though his heart might burst. A sense of emptiness, of being hollow, sometimes overcame him. At such moments he struggled to breathe. How could she betray me like this?

But at other times he imagined her lying on a beach on some Caribbean Island, drinking a piña colada, much as vamp Matty Walker (played by Kathleen Turner) did in *Body Heat*. But here the result would be different from Maddy's avoidance of justice. Very different. The authorities would quickly discover that Elaine's bankroll was counterfeit. She would be arrested, convicted, sent away for years. Just deserts to her!

Mike's upper body felt smaller, tightened, as though some unknown internal force constricted it. Too, he worried. Is there any way the counterfeiting can come back on me? Unlikely, but he could easily see Elaine trying to do that. Implicate him in return for lenience.

Not to worry; I'll think of a way out another day.

He switched gears, called Jeri Thompson on her mobile. "Jeri, Mike Ratigan here. Wanted to thank you for your help in putting that DVD together. I'm sorry I didn't get a chance to express my appreciation to you at the courthouse, but I had to get my client—"

She interrupted, speaking with enthusiasm. "A stunning victory, they said on TV. I was so happy for you when the judge decided to let Maguire go free."

"Yeah, that was terrific, and getting some press doesn't hurt."

"It's wonderful. Murder, too."

"Well, he's innocent . . . . Look, I was thinking maybe we should get together for a drink or something . . . ." The "or something" would be more like it. "What do you say? You busy tonight?"

"No, that would be great—I mean, No, I'm not busy tonight."

Barrister chose this moment to jump onto his desk and sit in front of him.

This prompted Mike to ask, "Say, you're not allergic to cats, are you?"

* * *

On the next morning when Mike came downstairs, Kaitlin immediately said, "Somebody keeps calling from the Bromfield Coin & Stamp Emporium. Says he's the nephew of a Mr. Weissman—needs to talk to you. Says you'll know what it's about."

* * *

Anne called to congratulate Mike on his victory.

"Thanks. I was going to call you anyway to thank *you* for your help."

"My help?"

"Yes. You remember that colorblindness test you had?"

"Sure."

"Well it was very useful in identifying the killer."

"My God! I can't believe it. How did it happen?"

Mike explained, and when finished asked, "Any further developments in that?"

"Things are at a standstill. As I told you, all the parents have sued the school board, and they're seeking an injunction against expulsion. It's a terrible mess, and nobody knows what'll happen."

"Did they sue you too, like you were afraid of?"

"They did, but I'm covered by the city, and the city lawyers are representing me along with everybody else."

"Well that's a plus, but sorry you got into that mess. I feel it's at least partly my fault."

"But it's not. Those boys are cheaters, and should be responsible for their own misconduct."

"True."

They arranged to meet for dinner.

* * *

Around 2:30 that afternoon Mike received a call from Tim Clough, a reporter from *Time* Magazine.

Clough said, "We ran a front-page story on Dr. Fessenden a few years ago when he won the Balzan Prize and some others too. My editor thought it might make an engaging cover story to tell our readers how a trial attorney brought down the man called 'Dr. Everlast'."

Jesus!—a *Time Magazine cover story!* Without pause Mike said, "I can see that."

"So I'd like to sit down with you, bring a photographer along with me."

"Sure. Let me know when."

They made arrangements for an interview in two days.

The reporter said, "You have to understand there's no assurance of a cover story—or any article at all, actually. That's entirely up to my editor."

"I understand."

"But I think it's very likely."

"Okay."

"Almost guaranteed."

"Good."

Mike hung up.

Time Magazine. Great!

Where's *Newsweek*?

END

ACKNOWLEDGMENTS

I gratefully acknowledge the enormously useful comments, critiques, and suggestions contributed by the following persons:

Thomas R. Bransten, author of *A Slight Case of Guilt*, and *Journey to Zembeylia*

Robin Stratton, author of *In His Genes, On Air, The Revision Process*, and other books

Members of the Meetup Writing Group, Bedford, Mass., chaired by Jennifer C. Lord

All of the writers in various writing groups in which I have participated over the years.

MISCELLANY

If you enjoyed this book, Don would appreciate your rating it online, and posting a brief review if you have the time.

Don Sweeney is also the author of *Uncalculated Risk*, and *Impelled*, thrillers soon to be published.

CPSIA information can be obtained
at www.ICGtesting.com
Printed in the USA
BVOW04*0427070617

485391BV00007B/4/P